Praise for
Of Water And Madness

"I highly recommend this whole series for anyone who wants to see magic, romance, and conflict woven together […] I guess my desire to see more of them speaks for itself."
— A.D. Trosper, author —

"Loved, loved, loved *Of Water and Madness*! I fell in love with these books from the beginning. What an amazing fourth book. I do love a happy ending. I plan on reading them again!"
— Jennifer, reader —

"I really enjoyed this series so much and this book was a great finale! You feel like you know the characters so well, like they're friends and you wouldn't mind visiting them in Euphora!"
— Angela, reader —

"Ms. Jennings is very, very innovative and I can't wait for each new book! It comes with my highest recommendations!"
— Sharon L. Divis, reader —

"... a satisfying end to this exciting series. It was as unique as Liam himself... quite the shocker...action packed."
— Natalie Gibson, author —

OF Water AND Madness

FOURTH OF THE DRYAD QUARTET

KATIE JENNINGS

Sapphire Royale
publishing

Published by
Sapphire Royale Publishing

ISBN-13: 978-0615722412
ISBN-10: 0615722415

Visit the author at:
www.katieajennings.com
www.facebook.com/katieajennings
www.twitter.com/dryadquartet
www.katieajennings.wordpress.com

For my family. We're at our best when we're together.

Thea & Sebastian
Mother Earth & Father Sky

Rohan & Serendipity
Earth Dryad | Muse

Rhiannon
Earth Dryad

Sienna
Muse

Clynn & Heidi
Air Dryad | Human

Capri
Air Dryad

Brock & Nyxa
Fire Dryad | Fate

Blythe
Fire Dryad

Lucian & Clarity
Water Dryad | Muse

Liam
Water Dryad

Cilla
Muse

Roarke & Erin
Fury | Enforcer

Rian
Fury

Trinity & Jean Paul
Muse | Human

Tobias
Muse

Balgaire & Nyxa
Fury | Fate

Nova
Fate

Balgaire & Olivia
Fury | Human

Brogan
Fury

Morgaine & Wynn
Fate | Enforcer

Mable
Muse

Angora & Alan
Fate | Human

Alastor
Fate

Dryads

Air
Clynn
Capri

Fire
Brock
Blythe

Earth
Rohan
Rhiannon

Water
Lucian
Liam

Muses ——— Furies ——— Fates

Muses
Serendipity
Sienna
Trinity
Tobias
Clarity
Cilla

Furies
Roarke
Rian
Balgaire
Brogan

Fates
Nyxa
Nova
Angora
Alastor
Morgaine
Mable

Prologue

I send my heart up to thee, all my heart,
In this my singing.
For the stars help me, and the sea,
And the sea bears part.

His name was Liam, and he was Water.

He had known destruction; had seen it rear its ugly head and attempt to consume all he cared about with a cruel, unrelenting fervor. But little could have prepared him for what he now witnessed.

Evil the likes of which he hadn't known could possibly exist in this world was waging war on those he loved, and he now found himself riding on the brink of this tidal wave of pure and maniacal madness, brought on by quite possibly the most evil being alive.

Well, momentarily alive. If he had his way, Dante would be snuffed out faster than he could utter his own name. But, as the circumstances currently were, revenge and ultimate justice were going to have to wait.

Liam stood on the cliff's edge, overlooking the valley where his family fought swiftly and valiantly.

Storm clouds raged overhead, beating back the sun that fought to shine through, a beacon of hope shadowed by a darkness even the Devil himself could be proud of.

And while they fought, he stood alone, prepared to take on the mastermind of this sinister battle.

But he was ready. Oh, he was more than ready...he was primed. Primed for revenge, thirsting for vindication...and not just for Dante.

For he had been fooled, had been used for a purpose so heinous, so vile that it boiled his blood and filled him with guilt and morbid horror.

Because while they'd been prepared for Dante's army, they hadn't been prepared for his secret, disastrous weapon.

And oh, what a devastating weapon it was.

Chapter One

His fingers skimmed along the nylon strings of his guitar, cruising down to coast over the hollowed wooden body, his admiring eyes following the movement. Who knew such a simple instrument could bring so much pleasure when the going was good and so much relief when the going was tough.

Music had always centered him, providing an outlet for the emotions that seemed to flood through his veins in a continual, forever changing stream. One minute he could be optimistic and cheerful, and then the next, almost unexpectedly, fear or resentment could come in to cloud his happy mood. Much like the rising, changing tides of the ocean, his heart and mind both yearned and shunned, dreamed and troubled, soothed and ached. But then he nearly always found his center again, usually with the balance of love and work.

Sure, they may have thought he was too laid back, too careless and therefore incapable of being a Dryad.

But that was because they only saw him when he was feeling relaxed and contented. Few but his father and Thea ever saw the way he devoted himself to his duties as a Dryad when he worked, and a part of him was disheartened by what the others said behind his back. But then he shrugged it off, knowing it didn't matter what anyone else thought. He knew the truth and that was what was important.

And love…well, he'd always known how to love. Ever since he'd been a young boy, he'd craved it with a passion he didn't understand and an unrelenting desire that he couldn't quite ignore. And when he'd at last discovered it, he'd held on fervently, refusing to let go. He had so much room in his heart for love and this need to share it with those he deemed worthy of its reception. That much he had learned from his father.

Lucian was a good man with an enormous heart, with an honest and caring nature that drew people to him for guidance and comfort. Liam liked to think that he got all of his best traits from his father and in a lot of ways he wanted nothing more than to be just like him. How could he not, when the man was his best friend, his confidant, and his mentor? He owed him more than just his life; he owed him the values and the attitude he carried with him day after day, and the fortitude and optimism that had been passed down to him along with the gift of Water in his blood.

He sat on the back steps of the castle, facing the gardens. Hazy morning sunlight drifted in through misty fog, casting rays of light through the birch trees to glow upon the grassy field of wild roses. Coming to this place meant long, thoughtful silences and reflection of purpose. And it reminded him of the girl—now a woman—that had stolen his heart all those years ago with something as simple as a laugh.

Rhia…just thinking of her made him forget everything else because nothing could ever be as important as her. And perhaps nothing ever would be. She was, and always had been, the object of his most latent desires. And now, finally, she was his.

Although it had been quite the road to get to this point, that much was certain. And it looked as though there was still more road to come—a bumpy one filled with unavoidable potholes and laden with potentially disastrous landmines. But they would pull through because nothing was stronger than love, and his love was even stronger yet.

She would never know how thrilled he was to see her and Blythe move past their differences and make a real, concerted effort to be friends. Capri understood, because she knew the importance of the four of them united just as well as he did.

And he had to hand it to Blythe for stepping up to the plate, though he had always had a feeling she would make the first move. She was assertive that way, and once her mind was made up she went at her goal full force, with no room for regrets. It was one of his favorite things about her, and he wondered if her passion and drive was the reason Jackson Murphy had stuck around as long as he had, clearly unable to let go of her. Liam smiled at the thought, and was willing to bet everything he had that it was exactly that which drew Jax in like a fish caught on a line. And he had to hand it to Blythe for bringing in one hell of a catch.

The bounty hunter had grown on him pretty quickly, despite Liam's natural aversion to the idea of anyone dating the girl who was practically his little sister. He had a right to be protective of her, though he knew damn well, despite her incessant reminders that she could take care of herself. But that didn't stop him from worrying about her or from making her see reason when she had some crazy idea in her head.

Fortunately for all involved, Jax was far from a crazy idea. In fact, Liam was fully ready to admit that the bounty hunter was an oddly perfect fit for Blythe. He swiftly and adeptly handled her fiery temper, could soothe away her manic bouts of sorrow and clearly loved her with a passion equal to her own. He handled her better than even Liam had ever been able to and that was saying something. That fact irked him a bit, but he was trying to get over it.

Just as he was finally getting over whatever grievances he'd had over Rian courting the lovely, guileless Capri, who was basically like his other little sister and therefore in need of his brotherly protection. Though she was anything but a fool and it looked as though she was a better gauge of character than all of them combined.

She had seen something inside of Rian that the rest of them had failed to see for years…this latent, quiet compassion and caring nature that they had all missed under his warrior's mask. Perhaps they had all been too quick to assume that because the man was a born and bred soldier that he lacked the capacity to feel. But it was evident to everyone now that he could indeed feel, and what he felt for Capri was obvious every time he looked at her.

And now they were getting married in just a few short weeks. He felt an instinctive swell of pride and affection at the idea, picturing Capri as clear as day, glowing with happiness and adorned in white. Who knew that the youngest of the Dryads would be the first to get hitched? He had certainly thought he would be first, with Rhia at his side. Of course, given the circumstances, perhaps it was foolish to have hoped that it would take less time than it had to release her from the bonds of her parents and her own mind. But even when it had seemed hopeless that she would ever be free, he'd reminded himself of what he was fighting for and then it would all seem clear once more.

Smiling, he reached into the front pocket of his jeans and pulled out a ring, inspecting it in the soft glow of the sun. The white gold band flashed brightly and the deep blue sapphire surrounded by twining, engraved leaves glowed like the depths of the sea. It was her birthstone, which was why he had selected it when he'd walked into the store a day earlier. And the square cut seemed to suit her practical, no nonsense nature. Combined with the leaves dotted with tiny white diamonds, the ring was nothing short of a masterpiece. He had only to wait for the right moment to give it to her.

But he could be patient, he thought as he tucked the ring away. Now would not be a good time, not when the entire castle was still reeling from the events of the last few days, and from the alarming awareness of the impending war they all knew was coming at some point in the near future…

Frowning, he stared at the waves of wild grass, remembering how Rhiannon had cried in his arms after they'd returned safely home. She'd had bruises on her neck, cuts on her wrists and ankles, and what he could only imagine would be hoards of emotional scars that could take years to heal. All of that was the doing of one man…Liam's fists clenched at the thought that he hadn't been able to exact the punishment he felt the asshole so rightfully deserved.

Burke Callahan…even the name made his blood boil and his mood sour. The man didn't deserve to live in his opinion, and if it were up to him, he would have paid dearly for what he had put Rhiannon through—what he had put all of them through—and for what? A grave misunderstanding as to what had truly happened to his son, Michael? Well, it was Michael's own damn fault he'd gotten himself killed by a demon. Burke had refused to even consider such a possibility and had instead jumped to the conclusion that someone on Euphora was responsible, namely Liam himself, Brogan…or Rhiannon, of all people.

And to think that Rhiannon's mother, Serendipity, had been convinced of Rhiannon's guilt and had assisted Burke in kidnapping her, knowing he had the full intent of murdering her. Good Lord, he couldn't even face that woman after what she had done. But Thea had been merciful, probably because she knew the woman would receive a suitable enough punishment from her own husband for her misdeeds. Rohan, rightfully so, was barely speaking to his wife and Liam wouldn't be surprised if she became an ex-wife sooner rather than later. After all, she had falsely accused their oldest daughter of being a murderer without any proof. If that wasn't enough grounds for separation, he didn't know what was.

But, all of that was behind them, at least for now. He was certainly not going to forget it and he knew Rhiannon wouldn't, but for now at least they could focus their attention on more pressing matters…such as Dante.

Even the name gave him chills, especially when he remembered being in the man's presence unknowingly and realizing afterward just how close to death they had truly been. Because there was no doubt in his mind that Dante was deadly, especially after what Blythe and Rhiannon went through with him. He was ruthless, cunning, and decisively evil. It wouldn't do to underestimate him, especially not now. If he really did have some kind of army at his disposal then they were all going to be in incredible danger.

But, until any of them knew for sure what Dante had planned, the best they could do was be watchful and hope they caught on to him before he could do any real damage.

Rising to his feet, Liam swung his guitar over his shoulder and stuffed his hands into the pockets of his casual, faded Levis, shrugging off any thoughts of Dante for the time being. But that didn't mean he was going to forget about the impending danger. He rarely forgot about anything, he just knew how to sort out priorities. And right now, getting some work done was at the top of the list.

Humming to himself, he strolled back into the castle and down the long corridor, his destination Water Tower. The entrance was conveniently located near the dining hall and near Air Tower, where he and his father routinely found themselves working with Clynn and Capri on developing and managing storm systems.

He pulled open the ancient wooden door that led to a winding, spiral stone staircase ending in a doorway one story up. Jogging up the steps two at a time, he opened the second door and swept in, a grin on his face the moment he saw his father.

"Hey," he greeted, slipping the guitar off his back and setting it on the wooden floor by the door.

Lucian turned from the large, scale model globe and eyed his son with humorous blue eyes.

"Late start this morning?" Lucian asked, his hands held out, palms spread, hovering over the surface of the globe.

"Lost track of time," Liam replied, reaching for an apple from the basket on his father's workbench and crunching into it. "Though it's probably a good thing for you to work alone once in awhile. Wouldn't want you to get rusty, old man."

Lucian's eyes flashed as one sculpted white eyebrow rose. "Boyo, I could do this job blindfolded. You, on the other hand, still have much to learn."

"If it makes you feel better to think I haven't surpassed your talents, then go right ahead." Liam winked, enjoying this time they had together. Joking around with his father was one of his favorite pastimes. "So when's Blythe coming back?"

"She and Jax are due back from Texas tomorrow," Lucian said serenely, turning back to his work. "And Thea wants to throw an engagement party for Capri and Rian as soon as they return."

"Cool." Liam bit into the apple again, then leaned up against the workbench and stared around at the tower that was as much his haven as his workplace.

The tower was large and cylindrical, with tall, skyward reaching walls that opened up with skylights at the top. Big, wide windows cut through the stone near the ceiling, sending rays of sunshine down into the room. The rest of the stone walls around them cried quiet, bubbling rivers of water that fell into a large pool filled with fish below, which was covered by a pine wood deck that served as a platform for their workbench and the globe his father was currently using.

All in all, it certainly wasn't a bad place to spend the day, Liam thought with a smile. As a kid, he'd loved spending time there, surrounded by the element that sang in his very blood.

Polishing off his apple, he chucked the core into the small garbage can beneath the workbench and proceeded to update his charts. He may not have been as studious as Rhiannon, but he knew his stuff. And when his father retired one day, he had full confidence that he could make the transition smooth and effortless.

As a Water Dryad, he was responsible for everything involving the largest body of water on the planet: the ocean. He managed every aspect of the sea, from the changing tides to the levels of algae, to the fish and other animal life that lived beneath its surface. But the extent of his duties didn't stop there. He and his father were in charge of providing the planet with rain, thus spreading fresh water throughout the world, benefiting all forms of life. Without water, the Earth couldn't survive.

He knew the weight of his responsibilities and he bore it well, with both time honored respect and humility. He truly cared about the impact he had on the world, and as such did virtually nothing carelessly where work was concerned. One slip up and entire towns could be wiped off the face of the map in a typhoon, or a species of fish could perish because their only food source had dwindled and disappeared.

It was a heavy burden, but he paid no mind to bearing it, just as those who had come before him had borne it for countless centuries. After all, as Rhiannon was apt to say, it was their duty…a gift as well as a burden.

A couple of hours later, there was a swift knock on the door. When Liam glanced up he saw Rhiannon peek her head in, a large wicker basket in her arms.

His smile was automatic and instinctive, and the pleasure he felt at seeing her smile in response couldn't possibly be measured.

"Hey, beautiful." He stepped toward her as she came into the room and stood on the little bridge that connected the platform to the doorway.

"Hello." Rhiannon nodded and then looked at Lucian politely. "Good afternoon, Lucian."

"Rhiannon," Lucian replied, glancing at his son before turning away to give them privacy.

Liam leaned in to tenderly kiss her lips before swiftly taking the basket from her hands.

"What's all this?" he asked nosily, already reaching in to see what she had brought.

"It's a picnic lunch…I thought we could go down to the courtyard and eat, if you're not too busy," Rhiannon told him, a bit miffed that he was rustling around her carefully packed dishes.

"I'm never too busy for you." He grinned, whirling around and nodding to his father. "Lunch break, be back later."

"Have fun." Lucian waved him away, pretending to be busy feeding the fish. When he heard the door click shut, he let out a contented sigh and smiled, pleased to see his son truly happy at last.

Liam lay back on his elbows, his long legs crossed in front of him as they sat comfortably in the grass beneath one of the large willow trees, the soft sunshine filtering down through the branches. His eyes followed Rhiannon's diligent, practical movements as she laid out their first course on top of buttercup yellow plates, complete with matching napkins and crystal glasses for the sparkling cider she'd brought.

"I've been experimenting with dill, so you'll have to let me know how you like these," she began, arranging small tea sandwiches topped with mayonnaise, smoked salmon, and some kind of green sprigs on the plates.

"I'm always the guinea pig," Liam grumbled, eyeing the sandwiches warily as she handed him a plate. "If this kills me, I promise to haunt you."

Rhiannon's eyes flashed to meet his as her lips curved a bit wickedly. "That wouldn't be such a bad thing."

"Me dying or me haunting you?" he asked, biting into one of the sandwiches. She only smiled, but he was instantly distracted by the incredible flavor fest in his mouth. "Hey, this is good."

"The dill isn't too strong?"

"Which part is the dill?" He gulped down the second half of the tiny sandwich and grinned.

"The green stuff was dill and there was more dill in the mixture beneath the salmon. There was also lemon juice, parsley, thyme, tarragon, and nutmeg."

"Mmm hmm, very interesting. Can I have another one?"

"I don't want you filling up on the first course; there are four more to go," Rhiannon chided, slipping one more sandwich onto his plate before taking a bite of one herself. Her brows furrowed in concentration as she chewed and her sage green eyes darkened a bit as she lost herself in the flavors, critiquing her own creation. He just watched her, as always fascinated by her serious, analytical nature.

"I feel it needs a bit more nutmeg," she said thoughtfully.

"I feel I need more food. Keep it coming, chef," Liam said playfully, poking her with his plate.

"Yes, master," she muttered, though her mouth curved as she unearthed another carefully packed container from her basket. "Next course, caprese salad."

She dished out basil leaves, tomato slices, and big chunks of fresh mozzarella onto his plate, and then drizzled oil over it. Handing him a fork, she sat back, sipped cider and watched as he sampled it.

He forked up a bite and groaned, the coolness of the cheese blended with the bite of the tomato and zesty dressing catching him off guard. "This is good, too. Why don't we have this salad every night?"

"Thea doesn't care for it, though I don't know why." Rhiannon filled her own plate and scooped up a bite, chewing delicately, again examining her own creation. When she swallowed, she smiled triumphantly at him. "This is just right, I must say."

Sitting up, Liam set aside his now empty plate and reached out to brush her hair away from her face, cupping her cheek and eyeing her intently. He saw the change in her eyes, from coolly in control to dark, nervous awareness in an instant.

"There are a lot of things that are just right now, Rhia," he murmured, tenderly stroking his thumb along her cheek, his deep blue eyes intense on hers. "Don't you think?"

She set her own plate aside without breaking eye contact with him and reached up with her hand to slide over his. She tilted her head and pressed her lips to his palm, almost experimentally, as if wondering if such a thing were alright, or expected. How little she knew just how powerful that one gesture was to him.

When she turned her head back to look at him, he leaned in and captured her lips with his, his hand trailing back to grasp her waves of dark hair. He felt her give in, felt her submit to him, and he knew it was a special kind of magic. For he was truly the one who submitted to her, all the time...all she had to do was ask and he would be at her side in an instant.

"I love you," he said softly against her lips, the words flowing as easily as a steady stream through a quiet forest.

"I love you too." She was still getting used to saying the phrase, even though her heart knew the emotion so well now. It had always been him, after all...

A sound to their left had them both turning, only to see Rohan, Lucian and Clynn strolling together, clearly in a deep discussion. They were all smiling, and Rohan let out a loud laugh at something Clynn said, filling the courtyard with the sound. Liam saw Rhiannon's eyes fill as she watched her father, who had been looking happier by the day.

The three men walked down the cobblestone pathway, and when they came across Liam and Rhiannon, they stopped mid-step.

"Is that caprese salad I see?" Lucian asked, leaning over to get a glimpse at Rhiannon's plate.

"Back off, old man, this picnic lunch is mine." Liam grinned, wrapping an arm casually around Rhiannon as he looked up at the older men.

Lucian wasn't swayed, however, and continued to examine the contents of their lunch. "Oh, and smoked salmon with dill!" he said excitedly, his eyes glittering with good humor. "Remind me again what you did to deserve this?"

"I made her fall in love with me," Liam responded, grinning ear-to-ear like a fool at his father's answering laugh.

"Rhiannon has always been an excellent cook." Rohan beamed, smiling down at his daughter proudly.

She blushed, flustered at having her father compliment her so easily. That was yet another thing Liam knew she'd have to get used to.

"Where are you guys off to?" Liam asked, enjoying the sight of the three of them together again, like how he knew the old days had been.

"Just out for a walk. We old folks can still do such things, you know." Lucian winked, earning another laugh from Rohan.

Clynn, being the most intuitive of the trio, turned to his friends with a knowing smile. "Perhaps we should get to it, give the kids some privacy."

"Mmm, yes." Lucian sent one last, contented glance at his son and the girl he loved, and patted both men on the back. "Come along."

Liam and Rhiannon watched their fathers walk away and resume talking and they both turned to each other at once with identical smiles.

"He's so happy to have his friends back." Rhiannon sighed, genuinely pleased.

"And his friends are happy to have him back, as well," Liam told her, pressing a kiss to her forehead. "Now all we gotta do is get your dad and Brock to make up, and then they will really be complete."

Rhiannon snorted, the idea of her father and Brock ever getting along a farfetched impossibility in her eyes.

"I wouldn't hold your breath, Liam," she advised, tilting her head up for another kiss. "Now, my darling guinea pig, I have more food to feed you."

Chapter Two

He was frustrated. Monumentally and hopelessly frustrated, and with no clear solution at hand.

There was a tremendous amount of flooding in the Tennessee River Valley, and it was all because the amount of water he had estimated for the storm had not been distributed as evenly as they had expected. Capri, for reasons unknown, had pushed the storm through the area at a much slower pace than they'd agreed upon, and now the valley was flooded well beyond what was needed.

He knew it was a simple miscommunication on his part with her, but damnit, now it made him look bad because whenever there was too much water somewhere, it fell on him. And when Thea got wind of it he'd have to explain himself and he wasn't looking forward to it.

With an irritated sigh, he stood before the globe and enhanced his view of the valley, enlarging it under a floating magnifying glass, deciding whether or not he could push some of the water down an available river canal. Sometimes these things could be repaired, with a little nudging. Thea didn't approve of using means that were less than natural, but this was important, and it was the only solution other than letting the poor people drown on his behalf.

He was neck deep in even more guilt and annoyance when the door burst open and his favorite distraction bolted in.

"I'm back!" Blythe announced cheerfully, racing across the little bridge and onto the platform, right into his waiting arms.

He grunted as she hefted herself up, and he spun her around playfully as he always did. Already he felt better, just by hearing her voice and seeing her infectious smile.

When he set her down, he cupped her smiling face in his hands and planted a big, noisy kiss on her lips.

"There's my girl," he greeted, feeling his frustration ebb away as if it had never existed. On impulse, he pulled her against him for a tight hug, realizing how much he had missed her. "How was the trip?"

She pulled away from him and beamed. "Excellent. I got to eat cactus and drink tequila with a worm in the bottle and everything!"

"Yuck." Liam grimaced, though he couldn't help but laugh at the same time. "That sounds…interesting."

"There's not much else to do in the desert." She shrugged, then grinned suggestively. "Except stay in bed all day, of course."

"Okay, I really didn't need to hear that." Liam wrapped one arm around her neck in a playful headlock and held her there as she squirmed. "Maybe I should tell you what Rhia and I did this morning…she's really quite flexible, you know."

"Ew!" Blythe shrieked, kicking her legs and fighting to pry his arm from her neck. "Please don't, oh God. I'll throw up on you, I swear to it."

Laughing, he released her and patted her on the head. "You don't waste food like that."

"True." She fluffed up her hair and blew at her bangs that had fallen into her eyes. "So I hear we're having an engagement party tonight."

"Just in time. The wedding is in three weeks."

Blythe rolled her shoulders, looking restless. "You'd think Capri would be more stressed out. God knows I would be. Sheesh, marriage? How…grown up."

With a laugh, Liam draped an arm over her shoulders and planted a kiss on the top of her head. "You're telling me you haven't given one thought to marrying the bounty hunter?"

Pouting a bit, Blythe shrugged. "I don't know. I don't think it's like that between us, not yet. I mean, I love him, and he loves me, but I don't know if I'm ready to be so grown up yet."

"Marriage doesn't automatically make you old, my love. It just proves you're in it for the long haul."

She chewed on that for a moment, then grinned at him. "This coming from the hopeless romantic. I bet you're just dying to ask Rhiannon to marry you, huh?"

Liam smiled sheepishly, then dug into his pocket, unearthing the ring. When he handed it to her, Blythe's mouth fell open.

"Jesus, Liam, that's one hell of a rock," she stammered, her eyes wide as she stared at the square sapphire stone.

"Do you think she'll like it?" he asked, stuffing his hands into his pockets now for lack of something better to do with them. The gaping look on his sister's face was unnerving him. "Is it too much?"

"Well, I don't know much about this kind of stuff, but I know it's gorgeous." She noted the leafy patterns engraved in the white gold and managed a flustered smile. "Someone like Rhiannon, being all noble and proper and stuff…I think she'll love it, Liam."

She rose on her toes to kiss his cheek, tears in her eyes. "God, I'm getting all mushy. Damnit."

He laughed and accepted the ring back, shoving it back into his pocket. "C'mon, let's go get some lunch. Wipe those tears away so your boyfriend doesn't think I upset you. I don't feel like getting my ass kicked today."

"Okay." She let out a watery laugh and wrapped an arm around his waist. "So when are you going to ask her?"

He pulled her closer as they walked to the door, his lips curving. "When the time is right. I've waited this long, haven't I? I can wait a little bit longer for her to be ready."

The night air was calm and comfortingly still. Music drifted lazily around the courtyard, soothing piano mixed temptingly with bluesy guitar, graced by a voice that was nothing short of timeless. Round white paper lanterns floated in the air over the dance floor, glowing with silvery light, and the stars in the sky glittered amorously, as if shining at their best and brightest just for this night.

For it was a night of romance, a night to celebrate love and laughter and joy. And while the moon shone full and alluringly bright in the sky, down below, the lovers swayed.

Liam held Rhiannon close, pressing her body against his as he brushed her cheek with his own, the woodsy sage scent of her intoxicating. He could feel her heart beating against his chest, and hear her breathing, slow and even. He knew she was just as mesmerized by the song and the mood of the evening as he was; just as seduced and blissfully entranced.

The music and the words seemed to float along beside them, as if through a smooth wave of cream, speaking of a woman as sweet as tupelo honey…

Pressing his lips to the smooth skin of her throat just under her ear, he murmured his love for her over and over, needing her to remember, needing her to understand just how much his heart yearned for her.

And when she held him closer and he could feel her lips curve against his collar bone, could hear her whisper the words in return, he thanked God for it.

As the song ended and another began, he pulled away from her to frame her face in his hands and kiss her.

"So beautiful." He grinned, kissing her again and again. She pushed him back slyly, her eyes darkening and her lips curving into a sultry smirk. He thought she looked like a woman who had just discovered the power of seduction and was thrilled by it.

"I bet you tell all the girls that," Rhiannon mused, letting him spin her around and bring her in close again, her heart jolting at the movement. He had that look in his eyes again, the one that still unnerved her with its outright and shameless intensity.

"No one compares to you," he told her, his hands cruising along her cream colored silk dress that dipped deliciously low in the back and came up to tie at her neck. "I'm the luckiest man here."

Rhiannon laughed, knowing that it was she who was lucky, not him. "My father's watching us, Liam, and you look like you want to devour me in one bite. It's not appropriate."

He grinned at her, chuckling at her carefully ingrained modesty. "If it makes him uncomfortable then he can look away."

She giggled as he spun her around again and the sound of it was sweeter than the bells of the angels.

"You look so beautiful, Rhiannon," Capri said as she approached them suddenly with Rian at her side, her eyes misty and sentimental.

Liam and Rhiannon parted, and she hugged Capri close and sighed.

"It's you who glows tonight, Capri," she murmured, pulling away to eye Capri with joy and feminine envy. The flowing silver gown she wore glittered in the soft light, and the pearls that graced the bodice and her neck and ears suited her delicacy perfectly. Her waves of pale blonde hair had been pulled back into a smooth, elegant up do, with tendrils escaping to surround her slender face. Beside her, Rian nodded to both Liam and Rhiannon, and his mouth seemed to be fixed into a permanent, satisfied smile.

When Liam turned to Capri, he pretended to look astonished. "I think an angel has been dropped into our midst from

Heaven itself. Don't you think?" He winked at Rian as he pulled Capri in for a hug as she blushed and giggled.

"Please, it's just plain old me." Capri broke away and brushed at the loose strands of hair near her face, feeling embarrassed but pleased by the compliment. "Are you guys having a good time?"

"Of course," Rhiannon replied, her eyes warming. "I can't believe that in a few short weeks you two will be husband and wife. It's...oh." She felt her eyes watering and her throat tightening so she turned away, letting Liam pull her against him.

"She's been sentimental about this ever since you told us," he explained as Rhiannon straightened her back and cleared her throat.

"I'm fine," she managed. "Gosh, look at Blythe's dress, isn't it just stunning?"

Knowing she wanted to distract both herself and the others from her tears, Liam held her closer and followed her gaze as Blythe and Jax came to the dance floor, hand-in-hand.

He had to admit, she did look stunning.

Her dress was rich gold silk, cut short just above her knees with a layered skirt and heart shaped bodice. Against the warm ivory of her skin and the deep red curls of hair that barely graced her shoulders, she looked like a candle burning fiery and hot. Beside her, Jax was dressed in jeans and a casual suit jacket, open in the front with no tie, just a vivid red shirt beneath it. He noticed that they both wore matching black leather cowboy boots, and he couldn't help but laugh.

"Are you going to go ride the range after the party or something?" Liam joked as they approached, earning a bold smile from Blythe.

"Well, duh." She winked and smiled at the others. "We gonna get this party started, or what?"

Within minutes, the music had been switched from soothingly romantic to rough and tumble, melody blasting country, complete with line dancing and a shuffling feet rhythm that made Liam feel like a complete fool on the dance floor. He was having the time of his life.

Brooks and Dunn rang out as a big group of them attempted to learn the moves, with Blythe leading the way. Clearly country dancing had become her latest obsession since her trip down to Texas and she was more than willing to share it. And Jax looked just right beside her as the two of them shuffled along and kicked together to the steel guitar and catchy drumbeat.

Liam imagined the only way things could be better was if they were in some dingy southwestern bar with smoke hanging in the air and a live band pumping out the music. Maybe he'd take Rhiannon to a place like that someday, just so she could see what it was all about. Just watching her attempt to learn the moves, mess up and laugh with him as they both struggled and had a good time made him extraordinarily optimistic for the future.

Maybe Dante had only been bluffing and nothing would happen after all. It just didn't seem possible that one man could destroy everything that his family had built, everything they had worked for and loved. Not when they were being so vigilant and cautious, and when they were standing as united and strong as ever. Sure, there were a few loose ends, like Rohan and Brock, but that could hardly pose a threat compared to how stable everything else seemed to be now.

When the song came to a close and a slower country beat replaced it, Liam noticed Rohan approaching.

With a polite nod, he turned toward the older man. Beside him, Rhiannon smiled warmly up at her father, pleased when he leaned in to kiss her cheek.

"Rhiannon, Liam." He pulled away and reached out a hand to shake Liam's hand, pleasure and pride in his eyes. Liam accepted the handshake, a bit confused but delighted all the same. "I just wanted to let you know that I am proud of both of you for finally coming together this way. You can't know just how happy it makes me to see it."

"Thank you, sir." Liam grinned, turning to look at Rhiannon. "It makes me happy, too."

Rhiannon flushed, embarrassed to have the two men in her life eyeing her. "Maybe we should go get some champagne," she suggested, beginning to edge away from them both. Her father reached out to stop her.

"I was actually hoping I could have this dance with you, Rhiannon. It's been so long since we've danced together."

Rhiannon looked momentarily astonished, but Liam merely smiled and pressed a quick kiss to her forehead.

"Great idea. My dad looks lonely, anyway. I'll go keep him company." With a wink at them both, Liam slipped away and left them, the image of Rohan's warm pride burned into his memory. For so long he had waited for that man's acceptance, knowing it was key to Rhiannon's freedom. And now he had it, at last.

Grinning, he plopped into the chair beside his father, who had been sipping champagne and reading a novel under the table. Lucian looked up guiltily, only to see it was his son and smile instead.

"Tired of dancing, boyo?" he asked with a wink.

"For now." Liam snatched the book his father had been reading, examining the cover. "Dickens? Really? We're having a party and you'd rather sit here and read boring old Dickens?"

Lucian straightened defensively and slipped the book out of Liam's hands, setting it on the table. "It was either that or watch your mother doting on Serendipity."

Because it was obvious he hadn't meant to say the words, Lucian sighed and took a deep sip of his champagne, silently cursing himself.

"What's this?" Liam asked, glancing over to where the Muses were sitting and spotting his mother and Serendipity both watching Rohan with hurt expressions. "I see...it upsets you that she isn't on your side?"

"Obviously." Lucian's lips pursed in annoyance, something Liam was not at all used to seeing on his serene father's face.

"But I don't want to worry you with my troubles, Liam. Go dance with that lovely girl of yours."

"Dad, I'm not a kid anymore, I can handle the truth. Do you want me to go talk to her?"

"Absolutely not. I won't have you getting involved in this. You have such a tentative relationship with her as it is, I would hate to see you destroy that. She and I will work it out, in time."

Liam's eyes narrowed as he glanced over again at his mother, who was whispering something to Serendipity, clearly soothing and placating to her. It boiled his blood to see it. Did she not remember the harsh words Serendipity had for both himself and his father? The criticism that had been so poorly placed, so brashly exposed with carelessness and utter disgust? But apparently those degrading words had been forgotten, replaced instead by a need to cater to a woman who he felt did not deserve an ounce of sympathy.

Turning back to his father, he patted his arm supportively. "This will all blow over. Maybe she just doesn't know you're upset about it."

"Perhaps," Lucian mused, barely able to hide the cynicism in his voice. The truth was, she knew his feelings perfectly well as they had discussed the whole situation in detail only hours earlier. But he didn't want to trouble his only son with that information. "Rhiannon looks pretty tonight."

"Yeah, she could make a paper bag look sexy," Liam replied, elbowing his father in the side with a grin. "C'mon, I know you're happy for me, old man."

Lucian chuckled and swung an arm around his son's shoulders before leaning into him, his eyes twinkling. "She's a treasure, boyo. Make sure you hold on to her."

"I will. Trust me." Liam looked over to where she was slow dancing with her father, and his smile softened. "I don't think I could ever let her go now."

"I don't think you ever could, period." Lucian leaned back to sip his champagne casually, enjoying himself. "I used to wonder if you were ever going to get over her. You've always been persistent, but I wasn't sure she'd come around. I'm glad to see that she finally has."

"You didn't like her for a long time," Liam remembered, eyeing his father sadly. "That used to make me so mad, that you couldn't see what I could see. She's not just pretty on the outside, dad."

"You're right, I didn't see it." Lucian's eyes drifted over to watch his old friend dancing with the girl. "Things weren't easy for her for a very long time, or for Rohan. I'm glad to see them both smiling for once."

"You mean he wasn't always so stuffy?" Liam joked, though his father was completely serious.

"No, he had humor once and he used to smile. Granted, he's never been good with expressing his emotions, but I wouldn't call him stuffy. But Serendipity changed him, and her influence over Rhiannon was, in my eyes, very much like a poison."

"But none of you intervened to try and stop it?" Liam asked, though he knew in his heart that nothing like that was ever easy.

"There wasn't much we could do. With the feud that formed between Rohan and Brock, we Dryads were divided. Clynn and I tried to hold things together for a time, but even we became disillusioned. Rohan made it expressly clear to us that we were not to interfere with his marriage to Serendipity, so we stayed back. I had no idea just how bad it would scar their child." Lucian downed the rest of his champagne bitterly and let out a heavy sigh.

Liam reached for a glass himself and sipped, lost in thought. "Well, it's over now, at least. Rhia and Rohan are both better, and I could care less what happens to that cold, frigid bitch."

To his surprise, his father laughed.

"My sentiments exactly."

Liam smiled, but it didn't quite reach his eyes as he looked over to his mother again, his little sister Cilla sitting with her. How long had his own family been divided by his mother's insistence to keep a safe, emotional distance from both him and his father? She committed herself to her duty as a Muse, and played the part of wife and mother, but clearly she was nothing but aloof.

As if she could sense he was thinking about her, she looked up and met his eyes. It was cool, clear green into his rich blue, and he felt his lips curve into a smirk as he raised his glass to her in acknowledgement. She smiled back, bowing her head slightly, before turning back to Serendipity. Beside her, Cilla glanced over to look at Liam as well, only to blush and turn away.

They had, to his deep regret, never been close. Blythe was much more of a sister to him than his own flesh and blood, and that fact saddened him. But Cilla had never embraced his brotherly advances, had never seemed to want much to do with him, and so he had given up. Though he knew that if she ever asked him for anything, he wouldn't hesitate to help her. She was his sister, after all, and he enjoyed helping people too much to not want to help her if she needed him. And his mother...well, she was kind, that much he knew. And she was soft spoken, lovely, and coolly distant without appearing cold like Serendipity. But it was still there, this emotional detachment toward everyone and everything. Sure, she could kiss and make it look loving, but he doubted whether there was really much sentiment behind such actions.

But his father had married her, so he must have seen something there worth taking. He'd never really asked him that question before, why he had married Clarity, but given the current circumstances now was probably not a good time.

Pushing the thought away, he turned back to his father, who had quietly begun to read again.

"You know, Jax looks like he could use a real drink...why don't you go take Blythe off his hands and I'll take him to our stash of booze in the parlor?" Liam suggested, grinning at the prospect. Maybe it'd be a good idea to snag Rian as well.

"I guess I could stretch out the old limbs for a bit." Lucian grunted as he got to his feet, smiling as he patted his son on the back. "You never could dance as well as me, boyo."

"That's okay, I can still kick your ass at checkers."

His father laughed as the two of them headed over to where Blythe, Jax, Capri and Rian were all sitting.

Both Jax and Rian looked more than a little bored, while the girls were chattering away about dresses. Content in his role as liberator, Liam leaned in between the two men, a hand on each of their shoulders while his father propositioned Blythe for a dance.

"There's real booze inside. Whaddya say, boys?" Liam asked quietly, keeping his voice down so the women wouldn't hear.

"Praise God, get me outta here, son." Jax grunted, rising to his feet instantly. "I can't take any more of these females."

"Yes, but where would we be without them." Rian shrugged, standing up as well. Capri looked up as she saw him leaving, concern in her eyes.

"Is everything okay?" she asked.

"I think we're boring the boys." Blythe grinned, standing beside Lucian and eyeing Jax with one eyebrow raised. "You gonna go get drunk somewhere, cowboy?"

"Maybe." He grinned in return, the thin scar that ran down the left side of his face shifting from the movement as his hands tucked comfortably into the pockets of his jeans.

"Bring me some whiskey, will you?" Blythe asked as she waved them off and turned back to Lucian, who led her onto the dance floor.

Clynn approached and handed Capri a fresh flute of champagne before sitting beside her. She smiled at him before glancing up at Rian.

"Have fun." She blew him a playful kiss and then laughed at herself. "I've always wanted to do that."

Rian's eyes softened as he leaned in to kiss the top of her head, his hand resting on her shoulder and squeezing gently.

"I love you," he murmured, earning a sweet smile from her as he walked away with Liam and Jax.

Jax rubbed his hands together, an excited gleam in his eyes as he turned to Rian. "We haven't had a real drink together since… well, shit, since that time in Transylvania. Remember that? Asshole demon thought he'd pretend to be Dracula and terrorize the tourists."

Rian snorted and stared up at his friend. "I can't believe you even remember that night." He grinned at Liam as he patted Jax on the back. "Murphy let the locals talk him into drinking an entire bottle of some crazy Eastern European liquor that was in an unmarked bottle. Needless to say, I had to drag him back to the hotel while he sobbed for his mother."

"Whoa, now." Jax stopped mid-step and pointed a finger at Rian in warning. "I thought we weren't gonna talk about that part of our little excursion ever again."

"Oops." Rian shrugged, grinning as Jax punched him in the arm.

"Hey now, no fighting till there's booze. That way it's fair," Liam laughed, leading the way into the parlor.

"I don't want to leave Capri alone for too long, so just one drink for me," Rian told them, earning an amused look from Jax.

"Son, this is your engagement party. I'd say you deserve more than one drink. She'll be just fine without you for awhile. Blythe will keep her plenty entertained."

Rian still looked uncertain, but he smiled at his old friend. "Just don't make me have to drag you upstairs to your bed this time."

Jax just slung an arm over Rian's shoulders and grinned.

"I could find Blythe's bed even if I was deaf, blind and stupid," he joked, earning a disparaging look from Liam.

"I'll pretend I didn't hear that." He shook his head as he stepped up to the wooden bar in the far corner of the parlor, pointing to the two stools in front of it. "Sit down, gentlemen, and tell me your poison."

"Jack Daniels, straight up," Jax drawled as he took a seat. "And get my boy here the same thing."

Liam obliged, pulling out the bottle of Jack with easy finesse and pouring three glasses. He set two on the bar top and then lifted his own in a toast.

"To Rian and Capri." He beamed, pleased when Rian nodded appreciatively.

"Rian and Capri." Jax grinned, tapping his glass against the others before taking a deep sip and sighing. "Reminds me of home."

"Is it strange for you, living here?" Liam asked, leaning against the bar top and enjoying the burn the whiskey left as it slid hotly down his throat.

Jax shrugged. "I never expected I'd live here, that's for sure."

"Funny how things change, huh?" Liam asked, turning to Rian. "And here we are, three very lucky men."

Rian chuckled, sipping more of his whiskey. "I never thought I'd love anybody, much less her. But I do." He paused, staring into his glass, his brow creasing. "She's my light."

"I know what you mean," Jax agreed, smiling at his friend. "Hell, I never thought you'd get hitched either, but here we are."

"And I never thought you'd let a woman hang around longer than a day," Rian put in with a knowing smile.

"Hey now," Jax started, wagging his nearly empty glass at Rian defensively. "She isn't like other women, okay? You both know that. She's...damnit, I don't know. But there's something about her that gets under my skin and stays there. She sticks, and she doesn't let go. But by the time you realize she's got you, you don't want to let go either. Does that make sense?"

Liam shifted his weight and nodded, pleased to hear the honesty in the other man's voice. "Perfectly. Blythe's never been one to do things halfway. It's all or nothing with her, and once she has her mind made up, she stays the course. I'm glad she found you, Jax, I really am."

"I'm the one who should be glad," Jax acknowledged, shaking his head. "That little redhead is the best thing that ever walked into my life."

"How is Rhiannon doing?" Rian asked suddenly, watching Liam with serious eyes.

"Better, much better. She's nearly herself again." Liam played with the glass in his hands, watching what remained of the whiskey slide around seductively. "I've waited my entire life for her, you know?"

Rian nodded, and Jax reached over to pat Liam on the shoulder. "I didn't give her enough credit at first, but she's tough as nails, that girl."

"Yes, she is," Liam agreed, lifting his glass for another toast. "To the women."

They touched glasses and downed what was left of the whiskey in an ancient and time honored male tradition.

"Another," Liam announced, reaching for the bottle and cheerfully pouring more dark amber liquid into the glasses.

"I should go back," Rian began, only to be halted by Jax.

"Oh no you don't. We aren't done with you yet." His mouth flashed into a wicked grin, and Rian took a deep breath and obligingly sat back down.

"One more. Then I'm calling it quits," he told them seriously as he lifted the now full glass up for another toast.

"Sure thing, pal. Whatever you say." Liam grinned, enjoying the sound of glass hitting glass as they toasted.

Chapter Three

So I told him, I said 'Jax, you gotta keep a level head if you're gonna date my sister, because she's crazy.'"

Rhiannon scowled at Liam as she tried to support his weight, rolling her eyes. "That's not a very nice thing to say about Blythe."

"What? She is crazy," Liam reasoned, dragging his feet as Rhiannon led him up the stairs to his room. "But that's what makes her so special."

"I can't imagine she'd appreciate you warning her boyfriend that way. Now he might think she'll try and poison him or something."

"Eh." Liam waved the thought away, letting out a whoosh of breath the second they reached the top step. "God, that's a lot of stairs."

"You're just a lot of drunk." Rhiannon sighed, her own head swimming slightly from too much champagne. "Now come on, you need to sleep this off."

"With you around, baby, who can sleep." Liam chuckled, his hand squeezing her waist playfully.

Rhiannon snorted out a laugh as she pulled him along the hallway, hoping she could make it to his room before he passed out. At least he was still awake, though, along with Jax. Rian had already passed out at the bar in the parlor by the time they had found them.

Rhiannon smiled to herself at the memory of Blythe bursting into the parlor, Capri and herself in tow, wanting to know where the hell they were. They found the two of them laughing like manic fools and falling over drunk, and Blythe's expression of both relief and spitting mad anger had been priceless.

Capri had soothingly awoken Rian and helped him up to his room, while Blythe and Jax had viciously argued and then lustily made up within a shockingly rapid two minute altercation. And she had been left to deal with Liam, who thankfully was the least drunk of the three. But, gauging by the way he kept swaying away from her and stumbling, he was still way drunker than she had ever witnessed.

"Promise me I won't have to haul you around like this ever again. It's so embarrassing," she managed, huffing a bit as he leaned into her and she had to support nearly all of his weight so he wouldn't fall to the floor.

"Hey, I'm fine," he said, attempting to straighten himself and walk on his own. "See?"

He ran headlong into the wall, causing her to laugh despite herself. By the time he'd righted himself, looking both embarrassed and confused, she had to cup her hand over her mouth to muffle her laughter. Others were already asleep, after all, and they had to at least try and be quiet.

She shushed him when he started laughing as well, and in response he rounded on her, pressing her into the wall, his hands running up and down her sides.

"You look good enough to eat, Rhia," he murmured with a slow smile, leaning in to trail his lips along her neck and nibble at her collar bone. It took all the control she had not to melt to the floor that very moment.

"You're drunk, and I'm tipsy, and this is probably not the best idea right now." She had to bite back a groan when he pressed against her, his lips finding hers hungrily.

"I'm not drunk," he told her, already reaching up to loosen the straps tied at the back of her neck. "And you're just—"

He was cut off by the sound of an opening door and harsh whispering around the corner of the hallway to their right, and both of them froze in stunned silence as they heard Lucian's voice, accompanied by what sounded like his wife. Even though they were as yet out of sight, Rhiannon and Liam parted like guilty children and looked at each other questioningly.

Down the turn in the hallway, they could hear both Lucian and Clarity stop just outside their bedroom door, and fortunately they didn't come any closer.

"We should probably go," Rhiannon whispered, beginning to lead the way back down the hallway. But Liam stopped her, concern in his eyes as he stepped a bit closer, hoping to hear just what it was his parents were fighting about. Rhiannon followed him, chewing her bottom lip anxiously.

"You care nothing for my feelings, Clarity," Lucian said, bitterness laced with frustration in his tone. Even though he kept his voice down, they could still hear every word echoing off the stone walls. "And, frankly, I don't know if you ever have."

"Lucian…" Clarity softly replied, her tone soothing but coolly unemotional. "Serendipity is like a sister to me, and she needs me right now. How can I refuse her?"

"You should refuse her because she had no qualms voicing her prejudices against your own son, our son, Clarity. Don't you see that she is only using your kindness for her own gain? All she ever does is suck the life out of whoever is nearest."

"How dare you," Clarity began, though there was little heat in the statement. "She has since explained to me that she feels Liam is a fine boy, but just not the right fit for Rhiannon. I completely understand, Lucian, and I'm not about to go ending my friendship with her because she wants the best for her daughter."

Lucian let out a harsh half laugh, and Liam met Rhiannon's eyes, stunned.

"That woman wants only what's best for herself, and that has always been the case. She was a poison to her husband, a poison to her daughter, and now you are letting her poison interfere with your own son's happiness."

"She isn't going to get in the way of Rhiannon's relationship with Liam, so you can stop worrying about that. She's only focused on getting her husband back," Clarity said firmly.

"She made a very grave mistake, Clarity," Lucian said, his voice hollow and mean. "I wouldn't be surprised if Rohan never forgives her."

Clarity gasped. "If you know something, Lucian, you need to tell me. She's realized just how badly she needs him, and if he's decided to separate from her for good..."

"It is not our place to get involved," Lucian replied, a tone of finality in his voice. "But I want you to understand that what you are doing is hurting me. I feel like you're not even my wife any longer, that you are married to your fellow Muses instead."

Silence hung heavy in the hallway and Rhiannon reached out for Liam's hand, feeling sorry for him. She knew firsthand how hard it was to see parents bickering this way.

He looked back at her, his blue eyes wide with misery. He had no idea that what was going on between his parents was this bad...

"When we got married, Lucian, you knew that it was more out of obligation than anything else," Clarity reminded him, her voice betraying no emotion. "Over the years I've come to love and respect you, but we both have our own lives, separate from one another. You have Liam for your own and I have Cilla. We each have our own duties, and part of mine is to support Serendipity and Trinity, just as I fully expect you to support your fellow Dryads. So please, don't fault me for doing what I have to do, what I need to do. I couldn't bear for you to hate me, Lucian."

"I don't hate you," he murmured, misery in his voice. "I guess I just need more from you than what you're able to give."

"Perhaps," Clarity quietly replied. "Or perhaps you don't need me as much as you think you do."

"Maybe not."

They heard the sound of a door opening again and the shuffling of feet.

"I'm going to bed," Lucian said.

"I'll be there in a moment. I want to check on Cilla and make sure she made it to bed alright," Clarity told him.

They heard the door shut and then heard Clarity heading directly toward them, her heels clicking on the stone floor.

Liam briskly backed up several paces with Rhiannon, and hoped it would appear as though they had just begun to walk down the hallway.

Rhiannon had her arm hooked in his, and took a deep breath to clear the emotion from her face.

Clarity rounded the corner and nearly ran into the two of them.

"Oh," she gasped, clutching a hand to her chest as she let out a trembling breath. Her lips curved into a kind smile as she looked at them. "I'm sorry. I didn't know anyone else was up here."

Rhiannon shot a quick glance at Liam, who was eyeing his mother with intense dislike.

For a moment, he seriously considered saying something to her, scolding her for being such a callous, and coldhearted wife. But it might hurt his father even further if he knew his son was privy to the disaster their marriage had become.

"We were just going to bed," Liam told her, forcing a nonchalant smile on his face.

"It's very late." Clarity smiled, her hands clutching together in front of her even as her expression remained politely indifferent. "Have a good night."

She brushed past them and strolled down the hallway toward the stairs, her footsteps echoing hollowly. Liam turned to watch her go, a mixture of sorrow and anger in his eyes.

"I'm sorry you had to hear that," Rhiannon said, squeezing his arm gently.

He shook his head as he turned to her, coldly sober after what they had just witnessed. "I had no idea it was like this. I mean, he told me a little bit, but not that he was hurting this way. I should have known. I should have found out so I could help him."

Rhiannon pursed her lips, weighing her words carefully. "He doesn't want you to be hurt by this as well. That's all. It's not that he doesn't want your help, he just feels he needs to deal with it on his own."

Liam wrapped an arm around her shoulders and began walking, knowing he'd feel better once he could sit down and really think this all through.

When they made it to his room and stepped inside, he shut the door and sat on the bed, beckoning Rhiannon to sit with him. He pulled her close, needing her presence as a cold, harsh reality settled bitterly into his stomach.

"She never loved him," he murmured, shutting his eyes and pressing his face into her hair. "My mother…she never loved my dad. They only got married so they could have Cilla and me. It was basically arranged. God…he's never told me that."

Rhiannon curled against him. "I think he thought that over time, she would love him as much as he loves her. But maybe she's just not capable of it."

"I just don't understand." He pulled away so he could look at her. "How can you fool someone that way? It's so damn cruel."

Rhiannon reached up to touch his face, a soft smile upon her lips. "You've never been cruel, Liam. That's why you don't understand it."

His eyes searched hers, his brow furrowing with frustration and pain and disbelief as his hands came up to frame her face. This was real, this love he felt for Rhiannon, what he had right in front of him. And she loved him in return. It wasn't fake, it wasn't make-believe…

"Tell me, Rhia. Tell me you love me. Let me know that you mean it. Please," he groaned. His hands fisted in her hair, bringing her closer. A sharpening awareness flashed in her eyes as her hands roamed over his chest.

"I love you, Liam," she told him, her green eyes serious and focused upon his. "I always will, I promise you."

And when he kissed her, he truly believed in his heart that his love for her, and her love for him, was all they would ever need.

Though he'd been upset about his parents and their marriage, there was little he could do about it. And Lord, it was frustrating.

During the next few days, his father was his normal, cheerful self, revealing none of the misery he must have been feeling. Knowing his father was holding back his emotions simply to save face was annoying the hell out of Liam.

Maybe there wasn't anything he could actually do, but he still wanted his father to know he was there for him if he needed to vent his frustrations. But every time Liam brought it up, his father would change the subject as if it were the least important matter in the world.

So what was he supposed to do? He wasn't as skilled as his father at concealing his emotions, and he was having a hell of a time not exploding at his mother over her insensitivity. He was certain she knew he was angry with her. Either she wasn't bothered by it or she simply didn't want a confrontation to find out why he was upset. Instead, she kept to herself and clung to Serendipity and the other Muses all hours of the day, a constant supporter for that horrid woman and her scheming to get Rohan back.

And that was another matter altogether…Rohan and his sudden insistence on expressing his emotions and living life to the fullest. It should have been a good thing. Hell, it was a great thing. But it was irritating Rhiannon and therefore affecting him as well.

On one ill-fated occasion he'd gone into the kitchen to grab a snack and drop in on her, and she'd been in a shrewish mood, irritable and exhausted. He had tried to comfort her but it only made her angry.

"I don't need to be coddled, Liam, I just need some time to myself," she spat, which only succeeded in making him defensive and irritable as well.

"Don't take this out on me, Rhia, I didn't do anything to you." He crossed his arms and leaned against the door jamb to the little greenhouse off the kitchen, eyeing her resentfully. "I can't control the way your dad behaves."

"I know that," Rhiannon shot back, annoyed with herself when she heard the prissiness in her voice. "I'm just sick of him getting into these childish, brutal arguments with Brock and then letting it sour his mood for the whole day. He's a grown man. He's supposed to be more mature than this. In fact, up until recently, he *was* more mature than this. I don't know what he's thinking."

"He's trying out this whole 'freedom of expression' thing," Liam reminded her. "Look, this will all blow over. He just needs time to adjust. I think he and Brock need to sit down and have a long talk about the past, and try and come to some sort of resolution."

Rhiannon frowned as she considered his words. "I just don't know if either of them will ever get over it. They are both too proud and convinced they are not at fault." She shrugged, though her mouth curved into a tired smile. "It's like a ram going up against a bull, both of equal strength and both too stubborn to give an inch to the other side."

Liam chuckled and shook his head wearily. "I don't want our parents' bullshit to come between us, okay? It's not fair to either of us to let them influence our relationship, whether they mean to or not."

In response she moved close to him and tilted her head up, meeting his lips as her arms circled around his back. "I'm sorry, you're right," she said as she broke the kiss, her eyes searching his, humor in them now. "If our family was the slightest bit normal, I bet we wouldn't have any of these problems."

He snorted out a laugh, still holding her against him. "Nothing about any of us will ever be normal, Rhia, even you and I."

"I think I'm fairly normal," she said stiffly although a bemused look crossed her face. "I'm definitely the most normal out of us all.'

"Not a chance. But you are by far the most beautiful. In fact…" Something wicked flashed in his eyes as they darkened to a deeper, more glorious blue, and a sly smile spread over his lips as he spoke. "I've been thinking about this all day."

He suddenly lifted her up by her hips and planted her swiftly on the surface of her workbench, his hands roaming over her body possessively. Her answering giddy laugh died the second he crushed her mouth with his own and took possession of it.

Her legs wrapped around his waist and she clung to him as he pressed against her, eager to devour her in one, delicious bite. The sudden urge to have her, then and there, was too much to resist, and by the way she responded to him, both with her body and her voice, he knew she was just as seduced as he was.

"Liam." She broke the kiss and looked behind her, a gasping laugh escaping her throat as she tried to breathe and regain some semblance of control. "There's a pot sticking into my back."

He reached behind her and shoved the pot, along with everything else, gleefully to the floor. The ceramic hit with a shattering crash and scattered rich brown soil across the tiles. He heard her laugh again, a bit deliriously, and couldn't help but smile. He loved it when she was like this, so caught up in a moment that she forgot to react in her usual, carefully planned out way, and consequently threw caution to the wind. It was the Rhia that was free, and being with her was a kind of drug to him. He absolutely and positively couldn't get enough.

"I'll clean it up, don't worry," he said, his hands nimbly opening the buttons of her soft blue blouse even as he shrugged out of his own shirt.

Her eyes met his as her lips curved, slow and dangerous. "You'd better."

That night, they sat on one of the long sofas together, holding hands and people watching.

Liam enjoyed the calm times like this, when he could simply be with her, comforted by her presence and centered by the knowledge that everything he'd ever fought for had now been won. She'd come to him, after all his years of waiting, and made him the happiest he'd ever been. And from the look in her eyes when she glanced at him, he'd say he was doing a pretty good job at making her happy as well.

Thinking of their rendezvous in the greenhouse earlier that day, he leaned in to whisper something in her ear that had her clutching his hand tighter and biting her bottom lip. He reached out to tilt her face toward his own, and kissed her lushly.

For over an hour, they sat and stared out at their family, whispering to each other and laughing, enjoying all the mini dramas that seemed so prevalent on Euphora. Clynn was arguing politics with Lucian, while Rohan was with Sebastian discussing some historical event Liam had never heard of. Clarity was with Serendipity and the other Muses, including his little sister, and they were all huddled together near the grand piano, with Trinity playing a soft, sweet song.

Thea was with Brock and the Fates, looking radiant as always. Liam had always admired Thea, and respected her with both reverence and wonder. She had really been his first love, until Rhiannon of course. But when he'd been a baby, his father said that he wanted nothing more than to be held by the lovely and powerful Thea. And then Rhiannon had come into the world, and he'd found the true love of his life.

Rian and Capri were on the sofa beside him, along with Brogan, who was busy discussing some sort of Fury business regarding an American Senator with Rian. Capri looked politely interested, but her eyes kept wandering over to where Blythe was sitting, looking agitated and sipping wine with Jax while he kicked back and quietly read a book.

When Liam followed Capri's eyes, he noticed why she looked so anxious. Blythe was glaring at both her father and her mother, and there was fire brimming under the surface, he was sure of it. She was clearly trying to reign in some kind of frustrated urge, and he could only hope she found a way to release it safely before she exploded.

"What's wrong?" Rhiannon nudged him, looking concerned at the apprehension in his eyes.

"Blythe's pissed off about something," he murmured, frowning. "I should probably go talk to her."

Rhiannon nodded as he began to stand up, but it was already too late.

Blythe shot to her feet and bolted straight for her mother, Nyxa, getting in the woman's face in a flash.

"*I'm sick of this!*" she snarled, angrily stabbing a finger into Nyxa's chest, her eyes on fire.

Jax tossed aside his book and was about to rise to his feet to stop her, but when she shot a warning glare his way, he hesitated. He wasn't about to get in the middle of that hell storm, not while she was still the aggressor. If she got herself in trouble, then he'd step in, regardless of what she said. He wasn't going to let her get hurt over her own fiery temper.

"Sick of what?" Nyxa growled in return, shoving Blythe's hand away, her own face twisted with haughty rage.

"Now Blythe, calm down," Brock said suddenly, placing his hands on his daughter's shoulders to steer her away from Nyxa.

She just smacked his hands away and turned on him. "I'm sick of both of you ignoring me like I'm not even around anymore. You guys got back together and now suddenly I don't exist!"

"That's not true, babydoll." Brock reached out to her again, only to have her back away furiously. Instead he simply tucked his hands into the pockets of his jeans and tried a consoling smile. "I come to work with you as often as you've asked me, don't I?"

Blythe dramatically rolled her eyes. "Sure, fine, congratulations. But that doesn't make up for blowing me off all the other times I want to hang out with you. We're supposed to be rekindling this father/daughter relationship that we never got to have, and instead you're giving all your attention to *her*."

"You selfish little brat–"

"Nyxa, stop." Thea stepped in, sending a warning look at the woman before she did something she'd regret. The three of them were hotheads so Thea treaded carefully to help resolve the issue. "Brock, your daughter is upset with you, and you should really listen to her and see if there's anything you can do to help."

He rolled his eyes before he could stop himself, which only infuriated Blythe more.

"*Are you kidding me right now?*" she exploded, shoving him with as much force as she could muster. He barely moved, but stepped back in shock. With tears in her eyes, she glared up at him furiously. "You just don't care about me, do you?"

From the sofa, Liam watched the scene unfold with a mixture of sympathy, pain and anger. And when he saw the hot tears of anger spilling over Blythe's cheeks, he started to get to his feet, unable to watch any longer. He hadn't even noticed she'd been dealing with this and for God knows how long. Had he just been too consumed by his own family drama to notice?

Before Liam could even get out of his seat, Jax was already at Blythe's side, staring Brock down fiercely, his arms wrapping around her in a sign of support and unity.

Thea, recovering from the shock of what she was witnessing, stepped between Brock and Blythe, her eyes stern. "I think it would be best for the two of you to work this out, peacefully, in private." She looked at both of them, keeping her voice level despite the thrumming adrenaline in her veins.

Brock nodded, anguish in his eyes as Nyxa came up beside him, wrapping her arms around him possessively. He barely seemed to notice.

Blythe wiped heatedly at the tears that had managed to fall, and thanked God Jax was by her side. Her knees were trembling from the emotions raging through her and she wasn't quite certain if she could stand on her own.

"Let's go, Jax," she murmured, steering him out of the parlor. He glared at Brock before shutting the doors behind them.

Liam sat back down, looking relieved, but hurt. Rhiannon reached for his hand, holding it gently.

"You're used to her needing you," she said gently, nudging him out of his reverie so he would look at her.

"It's always been up to either me or my dad to take care of her. She didn't have anyone else when we took her in. I guess it's weird to pass that torch to someone else…she doesn't really need me."

"It's not that she doesn't need you anymore." Rhiannon squeezed his hand supportively. "She just needs you in a different way now."

He nodded, understanding but having a hard time accepting. In a lot of ways, he still thought of Blythe as a little girl needing his protection. After Capri had been taken, and Rhiannon had been sheltered and distanced, Blythe had been all he'd had. It was hard giving a part of her up, even though he really liked the man he was giving her up to.

Attempting to smile, he released Rhiannon's hand and wrapped his arm over her shoulders instead, pulling her close to him so he could comfortably rest his head on hers.

When his eyes drifted over to Brock, they narrowed with disappointment. He'd expected better of the man, at least in regards to Blythe. As much as she loved Lucian, she still wanted to know her own father. Even if he was somewhat of an arrogant ass most of the time.

Maybe Rhiannon was right. If Brock couldn't even commit to being a father to Blythe, how was he ever going to commit to a peaceful understanding with Rohan over their rocky and bitter past?

Perhaps it was a simple answer…he wouldn't.

Chapter Four

Am I overdressed? I mean, we are going to New York City, but…"

"Honey, you look gorgeous, so shut the hell up." Blythe shot Capri a quick grin and a wink as she fussed with her hair in the mirror over the dresser in Capri's bedroom.

Capri pouted, staring down at her classic gray slacks and elegant white blouse, accompanied by a simple string of pearls Rian had given her a few months before.

"At least these shoes will be comfortable. I expect we'll be doing a lot of walking," she put in, smiling sweetly and admiring her simple black flats.

Rhiannon popped into the room, looking distracted as she ran through her trip check list in her mind. She had plenty of cash for their purchases, a cell phone she'd gotten from Thea in case there was an emergency, a map of New York City with prime wedding dress shops and highly reviewed restaurants circled, and…

"Aw, now see, this one's overdressed," Blythe declared, putting her hands on her hips and staring at

Rhiannon accusingly. "You look like you're going to a corporate business meeting."

Rhiannon stared down at her slender black pencil skirt and scarlet red silk blouse. "I always dress this way," she replied, tilting her head up defensively. "Besides, we are going to some very expensive stores since Capri deserves only the very best, and the clerks will expect a certain amount of class from their customers or else they will not take us seriously."

She stared at Blythe's cut up faded Levis and simple white t-shirt, complete with practical sneakers that had seen better days.

"What?" Blythe snapped, temper flashing in her eyes. "You think I care what some prissy bitches at some fancy dress store think? We're trying on clothes, ergo, it's best to wear something casual so it's easy to take on and off."

Rhiannon was about to mention how it would be in Capri's best interest to blend in with the high society crowd of Fifth Avenue, but held her tongue at Capri's look of distress. They were supposed to be getting along now and putting aside their obvious differences, and if she had to be the bigger person and give in this time then so be it.

"You make a good point," she said before turning to Capri, ignoring Blythe's derisive snort. "I have a map with the best bridal stores circled on it, and I was able to do some research and we should have plenty of dresses to choose from in the color you want."

"Perfect!" Capri excitedly clapped her hands together, smiling at the two of them. "Oh, I should grab some money...I think I have a little bit stashed in my dresser..."

"Don't worry about the money, it's taken care of." Rhiannon reached out to stop her, her lips curving into a warm smile.

"Yeah, you didn't think we'd make you buy your own wedding dress, did you?" Blythe slipped an arm over Capri's shoulders with a grin.

"I don't know what to say," Capri managed, her eyes filling as she looked from Rhiannon to Blythe.

"Just say thank you so we can get going." Blythe winked at Rhiannon before turning to Capri, who let out a shaky laugh and threw her arms around her.

"Thank you." She spun away from Blythe and hugged Rhiannon, who felt her own eyes welling with tears.

"You're very welcome," Rhiannon murmured, pulling away to smile at her friend.

"Hey, where're you guys going?" Liam shuffled in suddenly, a half eaten apple in his hand that he cheerfully took a bite of as he stood before them.

"Dress shopping in New York," Blythe informed him, already revved to go. "Wanna come?"

"Mmm…shopping's not really my scene," he began, getting that nervous male look on his face that came from dreading an onslaught of female pressure.

"Oh, but you have to come! Why didn't I think of this before?" Capri looked a bit embarrassed but beamed prettily at him all the same, her gray eyes sparkling with humor. "You still have to get fitted for a suit."

"I'm going with Rian and Brogan to get a suit."

"They already have theirs." Capri bit her lip, trying to hold back a laugh at the look of horror and betrayal in his eyes.

He glanced over to Rhiannon for confirmation, and she merely smiled. "I've seen Brogan's suit, it's very classy. He told me which store he purchased it from…it's conveniently also in New York."

"Well, damn." He looked properly deflated as he scowled at Blythe, who had let out a hoot of laughter.

"Come on, it's not so bad. You get to hang with three beautiful women all day," she told him, wrapping an arm around him. "Perk up, or we'll make sure to take extra time fawning over lingerie for the wedding night."

"Lingerie, huh?" His eyes lit up as he looked straight at Rhiannon, who let out an impatient sigh.

"Not for me." She scowled, crossing her arms over her chest. "We're just going to get a couple of things for Capri."

"Mmm hmm." He grinned, winking at her before turning to the other girls. "So, we leaving or what?"

Liam had only one word to describe New York City: exhilarating.

They'd arrived in a secluded section of Central Park, and had trekked their way out along winding pathways surrounded by enormous leafy trees and wide areas of open grass. It was a warm, sunny day in the Big Apple, and with the heavy humidity of lingering summer he knew it was going to heat up substantially during their visit.

Buildings sprouted up out of the ground all around them, bursting up toward the sky with windows that glittered in the morning sunlight. On the roads, cars honked and people sped swiftly down the sidewalks, heads down and content to be a part of the bustling madhouse that was city life. He personally preferred quieter and calmer scenes, but for the moment he was enjoying the speed and anonymity of urbanites. And with the three girls beside him, he could enjoy their reactions to the city as well as his own.

Capri was staring around in absolute wonder and excitement. She had never been to the city before, and the pleasure she felt just to be experiencing every little detail that was so foreign to her was obvious in her expression of pure, unadulterated delight.

Blythe, not unused to city life and accustomed to New York City in particular, was strutting around brimming with confidence and well worn city ethics. She scanned the crowds seemingly indifferently, but he knew she was looking out for possible danger. Cities harbored all kinds of strange and potentially harmful people, and a smart city dweller always kept their eyes peeled for trouble.

Rhiannon had her reading glasses on and her face buried in her map of the city, busy locating the shop they needed to hit first. He had to keep his arm around her to steer her through the crowded sidewalk, but he didn't mind much. Without her practical ways, they'd wander aimlessly through the city for hours and accomplish next to nothing. As she was fond of saying to him, someone had to be the responsible adult in the group.

"Okay, so we have to go several blocks south to get to the first store. I think the fastest and easiest way would be to take a cab. Our appointment is at ten, and it's already nine thirty, so we don't have much time," Rhiannon said suddenly, unearthing herself from the map to stare at them owlishly through her reading glasses.

"Oh, I've never hailed a cab before," Capri said nervously, glancing around at the busy street.

"It's no big deal." Blythe flashed a quick smile as she stepped to the edge of the sidewalk and threw her arm out aggressively, waving at a cab that was cruising through the traffic. It swung toward them and stopped briskly in front of her. "See, that wasn't so tough."

Liam let the girls file in first before he climbed in and shut the door. It was a tight fit for four people, but they had managed it.

Rhiannon read off the address to the cab driver, who immediately pulled away and skillfully maneuvered through the traffic to take them to their destination.

After they'd arrived and Rhiannon had paid the cab driver with exact change plus a generous tip, they poured out of the car and stared up at the first store on their list.

"Oh my." Capri held a hand up to her mouth to hide the giddy smile on her face. "Look at those dresses in the window!"

Blythe followed Capri to peer through the glass and marvel at the dresses on display, while Rhiannon hung back with Liam, recounting the money inside her purse.

"I'm sure you brought plenty of money, Rhia." Liam slung his arm over her shoulder casually and grinned around at nothing in particular.

"Well, I brought twenty thousand, I hope that's enough for all of us…these dress stores are quite expensive."

"Jesus, Rhia." Liam glanced around nervously, though in typical New York fashion, none of the pedestrians were paying any attention to them. "You shouldn't advertise having that kind of cash."

"I wasn't advertising it," she grumbled, though she immediately zipped up her purse and clutched it a little tighter. "Well, should we go in?"

He kept his arm firmly around her and turned toward Blythe and Capri, who were focusing on a wedding gown that looked like something straight out of Cinderella.

"Alright, stop ogling the merchandise. There's plenty more to see inside," Liam called out as he walked with Rhiannon over to the other girls, who shot him distinctively feminine dirty looks.

"Just like a man, wanting to rush everything," Blythe huffed, though her lips curved into a devilish grin. "C'mon, Capri, let's go find that dress in your size."

"We have to sign in first, they most likely won't take us until exactly ten, and it's only…" Rhiannon glanced at her watch dutifully, "nine-fifty two."

Blythe rolled her eyes and reached for Capri's hand as she glanced over her shoulder at Rhiannon. "You take care of signing us in or whatever, since you're so good at it. We'll just go walk around."

Though the comment was more than a little snarky, Rhiannon took it in stride. She'd had no intention of letting Blythe handle anything other than tending to Capri anyway. Blythe's tomboyish ways would do nothing but insult their dress consultant, she was sure of it.

Liam held her closer and kissed the top of her head. "If I know you as well as I think I do, you want her to stay the hell away from the dress people."

Rhiannon shot a glance up at him and smirked. "If she can manage to, we'll have a much more pleasant experience."

They headed into the store and approached the counter, and while Rhiannon was checking in, Liam took in the surroundings a bit warily, like a man entering some foreign land he heard harbors both beautiful and dangerous things.

The ceiling was two stories high and coffered, with gilded floral accents and Corinthian columns descending down to the pale gold polished travertine floor. The front desk looked like something out of a Greek palace, graced with miniature columns and flanked by decorative roses and gold leaves.

While the store was large, it was surprisingly calm and quiet, despite several groups of women strolling around looking at the vast displays of dresses on both racks and on mannequins. Soft, lilting music played overhead, and he could smell the distinct scent of jasmine flowers.

Feeling extraordinarily out of place, he shoved his hands awkwardly into his jeans pockets and waited for Rhiannon to finish signing in. A group of young girls that looked like they were barely out of high school walked past him and stared, and on instinct he smiled politely. When they burst into giggles and raced off, he frowned in confusion.

Rhiannon stepped toward him with a full catalog of all the dresses and accessories cradled in her arms, her eyes on the girls as they disappeared around a corner. Amused, she looked up at Liam's confused expression and couldn't help but smile.

"They think you're cute," she told him, surprised he looked so awkward. He had always been such a charmer and a flirt; she'd been convinced he was that way with every girl.

He managed a half smile, but shot a look over his shoulder toward where the girls had gone anyway. "All I did was smile at them."

"And you should know that any girl with a pulse would get weak kneed at the sight of that smile," Rhiannon purred, tilting her face up to his, inviting him in with a slow curve of her lips.

"Is that so?" His hands came around to grasp her waist, bringing her in closer until his mouth was brushing over hers. "And here it was I thought you fell for my sense of humor."

"It certainly didn't hurt." She sighed when he kissed her, and silently thanked God he was hers.

"Excuse me, Miss O'Connor?" A slender and elegant woman with cropped black hair and raven eyes questioned, one eyebrow raised at the couple before her. It was highly uncustomary for a client to bring her fiancé to a wedding gown fitting…but, then again, she'd seen weirder things in her time.

Rhiannon broke apart from Liam and faced the woman, fighting to regain her composure. For a brief moment she hadn't recognized the name, since it was only a name she used when in the human world.

"Yes, hello." She smiled politely, holding out her hand to take the woman's. "You must be Eileen?"

"Yes, it's lovely to meet you." Eileen shot a curious glance at Liam, who was lingering behind Rhiannon, looking more than a little nervous. "And are you the husband to be?"

Liam looked at the woman questioningly, his eyebrows raised, but Rhiannon cut in to correct her.

"No, no, the appointment isn't for me. I scheduled it for my friend Capri. We're not engaged." Annoyed that she felt flustered, Rhiannon cleared her throat and let out a calming breath. "She's over there, looking at the jewelry."

Eileen spun around and spotted the tall, willowy blonde and the spunky redhead browsing the earrings section before turning back to Rhiannon.

"Well, let's collect them and we can get started." She smiled, motioning with her arm before leading the way toward the private dressing rooms.

About an hour later, Liam sat comfortably on the guest sofa in their own private dressing area, looking laid back and entertained while the girls were locked in dressing rooms trying on the gowns Eileen had brought them. Capri had tried on three different dresses so far, none of which had passed the test, and Blythe was on her fifteenth dress. But Rhiannon had been locked in her dressing room with her one and only dress for over half an hour, and he was starting to wonder if she had fallen asleep in there.

But when the door cracked open slightly, and he saw her peek her head out cautiously, he grinned.

"You alright in there?" he asked, humor in his eyes at the scowl she sent his way.

"I'm just fine," she replied defensively, glancing around to be sure the coast was clear. "Can I show you this dress and get your honest opinion?" she asked, eyeing him pleadingly. "Don't lie if it looks bad, okay? I want the truth."

"Okay." He nodded, still smiling.

But when she stepped out of the dressing room and into full view, his grin faded and his eyes widened.

"Wow," he managed, sitting up to focus on her. "Seriously, Rhia. Wow."

She bit her lip skeptically and spun around so he could see the whole thing, all the while examining herself critically in the tall mirrors that covered the walls.

"I don't know, I think it may be a bit too long in the back. It should probably be taken up a few inches, and definitely taken in a bit at the waist…"

He was already rising to his feet as she continued to critique the dress, unable to take his eyes off her. He thought of the ring that was still tucked away safely in his pocket, and the desire to give it to her then and there washed over him in one all encompassing wave. But he pushed the feeling aside, knowing there would be more opportune moments to come…

The dress was made of dusty rose colored silk, and fell long to her feet. It hugged the slender curves of her hips and cinched in at her waist, tied back with an elegant oversized bow at the back. The bodice was v-necked and hung seductively low, with thin straps hanging on her shoulders. She'd swept up her dark hair with a clip on top of her head, revealing the smooth curve of her neck and the arch of her back.

Though she hadn't stopped talking, he stepped toward her and spun her around, capturing her mouth with his and cutting off her words instantly. She gave in, a burst of surprised pleasure coursing through her.

When he pulled away, he eyed her seriously. "If you don't get this dress, I might have to kill myself."

She laughed and laid her head against his shoulder, curling into him as his arms came around her.

"I guess I'll be getting it then." She looked up at him and smiled. "I wouldn't want to have to explain to your father why you couldn't stand to live anymore."

"Trust me, if he could see you right now, he'd completely understand." He grinned and kissed her again, his hands trailing down along her sides. She shivered beneath his touch and deepened the kiss as his hands made their way seductively to the open back of the dress.

"Ew, God, get a room," Blythe groaned, coming out of her dressing room and immediately covering her eyes as Liam and Rhiannon separated.

Capri came out at the same time, but what she saw had happy tears coming into her eyes.

"You guys are so perfect," she sighed, clasping her hands together with a bright smile.

But they were all suddenly staring in silent reverence at the gown Capri was wearing, which was the same one from the window display. It had a full tulle skirt graced with tiny white flowers, and a heart shaped, strapless bodice with a scattering of tiny pearls and more flowers on it.

Liam couldn't hold back a smile, and he was touched by the purity of her, the quiet loveliness that only she could capture with such grace.

"You look beautiful," he told her, walking over to kiss her on the cheek. "Rian's not going to know what hit him."

Capri blushed, brushing at the full skirt nervously. "Really? You guys like it?"

"Honey, you look like a dream." Blythe had to brush back the tears in her eyes as she walked over to hug Capri. "It's so perfect for you. I knew it the moment I saw it."

"I feel very...pretty." Capri laughed, turning around to look in the mirror. "Do you like it, Rhiannon?"

Rhiannon watched her friend and had to fight back the urge to cry. "It looks like it was made for you," she said serenely, resting her hand on Capri's shoulder as their eyes in the mirror. "I guess I should cancel our appointments at the other bridal stores."

"Yeah, I'm happy with this dress," Blythe said suddenly, twirling around to showcase the knee length dress made of the same dusty rose silk. It was strapless and whimsical, with a flower made of the same silk material pinned to the middle of the bodice. "Are you happy with yours, Rhiannon?"

Rhiannon nodded, and Capri reached out to wrap an arm around each of the girls. "We all look beautiful. Right, Liam?"

They all turned to look at him, each smiling in their own unique way, and he felt his heart fill with love for all of them. Capri with her quiet, caring nature and dry humor. Blythe, wild and restless but loyal to the bone, always ready to fight for what was right. And Rhiannon...serious natured but generous and kind, with a backbone made of steel and a sharply intelligent mind.

They were his family and he loved all of them.

And seeing the three of them, standing together with their arms around each other and smiles on their faces, he couldn't help but feel both pride and relief that they were no longer divided. Those days were in the past and all they had left was what would hopefully be a bright and glorious future.

"I have never seen three more beautiful women in all my life." He tucked his hands into his pockets and grinned at them. "So, do I get to try on tuxes now and have you girls fawn over me?"

Blythe rolled her eyes but laughed all the same. "Sure, if that's what you want. Now come on, we gotta get shoes and jewelry and then we can hit up the tux section for you."

While Blythe and Capri spoke with Eileen about accessories, Liam reached for Rhiannon's hand and kissed it, eyeing her suggestively.

"You know, since Eileen is so busy, maybe I could come on in there and help you out of this dress," he murmured, kissing her hand again before straightening and pulling her against him. "Whaddya say?"

She pursed her lips and frowned in Eileen's direction. "I'm almost certain that's a violation of store policy. We wouldn't want them to kick us out."

"No, I guess we wouldn't." He leaned in to kiss her nose playfully. "Well, then I fully expect you to slip into this thing the moment we get home so I can get you right back out of it again."

She laughed and smiled up at him, one eyebrow cocked questioningly. "And if I say no?"

Humor flashed with the desire in his eyes. "I can be very persuasive."

After the shopping was complete, they treated themselves to a late lunch at an elegant café, which according to Rhiannon's carefully studied research, was one of the most popular spots in town. And Liam had to admit, it had great atmosphere.

The entire place was decorated like a Parisian café, with lush pink flowers hanging from baskets on the walls and wrought iron adorning the tables, chairs, and fencing in the outdoor patio. Well worn rustic tiles the color of sand laid on the floor, and a live band played soothing piano and violin in the corner.

They sat at a round table beneath a rustic chandelier with dripping crystals that caught the light, surrounded by people happily chattering away while they feasted on exquisite French cuisine.

Liam scanned the menu, passing over any item with a name he couldn't understand. Settling on a sandwich, he ordered a beer to go with it and sat back to enjoy himself.

"I don't know…." Capri was saying, eyeing the glass of champagne Blythe was forcing on her apprehensively. "We still have to get back to Central Park, and I don't think me being drunk is going to help any."

Blythe snorted out a laugh and shoved the glass into Capri's hand. "Worse comes to worse, Liam will carry you. Now drink up and enjoy yourself, this is your day."

Capri shot an embarrassed glance at Liam. "I won't do that to you."

He only grinned. "As long as I don't have to carry more than one of you at a time, I'll be fine."

She still didn't look convinced, but took a tentative sip of the champagne anyway. The bubbles burst on her tongue as she swallowed, and she took another quick sip before setting down the glass on the table. "Champagne has grown on me. I really didn't like it at first."

"Your tastes are more refined now," Rhiannon said, taking a sip from her own glass.

"I still prefer beer, but because we're celebrating getting our dresses I'll stick with the bubbly." Blythe downed her glass and grinned. "So, who wants to hear my plan to get Brogan laid?"

At Blythe's words, Rhiannon started choking on her champagne, coughing into her hand as Liam patted her back and laughed at Blythe.

"What's this, now?" he asked, rubbing Rhiannon's back as the coughing fit subsided. She glared at Blythe with watery eyes, unsure if she was amused or mortified.

Blythe simply grinned. "Well, now that we're getting along or whatever, I figured it was my step-sisterly duty to help him out. I don't think he gets to meet too many people, and Jax knows some good girls down in Texas that I got to meet when I was there recently. I think there's one or two of them that he might click with."

"I don't think Brogan would appreciate you playing matchmaker," Rhiannon began, shaking her head and fearing for her quiet, good natured friend. "He's very shy, I don't know if he could handle you springing some girl on him."

Blythe waved the thought away. "He'll be fine. Besides, he's gonna have to put himself out there eventually."

Rhiannon looked momentarily stumped, and Liam had a feeling that she agreed with Blythe at least on that part. He shifted his gaze to Capri, who was sitting between the two other girls, glancing curiously from one to the other.

"I think it could do him some good. He's gotta break out of his shell at some point," Liam added, absorbing the skeptical look Rhiannon sent his way.

"I don't know." Rhiannon took a deep breath and let it out, working through all the angles of it in her head. "Maybe you should let me talk to him first. I think he'd be more willing to go along with this if I present the idea."

"Good point," Blythe conceded as the waiter came by to refill her champagne glass. Lifting it up for a toast, she smiled to all of them. "To working together for the first time in fifteen years."

Rhiannon laughed, shaking her head as she held up her glass as well. "To working together, period."

Liam sipped his beer and watched his fellow Dryads talking, laughing, and enjoying themselves in each other's company. Just how long had he waited for moments like this? Too long, he thought regretfully. But now, everything was so perfect that it appeared as though nothing could destroy the peace they had finally found.

If only he had known then just how wrong he was.

Chapter Five

As the days went by, everyone was more preoccupied with the upcoming wedding than with thoughts of Dante. Liam was certain it was because it had been over two weeks without any real update on his whereabouts and therefore many of them simply brushed Dante's threat off as nothing more than empty words.

He knew that Jax, Brogan and Rian had all been diligently working with the Enforcers to hunt him down, but little had been discovered. Clearly, he had dropped off the radar for the time being, either because he was plotting something or because he had decided to go into hiding.

He sincerely hoped it was the latter.

They'd eventually find him. That much he could believe in. But whether or not the shit would hit the fan before they did was what worried him most.

Thea was working with the Muses on how to decorate the courtyard and the castle for the wedding, and was focusing nearly all of her attention on it. He worried about that, thinking her being distracted was foolish, but he figured that she had been around long enough to know best. And Sebastian was still keeping an eye on the Dante situation, so if anything came up it would likely be snuffed out before it could cause real damage. At least he hoped that would be the case.

And so he started his day just like any other day, only to notice his father wasn't present during breakfast. Curious, but not overly concerned, he made his way to Water Tower, an extra cup of coffee in his hand to stem off his restlessness from the night before. Worrying over Dante had him losing sleep, and this impending doom that had come over him the last few days was weighing on his mind. Why did he have this sickening feeling that something bad was going to happen...and soon?

Attempting to shrug it off, he jogged up the steps to the tower and opened the door, relieved when he spotted his father inside, working with the globe.

"Hey," he greeted, sipping his coffee as he crossed the little wooden bridge.

Lucian let out a huff of breath and looked extraordinarily stressed, his long white hair sticking up in places and his eyes hard as steel as he focused on the globe, his hands working to enhance the view of what looked like the Gulf.

"Mini crisis this morning, boyo," Lucian said, meeting his son's eyes solemnly. "An oil rig in the Gulf of Mexico sprung a leak. We've got oil everywhere."

Liam cursed under his breath and set his coffee aside on the workbench, approaching the globe to see what his father was looking at. "How bad is it?"

"Not too bad so far, as they appear to have capped it off already. But I have to go down there to evaluate the damage and repair what I can onsite."

"Don't worry about it, I'll go." Liam placed a hand on his weary father's shoulder, concern in his eyes. "You don't look so hot, old man."

Lucian sighed, wiping at the sweat that had begun to bead on his forehead. "I didn't sleep very well, but I'll be alright."

"Stress?"

"A feeling of dread." Lucian shook his head, feeling foolish for even saying it. He looked at his son and tried to smile. "Tell you what, you go on down to the Gulf and I'll let you play hooky for the rest of the afternoon. Maybe you can take that girl of yours out to a late lunch."

Liam grinned. "Deal. Now you go lie down, take a break, whatever. When I get back I don't want to hear that you've been working."

"Mmm." Lucian smiled and turned around, preparing to close out his work for a couple of hours, thinking that perhaps a nap would indeed rest his nerves. "Be careful down there, Liam," he said with his back turned as Liam started to leave.

"Don't worry. I'll be back before you know it," Liam assured him as he swept from the tower and shut the door.

Though neither knew it, both father and son felt an abrupt, unnerving shiver run over them the minute the door shut, as if the hollow echoing sound of it foreboded what both of them had been sensing for days.

When he arrived in New Orleans, the sun had barely begun to rise in the east. He walked along the coastline, enjoying the sultry southern air and the sound of the salty waves coasting to the shore. In the distance he could see the oil rig, lit up with shimmering lights as the crew continued to tirelessly manage the spill. If his father was right, then they had the leak fixed by now, but there would still be more to do in the days to come.

A lot more, he thought as he glanced down at the water. Though he couldn't see it yet, he knew oil was floating over the surface of the waves in the distance, and would eventually make it to the shoreline. He would need to test the water and see just how much oil had leaked, and then decide what he could do to help.

Kneeling down beside the water, he slipped his hand in and closed his eyes, letting the images flood his mind of the spill and the levels of oil currently contaminating the water. Because it appeared that very little had leaked before they had stemmed the flow a few hours before, he let out a relieved sigh, pleased it wasn't as bad as he had been expecting.

Glancing at the oil rig with a knowing smile, he set out to help the men even though they would never know what he had done.

Focusing on the algae below the surface and along the ocean floor, he instructed it to absorb and devour the oil, thus over time cleansing the water. It was really the only way to fix the problem, and would help the humans as they tried to solve it using their own methods.

When he was finished, he rose to his feet as the sun crested over the horizon, bright and golden. Holding his hand over his eyes to shield them from the light, he watched the oil rig, feeling sorry for the humans onboard. Such things were a liability on the entire area, and many people would be affected before the algae and the humans were able to clear out the spilled oil. But at least he had done his part to help.

Turning around to head home, he stopped short when he spotted a woman watching him from a few yards away, her long honey blonde curls glowing gold in the sunlight. For a brief moment, it seemed almost as if she were ethereal, with a soft, silvery glow emanating from all around her, thrumming with power and an aura of intensity. But when he blinked, the impression was gone, and all he saw was a human girl, likely around his age, with sun kissed skin and a charming smile.

"Hi," she called out, waving to him as she approached. "Did you hear about the oil spill, too?"

She had a lilting southern accent and pretty blue eyes that fluttered flirtatiously at him. Sensing her intent, he shoved his hands into his pockets and smiled politely.

"Yup. Just came down to take a look," he told her, staring over her shoulder toward the trees where he had arrived only minutes before. He tried to work out in his mind a polite way to evade her and get home, but she spoke before he had the chance.

"It's a shame, all those poor little creatures in the water that are gonna die from all that oil." She eased toward him a bit more, her eyes focusing intently on his face. "Don't you think it's sad?"

"Everything will be okay, don't worry." He felt bad that she was so distraught, so he turned to her and smiled. And when his eyes locked on hers, he found it very hard to look away or even move, as if his entire body had almost instantly gone numb. His thoughts were frantic for a brief moment, before those too seemed to slow, as if his head was suddenly full of thick molasses, and all his thoughts were jumbled around inside, floating in chaotic disarray.

Her luminous blue eyes held his as her lips curved into a smirk, and suddenly he heard a voice inside his head that sounded like his own.

She's beautiful. I wonder what her name is?

As if on cue, he felt his mouth open and the question pour out. "What's your name?"

"I'm Stella," she replied, smiling again and holding out her hand for his. Instinctually, he took her hand and heard himself tell her his name, even as he stared down at their joined hands dully. What was happening to him? He had to get home…

"Are you from around here, Liam?" she asked, not releasing his hand immediately, as if she enjoyed his touch too much to let go. "I've never seen you before."

"No," he heard himself say, though he seemed to be floating in some kind of foggy haze inside his own mind, and even though part of him knew he should be concerned, he couldn't quite seem to summon the emotion. He couldn't seem to do much at all, except listen to the voice inside his head and listen to the words leave his mouth, without any concept of where they'd come from.

I'm just visiting....but I'd love to see New Orleans. Maybe she can show me around...

"I'm here visiting. I've never been to New Orleans before," he said as she finally released his hand. The skin where she had touched him felt odd, as if his hand had fallen asleep and the blood was finally working its way back into his fingers.

"I could take you on a little tour if you'd like, if you're not too busy?"

Not at all. I have nowhere to be today.

"No. Let's go."

Rhiannon sat at the butcher block island in the kitchen, working out a new recipe she wanted to try. Beside her were samples from her herb collection and a compilation of spices.

Since fall was just around the corner and it was Thea's favorite season, it was expected that there would be the usual dishes that came with the late harvest. Butternut squash, apples, cinnamon, sweet potatoes, pumpkin...she wanted fresh new ways to incorporate them all and still somehow maintain a healthy menu.

She sampled a bite of boiled squash with a mixture of a few herbs and some cinnamon, and was pleasantly surprised. It could make a good casserole, she mused, jotting down notes as she went. Liam loved squash...

She heard the door open and glanced up to see Brogan come in, a quiet smile curving his lips.

"Good afternoon," he said, bowing his head slightly as he walked toward her.

"Good afternoon," Rhiannon repeated, pointing to the chair beside her. "Have a seat."

He did as she requested, his eyes fixed on the ingredients in front of her.

"What are you working on?" he asked curiously, unsure he could even name half the things on the table.

She smiled warmly at him. "Fall recipes. I'm getting an early start so I don't have to worry about it later."

"We're barely through September yet." He chuckled, his dark eyes amused as he watched her. "But I know how you like to prepare."

"Indeed," she mused, swiftly putting together the same sample of squash she had just tried and handing it to him. "Tell me what you think of that."

He sniffed at it before eating it, less apprehensive than Liam usually was. Brogan had more faith in her culinary abilities. As he chewed, he nodded and met her eyes. "It's good, I like it."

She beamed. "I think it'll be good in a casserole, maybe with some sweet apples and raisins."

"How do you come up with all this stuff?" he asked, resting his chin in his hand and watching her with wonder. Whenever he looked at her that way she couldn't help but feel he was giving her more credit than she deserved.

"It's just knowing the flavors and experimenting with them, that's all," she told him, eyeing the ingredients as she did. "There are limitless possibilities."

"I see," he murmured, suddenly looking sheepish. "I came up here because Rian's been restless all day. It was driving me crazy." He laughed, embarrassed. "I hope you don't mind, I had to escape for awhile."

"Not at all," Rhiannon assured him, pushing aside her notebook and resting her elbows on the table. "What's he anxious about?"

He shrugged. "The wedding, I guess. It's a big step for him, and he's thrilled, but worried too in some ways. He hopes that he'll be good enough for her."

"Why wouldn't he be?" Her brows drew together in confusion as she shook her head. "She loves him."

"I think he just hopes he can give her everything she needs emotionally. He's devoted to her, but part of him worries that she deserves someone better than him. Someone who doesn't take everything so seriously."

"That's nonsense," Rhiannon huffed, looking insulted. "You can tell him that I have full faith in his ability to take care of Capri and that I would not approve of this marriage if that were not the case."

"Alright." He grinned, amused by the heat in her eyes. "Don't worry about it, though, he's crazy about her. He's not going to blow this."

"I'd hope not." She let out a sigh and then suddenly remembered the conversation she'd had with Blythe while they were in New York. She felt her face flush with embarrassment. Well, here was her opportunity to ask him… "Brogan, this is kind of embarrassing, but Blythe had this idea that maybe we could set you up on a date…"

"Excuse me?" he managed, surprise and alarm in his eyes as he stared at her, eyebrows raised incredulously.

She shrugged, hoping not to come across as nosy and insistent, which she was sure she was going to anyway. "She says that Jax knows some nice girls down in Texas and if you're interested maybe we could arrange something."

He gaped at her, caught off guard. "Well…I don't know what to say, Rhiannon."

"Oh, forget I said anything. I knew it would sound meddlesome." Rhiannon waved it away, embarrassed. "I'll tell her you said no."

"But I didn't say no," he said softly, his mouth curving into a shy smile.

She froze and then let out a shaky laugh. "Okay, good. Well, give it some thought and when you're ready let me know and we'll figure it out."

"Okay." He reached out for her hand, amusement in his eyes. "I'm humbled that both of you even thought this up. It's… strange, but maybe worth giving a shot."

"I know, it is strange." Rhiannon laughed, squeezing his hand. "But maybe it'll be—"

The door burst open suddenly and Lucian peered in, looking distraught.

"He's not here?" he asked, concern in his eyes as he glanced around despairingly.

"Who?" Rhiannon felt a jolt of fear pulse through her at the anxiety in Lucian's eyes.

"Liam. I don't think he's come back from New Orleans yet," he informed her, coming into the kitchen fully and shaking his head. He looked exhausted, and more than a little worse for the wear. "He was supposed to have been back hours ago."

Rhiannon glanced nervously at Brogan, who rose to his feet and eyed Lucian questioningly. "Have you seen Blythe? He could be with her."

"No, she's with Jax. She hasn't seen him since he left." Lucian wrung his hands together nervously. "It's possible he chose to make a day of seeing the city, but it's not like him to not let me know first. I'm probably just overreacting…"

"Lucian…" Rhiannon rose to her feet as well and went to him, fighting back her own anxiety. "I'm sure he's fine."

She placed a comforting hand on his shoulder, even though she knew it would do little to help since her own nerves were now pulsing through her system on high alert.

"I just can't shake this feeling of dread that I've had these past couple of days." Lucian scrubbed his face with his hands, feeling helpless. "I should have gone with him."

"Maybe we should go looking for him," Rhiannon said, shooting a nervous glance over her shoulder at Brogan.

He nodded, concern in his eyes. "I'd say if he's not back by dinner, then yes, we should."

When Liam still hadn't returned, they got together and went to look for him.

Rhiannon was sick with worry. She could only imagine the host of things that could have happened to him…he could have been hit by a car, shot at, in jail…he could be lying in a hospital bed somewhere, calling for her and she would have no idea. Feeling helpless was doing nothing but causing her grief, and as much as she tried to push it aside and stay positive, there was a portentous cloud shrouding her mind.

Tears burned behind her eyes as she rushed into the meadow with Lucian, Blythe and Jax, praying that it was all just a misunderstanding and that he was okay.

She had to hold on to that, couldn't let herself dread something worse. What would she do without him?

When they arrived on the shoreline in New Orleans, they had no idea if they were in the same spot as Liam or if they were miles from it.

Night was settling in on the Gulf and it was dark now. Overhead, the moon hung ominously heavy and full in the sky.

"Where should we start?" Blythe asked Jax, who'd already taken out his sensor that Rian had given him. He set it to Dryad and immediately began to scan the area.

"The coastline would have been his destination, so we should walk around here and see if we pick up anything," Jax said as he began to walk down the beach, watching the scanner for any sign of a Dryad other than the three behind him.

Blythe had her arm around Lucian and was trying to be positive, even though Rhiannon could see the panic in the other girl's eyes.

"Maybe he just fell asleep on the beach. Lazy bum," she was saying as she glanced all around them, trying to see through the darkness. She held out her palm and created a small ball of fire which acted as a torch to light their way.

Rhiannon said nothing as they walked, her arms crossed tightly around her chest as she looked out across the waves. She could see the lights from the oil rig far in the distance, and part of her wondered if somehow he was out there, working with the men to clean up the oil.

But no, he wouldn't have done that…Lucian said all he had to do was test the water and mend what he could from the shore. There would have been no need to go out on the water, much less to the rig itself…

A sudden beeping sound on Jax's device had her heart leaping into her throat as they all gathered around him, eager to see what he'd come across.

"It's faint, but there was a Dryad here hours ago," he told them, pointing to the strip of sand where the waves lapped onto the shore. His eyes then shot to the city streets not too far away. "It's possible he went into town."

"Maybe he wanted to get a beer at the local bar. I could see that," Blythe put in, nodding to Lucian. "Let's go walk the streets, see if we pick up anything else."

They trekked up the beach toward the street and headed into town. Though it wasn't as busy as New York City had been, there was still enough of a crowd to grace the sidewalks and enough cars to populate the streets. But Rhiannon saw none of it, could process none of it. All she could do was scan the faces of the crowd, and hope she'd see Liam among them, smiling at her.

"If he's been on the move, the sensor won't pick up on him. He'd have to stay in place for at least five minutes for it to detect his signature," Jax said, his eyes still focused on the sensor.

"I'm sure he wouldn't have gone that far," Lucian said out loud, glancing around at the people walking the streets, at the bustling night clubs and noisy restaurants.

"We'll find him, Lucian. Don't worry." Blythe rubbed his back as much to comfort herself as to comfort him as she stared around anxiously, her entire body thrumming with nerves and adrenaline.

Rhiannon walked beside them, feeling oddly alone and out of place. Without Liam with her, she didn't feel right being with Lucian and Blythe, much less Jax. But they were here because they loved Liam as much as she did, and were committed to finding him. So, she supposed that in some small way, perhaps she did belong with them...

"I should call the local hospitals, see if he's been admitted. There could have been an accident," Rhiannon said suddenly, unearthing the cell phone from her bag that Thea had given her days before.

"Good idea." Jax nodded at her, turning his eyes back to the sensor.

While Rhiannon spoke on the phone with the hospital staff, Blythe distanced herself from Lucian and went to Jax, lowering her voice so only he could hear her.

"Have you been checking for demons, too?" she asked, brushing against people walking on the sidewalk with them.

"I have. Nothing so far," Jax solemnly replied, glancing down at her sympathetically. Wrapping an arm over her shoulders, he planted a quick kiss on the top of her head. "He's around here somewhere. And when we find him, think of how much fun you'll have yelling at him for making you worry."

"True." She tried to smile, but couldn't fight back the uneasiness she felt. "Why do I have a feeling that Dante is behind this somehow?"

"Believe me, I've thought about it." Jax released her and looked back down at the device, which had begun to beep again. "It's picking up a strong signal from over there."

He pointed across the street to a rowdy nightclub, with sultry jazz and blues pouring out into the heavy summer night air. Blazing neon signs glowed in vivid blues and greens over the door, declaring the club as The Holler.

"Let's go." Blythe grabbed his hand and sprinted across the street, not waiting for Lucian and Rhiannon to get the hint and follow. She didn't have time for that; she had to find her brother...

They had to show ID's at the door, and thankfully Rhiannon had thought to bring not only hers but Blythe's as well, which handily labeled Blythe as twenty two year old Blythe Collier from California. Anyone who spotted them would simply see two anxious young women, a rough and tumble looking Texan, and a harried looking older man with a shock of white hair and weary eyes.

After the usual questioning looks from the bouncers, they managed to get inside.

They let Jax lead the way into the club, which was packed to the brim with people of all flavors...sultry looking women with gypsy faces, businessmen, gamblers, drunkards, pert college blondes...and the list went on and on. They maneuvered their way through the crowd, Jax glancing from the sensor and up again to the scan the room, hoping to spot Liam in what he had a hunch would be the back corner of the lounge area.

Rhiannon walked behind the others, chewing on her bottom lip anxiously and wringing her hands, uncomfortable with the environment and worried that the little ball of hope that had blossomed in her chest would burn out if they somehow had not found him...

When Blythe, Jax and Lucian all came to a screeching halt, she nearly ran into them. She couldn't see what it was they saw, but she heard Blythe's words loud and clear over the boisterous jazz.

"You have got to be kidding me..."

Pushing her way through, Rhiannon came up beside Blythe and followed her line of vision, which was on the lounge area filled with sofas and chairs and hoards of people, laughing and talking loudly over the music. And when she saw what Blythe had seen, she felt the color drain from her face and a cold shock freeze her entire body.

Liam was sitting on a leather lounge sofa the color of spicy red peppers, seemingly unscathed with a broad smile on his face. And cuddled up with him was a lushly built blonde with summer tanned skin exposed in all the right places. Rhiannon saw the strange woman lean in to kiss him, and watched with painful disbelief as his hands trailed up her body, holding her against him. She felt instantly sick to her stomach.

Lucian whirled around to face Rhiannon, shock in his eyes. His mouth opened as if he wanted to say something, but no words would come. She saw that he didn't want to believe what they were all witnessing, but that didn't make it any less real. It was obvious what was going on.

"Goddamnit," Blythe spat as she suddenly surged forward, getting over her initial shock and disbelief. The Liam she knew would never do something this careless, this cruel…

When she reached them, her hands fisted on her hips and she glared accusingly from him to the woman.

"What's going on?" she demanded, pleased by the look of complete and utter shock on his face when he saw her.

"I…" Liam began, for a brief moment looking lost and confused as he stared around him, as if he didn't know how he'd arrived there. But then he heard the voice inside his head, reminding him that he was there with Stella, and that Blythe was probably just worried. He looked back up at his sister and grinned. "Hey, Blythe. What's up?"

"What the hell are you doing?" Blythe shouted, her anger blinding her to the dull confusion in his eyes. "We've been worried sick looking for you, and you have the gall to be in some trashy bar, cozied up with some bimbo?"

Stella looked to Liam with eyebrows raised. "Is this your girlfriend, Liam?" she asked, snuggling up to him closer and batting her eyes at Blythe.

"No, but she is." Blythe whirled around and pointed at Rhiannon, who was standing between Lucian and Jax, her arms crossed over her body as she stared at him in disbelief. His eyes met hers, and for a flickering moment a memory flashed in his mind of her smiling up at him, his lips warmed from touching hers as he cupped her face in his hands and felt his heart fill from the sight of her. And, as quickly as the memory had come to him, he felt as though someone had invaded his mind and snatched it away again. The haze crept over him once more, and he heard the voice echo loudly in his mind.

She doesn't mean anything to me anymore...just a girl, I don't want to be with her now, she didn't make me happy. Stella is so much more beautiful...

"I wasn't happy." he heard himself say hollowly, and the second the words came out of his mouth he felt a stinging pain stab through his heart, and he reached up to clutch his chest, momentarily confused and startled. But words kept pouring out of his mouth before he could stop them, and he had no grasp on what it was that he was saying. "I met Stella on the beach, and we really hit it off. She's everything I've ever wanted. I told her about Euphora, and she thinks it's great."

"*What?*" Blythe shrieked, her eyes bulging as she spun back around to face Lucian, throwing up her arms in complete and utter disillusionment.

"Liam..." Lucian stepped forward then, meeting his son's eyes cautiously, unsure just what was going on.

"Damnit, Jax, check the sensor and see if he's possessed. Something's wrong here," Blythe barked out, her temper flaring viciously to mix with the fear in her gut. What the hell was going on with her brother?

"I've already checked, he's clean. So is she," Jax confirmed, nodding to Blythe. While she launched herself back at Liam, he stayed quietly beside Rhiannon, though he had no clue what to do for her.

So far, she hadn't moved an inch; she'd only stood there, frozen in place, feeling God only knows what. Jax felt disgusted and helpless all at once, knowing just how difficult it had been for her to give her heart to Liam in the first place…and now this?

"Dad, I'm fine, why are you looking at me that way?" Liam asked, shaking his head. "I don't see what is so difficult to understand here. I met this girl and we're enjoying each other's company. End of story."

Rhiannon decided she had heard enough. She whirled around and fled, pushing her way through the crowded club and out onto the dark street, clutching her chest to will away the pain.

This had to be a nightmare, it just had to be…there was no way this was real. Liam couldn't possibly be doing this to her, not this way. He hadn't been happy? How was that even possible?

While she raced off to the nearest tree, needing to disappear, to get away from the memory of him kissing that beautiful blonde, back in the night club Blythe grabbed Liam by the arm and yanked him off the sofa.

"You're coming with us, buddy. Your little slut can stay behind," she ordered, glaring down at Stella, who looked amused and ridiculously entertained. "I'm glad to see you find this all very funny, bitch."

Stella made a point to make eye contact with Liam as Blythe dragged him out of the club, and he was stuck with the haunting memory of those cornflower blue eyes as his family led him away.

Chapter Six

When she reached Euphora her father was waiting for her.

"Did you find him?" Rohan asked, instantly alarmed by the dull shock and pain on his daughter's face. "Rhiannon, what's wrong?"

For a moment she stood completely still, the surrounding meadow glowing like always with soft sunlight, the cheerful sound of birds filling the air. She met her father's eyes and felt the first tear slip down her cheek.

"He's fine," she heard herself say, her throat tightening around the words like a fist. Her knees trembled beneath her and the words Liam had spoken resounded in her mind. *I wasn't happy...*

Troubled, Rohan stepped toward her and wrapped his arms around her, unsure what was wrong. He only knew that she looked paler than the dead.

When her father pulled her against him and held her close, she gave in to the pain and cried, deep shuddering sobs that wracked her body and hurt so deeply that she wondered if she would ever recover from the pain.

Curse this heart and curse Liam for encouraging her to feel, only to annihilate everything so callously, so cruelly.

She didn't care now what happened. She only wanted to stop feeling.

"I don't understand all of this." Liam shook his head, a confused smile curving his lips. "What's the big deal?"

"What do you mean, what's the big deal?" Blythe spat, rounding on him where he sat on one of Thea's long sofas. "What the hell is wrong with you?"

Liam stared at her, though for the life of him he couldn't grasp just what it was that he was saying. He knew he could see, knew he could hear...but words were flashing in his mind that weren't his own, at least he didn't think they were. And when they poured out of his mouth, he wasn't sure just why he was saying them. He was unhappy...right? Had he been unhappy? He couldn't really be sure, but his mind seemed to have decided that, so it must be true...

But he couldn't shake the ache in his heart, as if that part of his body was rebelling against his brain, attempting to fight back. And yet he had no grasp on just what it was that he was fighting for. In truth, he felt like he was nothing more than a mere shadow of himself, hiding out inside his own body but unable to control his actions. He had thoughts...at least, he thought he could distinguish between what he was thinking and what the voice was telling him. But why did the voice sound like his own, even though he couldn't seem to control it?

"Nothing's wrong with me, Blythe," he heard himself say, even as the voice flashed in his mind again.

I thought I was in love with Rhiannon, but I realized that I was just fooling myself. I'm moving on now.

"I realized that I don't love her," he told her, earning a skeptical look from Blythe and a concerned look from his father and Thea. He stared at all of them, unsure why they looked so upset. "I'm sorry it had to happen this way, but it is what it is."

Blythe's face flushed an angry red and she whirled around furiously, searching for something breakable to throw. She had to smash something, or the urge to punch her own brother in the face was going to come to fruition swiftly and violently. Her eyes landed on a platter of tea cookies that Thea kept on a small table beside the sofa, and she grabbed it and smashed it aggressively at Liam's feet, shattering porcelain and cookies everywhere. The look of stunned surprise on his face only made her angrier.

"The Liam I know wouldn't do this," she snarled through clenched teeth, ignoring Lucian as he tried to clean up the plate she'd shattered. She felt no remorse over it, not one bit. Leaning in to jab a finger into Liam's chest, she met his eyes and silently vowed to Hell and back that she'd uncover whatever it was that that human woman had done to him. "You disgust me."

With that, she whirled around and fled the room, furious tears suddenly streaming down her cheeks.

Liam watched her slam the door behind her, and he sat still and silent for a moment, as if he couldn't think of what to say. Inside, his heart throbbed with pain, but his mind was oddly clear and calm. The voice crept in to offer words of comfort.

Blythe will get over it. She'll see, Stella is a great girl.

Feeling his lips curve, he smiled up at his father and Thea. "Can I go now?"

Thea stood with her arms crossed tightly over her chest, her face grim. Something was wrong with him, that much was certain. But just what it was she couldn't say. She'd never seen something like this…Liam wasn't possessed, and appeared to be acting of his own will. But every word out of his mouth seemed so out of character, as if his soul had been swapped with another. But at the same time, he seemed to have the same feelings toward everyone except Rhiannon. It was like his love for her had quite simply evaporated into nothing.

"Liam, tell me about this human girl you met." Thea took a seat beside him, her eyes never leaving his.

Liam grinned. "Her name is Stella and she grew up in New Orleans. She's twenty years old, has blonde hair and these stunning blue eyes...I had the hardest time looking away from those eyes of hers." His gaze drifted over Thea's shoulder as the memory of Stella's eyes flashed over him, halting all thoughts for a moment as the image penetrated his mind.

I have to see her again...she's everything I've ever wanted.

"I want to go see her again," he told Thea, focusing back on Mother Earth hopefully. "It's like I've waited my whole life to meet her...she's perfect."

Thea's brows drew together as she glanced up at Lucian, who looked deeply disturbed by his son's behavior. Both of them knew that they had time and time again heard Liam say those same words about Rhiannon.

"Do you know who Rhiannon is, Liam?" Thea asked, making sure to meet his eyes to see if anything changed at the mention of the Earth Dryad's name. But there was nothing.

Instead he simply grinned and laughed. "Yeah, I've known her my whole life." He looked up at his father as if it was an old joke. "She's a nice girl, but I just don't feel anything for her anymore. We had fun, but it's done."

"And were you planning on telling her that you wanted to end the relationship?" Thea's hands clenched in her lap, her worst fears confirmed. Liam appeared to have truly just stopped loving Rhiannon. "She's very hurt that you chose to move on without telling her."

For a brief moment, he felt that stabbing pain in his chest again, but his mind refused to comprehend the feeling. "I know, it was rude of me," he said casually, the voice in his head feeding the words to him on cue. "I'll go talk to her, make her see that it's for the best."

He rose to his feet, and Thea did as well, turning to face him. She was nearly the same height as he, and as she stared into his face, one she had thought she knew so well, she felt a violent fury rising within her. Her disappointment with him enveloped her like a cloak until she lost all reason, and without thinking her hand whipped out and struck his face in a swift slap, one that left the three of them stunned into silence.

Liam reached up to touch his cheek as his eyes met hers. He suddenly had a flashing memory of her smiling with wisdom and ethereal beauty, with power emanating from her very body in shimmering waves. His heart opened to the image, yearned toward it, and he knew his eyes had widened with the knowledge of what he had felt for her. He had never upset Thea, not once... God, what in the world had he done?

But the voice slapped sharply back into his mind as the image faded, and he tried to cling to it but within mere seconds, it was gone. His mind was wiped clean of all thoughts, and his face went calmly blank.

"Do you know where she is?" he asked, the old memory of Thea long gone.

Thea, chest heaving and pain and fury in her eyes, looked to Lucian incredulously. Lucian placed a tentative hand on his son's shoulder, and urged him to turn around and look at him.

Both he and Thea knew it was very unlike Liam to ask for Rhiannon's whereabouts. He usually had a kind of sixth sense in regards to her...

"I believe she's in the back gardens," Lucian murmured hollowly, his hand clenching on his son's shoulder as a sudden urge to shake the sense back into Liam washed over him. But he refrained, and simply released him and watched Liam smile before walking away, as though he had no care in the world.

He found her on the back steps of the castle, sitting with her hands clenched in her lap and her face smoothly blank. He stepped toward her and sat at her side, a carefully prepared sheepish smile already on his face.

But when he turned to look at her, his heart clenched and thundered with pain, and he let out a sharp hissing sound as his hand came up to rub his chest.

Rhiannon immediately glanced over at him, worry in her eyes at seeing the anguish on his face.

"What's wrong?" she asked, reaching out to him, her hand covering his as it clutched at his heart. At her touch, he met her eyes and saw the tears in them, and the memory of her collapsed in his arms in that very garden, sobbing against him as he held her tight and comforted her hit him like a stone cold wave.

She saw what she assumed was guilt on his face, and seeing it had her pulling her hand away and turning from him. She said nothing as she closed herself in, shutting all doors and locking them tight. She wouldn't let anything he said upset her, couldn't let it creep in to hurt her, not now, not ever.

Whatever excuses or reasons he had, she would listen to them objectively, and accept. But she wasn't sure if she could ever forgive…

When he lost eye contact with her, he struggled to hold on to the image of her in the garden, but it slipped away as if blown by a swift and careless breeze. He tried to grasp the lingering remnants of it, but felt the fog settle in once more over his thoughts and shroud him in emptiness.

All that remained was the misery in his heart, but he had no idea now just what had caused it…surely it didn't have to do with the girl?

What was it that I ever saw in her anyway? She's so cold…

"I'm sorry you're hurting, Rhiannon," he told her, smiling as he rested his arms on his knees casually, ignoring the pain that continued to throb in his chest. She refused to look at him, and sat in silence as he continued. "Things just weren't working out. I hope you won't hate me too much…we can still be friends."

She absorbed his words and felt the chill set in, covering her in frosty shivers that encased her in a shield of ice. So cold…she would never, ever be warm again.

"I think you'd like Stella if you met her, she's great," he continued, not seeing the single tear slip down her cheek. "Anyway, I'll leave you alone, I'm sure you have work to do. Thanks for understanding."

He patted her shoulder and got to his feet, leaving her to emotionally crumble to pieces on the steps behind him. If only he knew what he had done; it would have killed him.

When morning arrived, Liam woke to the voice in his head, telling him to go to Stella.

A sense of urgency accompanied the voice, so he didn't even wait to have breakfast or tell anyone where he was going. He simply left.

He arrived in New Orleans and wandered into town, his hands tucked into his pockets and his mind filled with Stella's face. In his head the voice kept repeating her name, over and over, until the excitement to see her consumed him. He couldn't stay away from her that much he knew. She was just so wonderful…

Without even realizing how he knew where to find her, he wandered to a coffee shop in the historic French Quarter, and there she was, sitting at one of the little café tables on the outdoor patio, sipping a latte and reading a book.

Although his mind told him to be happy to see her, he felt quite the opposite feeling in his heart. But something told him not to worry about it, and so he simply didn't.

"Stella," he greeted as he sat across from her, the little voice instructing him to smile.

She glanced up from her book and smirked, closing it and setting it aside as her eyes met his.

"Hello, handsome." She held her hand out gracefully, and he took it in his own and pressed a soft kiss to her skin, his eyes holding hers. It wasn't until he'd made the gesture that his heart rolled over horribly and he had a brief moment of wondering why he had done it...but seeing her eyes had the question subsiding.

"Can I get you anything?" a waitress said suddenly as she approached, her sunny smile distracting him momentarily.

"I'll have whatever she's having." He grinned back at Stella, although he had no idea why he was smiling.

Stella smirked again and took a sip of her drink, eyeing him over the rim of her coffee mug. When she pulled it away, she licked her upper lip delicately, pleased when his eyes followed the movement.

"I wasn't sure I'd see you again," she told him, setting her mug down and leaning in to grasp his hands in her own. "I had such a good time with you yesterday, until your family stole you away."

They just don't understand.

He grinned. "It's okay, I've explained it all to them. They'll get over it."

"So what's it like, this Euphora place you were telling me about?" She smiled up at the waitress as she dropped off Liam's coffee, but made sure to meet his eyes again the moment the woman was gone. "Could you take me there?"

Why not? That way everyone could see how wonderful Stella is...

"Sure." He took a sip of coffee as his face lit up with pleasure. It really was a grand idea, wasn't it? Then they would all see...

Stella smiled and leaned over the table suddenly, tilting her face so that her lips brushed his seductively. He froze for a moment, something deep inside of him hesitating, before his mind urged him forward.

Kiss her...

He did, pressing his lips to hers. The kiss was gentle and sweet, but when he pulled away he had a fleeting thought about how he had felt nothing but an odd emptiness in his heart. He couldn't really remember how it had felt to kiss anyone else, but something inside of him knew there should be something more than this eerie emptiness...

But even as the thought occurred to him, it vanished and he smiled, his mind cheerfully blank.

"So, when would you like to go?" he asked her, his mind suddenly deciding that this had to happen. He had to bring her home, had to introduce her to everyone so that they could understand.

Stella smiled and tapped her lips with one perfectly manicured fingertip, her eyes flashing with feminine power. "I'm ready when you are, handsome."

They walked up the cobblestone walkway together, hand-in-hand. It hadn't even occurred to him to wonder why Stella had so easily accepted his explanation of what he was, and where he came from...instead it had all seemed so natural and perfect, as if it was meant to be.

At least, that was how the little voice justified it, and he didn't have the willpower to question the voice. Instead he was floating along in the dark recesses of his old self, barely aware of what was happening to him and content with what the voice told him was reality. And if his heart strained away from Stella, and ached bitterly whenever he looked at her, he didn't understand the feeling and therefore brushed it off.

They came across Capri and Rian first, who were both sitting beneath one of the large willow trees, reading to each other and talking. When they saw Liam and Stella approaching, they both froze and stared in stunned silence.

"Hi guys," Liam greeted, waving a hand at them cheerfully. Capri's eyes shot to Stella almost immediately, and the disbelief and uncertainty she felt was obvious.

Rian instinctively shifted closer to Capri, eyeing the human girl coldly. He didn't trust the gleam in the girl's eyes, or the way she kept her hand clasped firmly in Liam's, almost possessively.

"Liam, is this the girl…Stella, right?" Capri asked, sincerely in her heart wanting to give him the benefit of the doubt. If this girl really made him happy, then who were they to judge him?

Liam beamed down at her before glancing at Stella, meeting her eyes. For a brief moment he said nothing as he stared at her, as though losing himself completely in the moment. Capri's eyebrows raised curiously while Rian's eyes narrowed suspiciously.

Suddenly Liam shifted his gaze back to Capri and grinned. "Yes, this is Stella. Stella, this is Capri and Rian."

Stella smiled politely. Capri took the cold strain in the other girl's eyes as nerves, so she tried to return the smile in a show of good faith.

"So, um, how did you two meet?" Capri questioned, only to be momentarily distracted when she realized Rian was as still as a statue beside her. The tension in the air was unbelievably palpable, and she worriedly bit her lip.

"She was walking on the same beach I was and we just stumbled across each other."

"I just thought he was the cutest thing I'd ever seen," Stella said, looking at Liam fondly. "So when he told me about this place, I wasn't too surprised. He seemed…otherworldly, if you will."

Liam grinned and leaned down to kiss her nose affectionately, his eyes filled with humor and happiness. If only those watching knew how violently his heart was retaliating or how hard his mind was working to try and convince him not to listen.

"Isn't she cute? I can't get over that accent." He laughed, wrapping an arm around her and winking at Rian. "We should probably head inside. I want Stella to meet everyone."

They started to walk away, but before they could, Blythe and Jax appeared at the entrance to the castle, and when they spotted Liam and Stella, they both started forward.

As Blythe got closer, she suddenly broke into a run. Jax had to try and keep up with her, knowing she'd do something drastic. He barely managed to catch her by her arms moments before she launched herself at Stella, fists flying.

Blythe snarled like a spitting mad cat, her hair flying around her face as Jax restrained her, struggling against her wrath.

"How dare you bring her here?" Blythe shrieked, furiously kicking her legs to try and free herself from Jax's iron grip.

"Stop bucking like a bronco and maybe I'll let you go." Jax grunted as he fought to maintain his hold on her. For a little thing, she was unbelievably strong.

For a moment Blythe wanted nothing more than to fight her way free, but she wore herself out and ended up collapsing against him, her eyes glued to Stella, full of bitterness and hate.

"Blythe, you remember Stella." Liam kept his arm around Stella protectively, the voice in his head urging him to keep Blythe at a safe distance.

Blythe let out a strained laugh as she straightened, fury coursing through her. "How could you do this? Huh? How could you bring her here when you know how upset everyone is right now?"

"I…" Liam froze, his heart thudding painfully hard in his chest at the look of disgust in his sister's eyes. "I don't know."

He turned to look at Stella, momentarily lost again. But once his eyes met hers, his face cleared and his mind was filled with the little voice, instructing him on what to say.

"I wanted you guys to see that she's a nice girl," he told them, glancing back down at Capri and Rian as well, who were still sitting apprehensively beneath the tree. "You're going to have to give her a chance, because she means something to me."

"You've only known her for one day, Liam," Blythe spat, furious tears burning in her eyes. "And you knew Rhiannon forever. Goddamnit, I never even liked her, but I was still happier to see you with her than I am to see you with this bitch."

"Blythe," Liam growled defensively, a warning in his tone. "It's not up to you to decide who's right for me and who isn't."

"Clearly." She crossed her arms over her chest haughtily and scowled down her nose at him. "You know what, I need to see something for myself."

She spun around and reached into Jax's pocket, unearthing the sensor and swiftly setting it to demon. She then aimed it right at Stella and glared down at the screen, her eyes hardened and ruthless. When the sensor picked up nothing, she growled and shoved it back at Jax.

"Fine, whatever. So she's a human. I still don't trust her."

"I don't think any of us trust her just yet, darlin'," Jax drawled, stuffing his hands into his pockets and frowning at the girl from Louisiana. He knew the state well, knew the people from it... and this girl didn't fit the mold. She had an upper-class refinement to her that was carefully disguised as home grown, but he wasn't buying it. "C'mon, let's get away for awhile."

He reached out and wrapped an arm around Blythe and led her away, leaving the others behind. He wanted to go down to New Orleans to check up on this girl himself, before it was too late. Blythe would appreciate the gesture once they were far away enough to discuss it.

Because he was certain of one thing, and one thing only: Liam was not acting on his own accord.

The first thing Capri did once Liam and Stella disappeared inside the castle was to go see Rhiannon.

Rian let her go, troubled over what they had witnessed. It was because of this that while his fiancé went to comfort her friend, he headed straight to the Furies chambers and went to work, researching possible reasons for Liam's bizarre behavior. He went through all of his father's old books on demons, on the Underworld, and everything related in any way to evil.

On the outside, Stella had appeared to be a polite, healthy young woman. But there had been something in her eyes that had irked him, and he was determined to find out what was behind it.

So he dove headfirst into research, knowing he had to do something about what was happening to Liam, if only for Capri's sake. He'd seen the worry cloud her eyes, and the strain it took for her to try and see Liam's point of view. It was, after all, one of the things he loved most about her. She had the biggest heart, and was always the last to judge anyone, including himself. And if it hadn't been for her…he might have never had anyone to call his own.

While Rian searched for answers in books, Capri knocked quietly on Rhiannon's door, hoping she could provide some kind of comfort.

When she heard only silence, she knocked again, her fingers aching over the doorknob, wondering if she should just open it. Because she knew it was rude, she tried calling out Rhiannon's name. When she still didn't get an answer, she sucked in a quick breath of air and, her mouth set in a grim line, pushed the door open just enough so she could peek inside.

She spotted Rhiannon sitting at an old fashioned writing desk in the corner, ferociously scribbling in a notebook. The shades were drawn, but a single lamp shone brightly over the desk, pointed directly at the work surface and casting a shadow of her hand as it swiped efficiently across the paper.

Capri's heart broke when she noticed Rhiannon's bridesmaid dress, covered carefully in plastic and hanging on the door of the armoire, unopened. She'd been happy that day, Capri thought painfully as she fought back tears and focused on her friend. Surely she'd be happy again someday...

"Rhiannon?" Capri left the door open behind her and stepped into the room, her hands clutched together anxiously.

Rhiannon continued to write, her eyes hard and cold behind her glasses and her back rigidly straight. When she spoke, Capri wasn't sure it was even Rhiannon speaking.

"I'm busy, Capri. Now is not a good time."

Capri glanced around and spotted a side chair by Rhiannon's bed. She walked over and pulled the chair up beside the desk and took a seat, trying to put as much stern resolve into her expression as possible. She didn't want to be pushed away, not now. She wanted to help Rhiannon, no matter how badly she fought back.

"I wanted to let you know something...I didn't want you to stumble in on it, I wanted you to prepare yourself..." Capri began, her gray eyes soft with sympathy and sorrow.

When Rhiannon said nothing and only continued to write, Capri took a deep, steadying breath and continued. "Liam has brought that girl here. They're downstairs."

She saw Rhiannon's hand falter and freeze, and her breath hitch in her lungs in a startled gasp. For a flickering moment, unbridled misery flashed in her eyes.

"I don't have any desire to meet her," Rhiannon whispered, her eyes lifting from the page to stare unseeingly straight ahead. "Please let me know when they leave again."

Capri felt tears spring into her eyes as she nodded, and on instinct she rose to her feet and wrapped her arms around Rhiannon.

"I wish I knew why this was happening," Capri murmured, pressing her face into her friend's dark hair. "I just don't understand it."

Rhiannon inhaled slowly and deeply, forcing back the feelings that threatened to consume her. Because she knew Capri was only trying to help, she patted her friend's arms and tried to stay neutral. Anything else and she'd surely give in to the pain.

"He said last night that he was unhappy," Rhiannon said quietly, tilting her head up to meet her friend's eyes. "I'm not going to hold him back."

"But he loves you, I know he does," Capri countered, kneeling down and cupping Rhiannon's hands in her own. "You have to fight for him, tell him you want to talk things over. I know he'll listen to you."

Rhiannon shook her head slowly, averting her eyes in an effort to avoid the anguish on Capri's face. "I won't do that to him. He's made it clear he doesn't want me, and that's the end of the story."

"Rhiannon?" Brogan appeared in the doorway to the bedroom, visibly distressed. It was the first time he'd seen her since she'd returned from New Orleans, and it was clear on his face that he was deeply troubled by the news.

"Brogan," Rhiannon managed, feeling a single tear escape and slide down her cheek as she stared up at him, her chest clenching painfully.

When he started toward her, she rose to her feet and went straight to his arms, not even realizing until that moment just how badly she needed to be comforted by someone who would only give her solidity and not outrage.

"I'm so sorry," he whispered, holding her close and suffering as she suffered. He hated knowing she had been fooled, had been used.. and he especially hated knowing there was so little he could do to help her.

Except, of course, confront the bastard himself and give him a piece of his mind. But because he knew that it would only hurt Rhiannon more if he did so, he knew he'd have to refrain and keep his opinion to himself.

For now, at least.

Chapter Seven

At dinner that evening, no one questioned why Rhiannon was not present. Instead, tension hung heavy in the air like an impending storm, hovering low enough to darken everyone's mood.

No one could grasp what was going on with Liam, but he continued to reassure those around him that this was his decision and that Stella was going to be a part of his life now. He insisted that they would all be happier just to accept it.

Stella sat beside him at the dining table, smiling sweetly and playing the role of the curious human embarking on unfamiliar and exciting territory. To all she spoke, Stella appeared to be charming, beautiful, and well mannered. But to those who could sense such things, there was something behind her eyes that indicated a calculating and careful mind, one that had honed in on Liam and appeared committed to not letting go.

Thea was one of those who could sense it, and it did not please her at all. Nor did it please her to sense something more about the girl, something oddly familiar that she couldn't for the life of her place. Stella did not look physically familiar, nor did she behave quite like anyone that Thea had known. But there was just something there, something residing deep inside the girl that struck a hauntingly familiar chord with Mother Earth, and it made her even more apprehensive.

Blythe and Jax had come and gone, ignoring the others while they quickly ate before leaving without a word. Thea didn't blame them, nor did she fault Rian for his probing questions disguised as polite inquiries, or Brogan's constant vigilance of the girl's every movement, as if waiting for some kind of sign that would explain everything. Though from the look in his eyes, he deemed Liam just as guilty as the girl in terms of hurting Rhiannon, a fact which Thea found hard to disagree with.

But from what she could see, there was nothing out of the ordinary about the girl except this odd feeling she had. Stella appeared to be very nice, open and smart without being overly opinionated. She smiled at everyone and seemed to genuinely fit in despite how most humans would have reacted to Euphora. It bothered Thea that the first thing she had thought of when noticing this about Stella was that Heidi had been the same way. Heidi had accepted Euphora and Clynn as easily as she accepted the color of the sky or the scent of a rose. It came naturally to her, and had made her transition to marrying Clynn all the more appropriate.

But the last thing Thea wanted to do was compare Stella to someone as loving as the late Heidi, who had been such a blessing to all of their lives. Because she knew, deep down, that Stella was nothing like Heidi. There was something darker there that she couldn't place, but she certainly found she did not trust. There had never been trust issues with Heidi. Not once.

Rohan was edgier than usual, which wasn't surprising. He'd just come down from bringing his daughter a plate of food with Capri, and what he had seen had devastated him.

Rhiannon wouldn't smile, though he could understand that. She seemed to have drawn in upon herself, just as she had for most of her life, and was carefully reconstructing the wall that Liam had so ardently torn down only months before. Brick by brick, she was shielding herself from the reality of what had happened, and dismissing it without any emotion. His daughter, who recently had blossomed so beautifully, was shutting down and encasing herself in a cocoon made of steel.

It broke his heart to see it, to know that the pain she had inside would never release itself. It was in her practical nature to simply bury it deep and ignore it, and move on without a word or a care.

Other than the moment she had returned from discovering Liam in New Orleans, Rohan had not heard or seen her cry. And he knew that if what was happening with Liam became permanent, his daughter was likely to never open her heart again.

She'd thought it was safe to venture down to the Greenhouse the next morning and resume her work. Certainly she'd gotten a lot done the night before at her writing desk in her room, but there was always more to do, and she knew it was impractical to stay away for long, despite the circumstances.

Rhiannon had convinced herself that she was over it, and that she was ready to move on with her life as it had been planned before Liam had pried open her carefully protected heart and convinced her to love him. She had come to terms with the notion that she simply had to act as if those months had never happened, and that she was the same person she had been before.

She was strong, capable, intelligent, and an excellent Earth Dryad. She had grace, class, and ambition enough to power her through anything. Work was all she needed, after all, and in a few years when it became prudent to marry, perhaps she would have her father choose an Enforcer for her.

Because she had to admit, following her heart had been fool-ish, and look where it had gotten her. She would never, ever make that same mistake again.

And so she got out of bed as she did every morning, got ready and dressed in pressed slacks the color of walnuts and a floral print blouse in shades of pink, and slipped on heels and her glasses and gathered her notebooks and charts. She neatly packed her bag with her calculator, pencils, and every other item she'd used while working the night before.

With a deep, calming breath, she checked her watch and noted that it was still very early. With a tiny prayer that she would not run into anyone else, she opened her bedroom door and stepped out into the hallway, cautiously looking around. It was empty.

She shut the door as quietly as she could and proceeded toward the stairs, clutching her books to her chest and keeping her chin held high. She was strong, very strong. Nothing and no one could reach her now.

She made her way down the steps and out into the corridor, which she was also pleased to note was empty.

But as she continued along toward the Greenhouse, think-ing she was home free, Liam and Stella appeared out of the dining hall, arms wrapped around each other with giddy smiles on their faces.

Rhiannon felt a sharp jolt shake her heart, but she didn't falter. Instead she just averted her eyes and prayed they ignored her as she walked past them.

But she wasn't so lucky.

"Good morning," Liam called out, grinning at Rhiannon cheerfully.

Rhiannon nodded politely to him, avoiding looking at Stella, who's lips had curved into a cruel smirk as she tilted her face up to Liam's.

Despite herself, Rhiannon was mortified to see Liam lean in to kiss the girl, as if she wasn't even there to see it. Offended by his callousness, she turned and walked as quickly away as she could.

But as she left, she heard Stella's southern lilt echo off the stone walls of the corridor, as if the girl purposely wanted Rhiannon to hear.

"What in the world did you ever like about that nerd in the glasses? She's awful cold, don't you think?" Stella chimed, laughter in her voice.

Liam's own laughter resounded through the corridor as he responded. "You're right! She is pretty cold."

Rhiannon felt the insult rise in her even as tears sprang hot into her eyes. She disappeared inside the Greenhouse and slammed the door as hard as she could.

"This is where I work," Liam said cheerfully as he led Stella into Water Tower, motioning with his arm to showcase the vast room. The sound of water dribbling down the walls and into the pool below echoed off the stone as light poured in through the skylights at the ceiling.

"My, my, handsome. It's beautiful." Stella wandered forward, her head tilting as she looked skyward and marveled at the room.

Liam watched her, feeling his mouth curve into a smile. But being in this most familiar of surroundings had something passing through him, some kind of rekindling of his true self, that had him feeling dizzy and disoriented. What was happening to him? Why was he smiling?

And looking at Stella, his hands started to shake as her image blended with that of Rhiannon, blonde curls morphing into straight bark brown, and when she turned to look at him, her face flickered once into Rhiannon's face, and he felt a shudder race down his spine at the sight of it. Good God...what was going on?

But even as the question surfaced somewhere deep inside of him, it was immediately squashed into nothingness, and then gone. He felt his body release a whoosh of breath, as if he had been stunned into holding it. His mind cleared into blissful nothingness as he smiled again.

"Isn't it great?" he heard himself say, his voice echoing dully inside the shell of his body.

"Yes, it is." Stella sauntered toward him, holding his eyes with hers, penetrating into them with every step. He felt himself lean into her as she wrapped her arms around his neck and pressed her lips to his. "You are mine now, Liam," she murmured, a humming purr in her throat as she enjoyed the feel of his hands running over her body. "You have no idea just how important you are."

The real Liam crouched inside the shadowy recesses of his own heart, rocking back and forth and revolting against what was happening to him. This was wrong, oh so incredibly wrong...but while his heart knew it was wrong, his mind couldn't wrap around the concept, so clouded was it with Stella's face and her voice...the voice that in his head sounded so very much like his own...

"Ahem." Lucian cleared his throat noisily behind them as he came into the room, his eyes narrowing at the sight of his son kissing Stella. His disapproval was obvious.

Liam whirled around and grinned, looking embarrassed. "Good morning."

"Indeed," Lucian returned coldly, eyeing the girl.

"I was just showing Stella around," Liam explained, pulling her closer. "But we'll get out of your way if you want."

Letting out a huff of breath, Lucian stepped across the little bridge and onto the main wooden platform, his footsteps thudding over the planks. He stared into his son's eyes carefully, as if trying to see if it was really Liam he was looking at. But those eyes were the same, vividly blue and cheerful, and he felt the guilt creep in to mix with the uncertainty. Perhaps he was being cruel to his son by being so cold this way, by not accepting what was clear on the surface. Liam had chosen this girl over Rhiannon, and so there must be a valid reason. Maybe she wasn't really as bad as they all wanted to believe...

Attempting a smile, he turned to look at Stella, who smiled sweetly in return.

"My dear, I hope you are not too overwhelmed by all of this." He held his arms out to emphasize his point, warmth returning to his eyes. "It is a lot to take in."

"It is, but I've always been open to new things," Stella replied, tilting her head to smile up at Liam, who was staring at her intently, his lips fixed into a permanent grin. Lucian noticed this, and a part of him darkly questioned it. His son seemed utterly captivated by this girl...but why?

"I apologize for the less than gracious reception you have received from all of us," Lucian said, focusing back on Stella. "But I hope you can understand that this is quite a surprise."

"I do. And I'm sorry for intruding this way...I didn't mean to get in the middle of things like this. It's just that...well, when I saw Liam, I knew I had to have him." Her lips curved into a wickedly feminine grin that should have sent warning signals off in his brain. But he was distracted by the door bursting open behind him, and Rohan's jolting presence.

"I can't hold this in any longer," Rohan declared, surging toward Liam and getting directly in the younger man's face, his mellow green eyes hardened with hate. "You've destroyed my daughter. Have you nothing to say for yourself?"

"Rohan–" Lucian started forward, placing a hand on his friend's shoulder only to be shoved off.

"Back off, Lucian, this doesn't involve you," Rohan growled, glaring at his old friend before turning back to Liam, his fists tightly clenched at his sides. Lucian's eyes widened with the realization that Rohan could very well choose to use them.

Liam stared into Rohan's eyes, and his entire body trembled as the memory of that same man standing before him, beaming with pride and joy and thanking him for being so good to his daughter, flashed through his mind. And when the look of pleasure faded in a snap to reveal Rohan's current expression of misery and hate, Liam subconsciously backed away, fear circling viciously with the guilt in his stomach.

"I..." His mouth fell open as he shook his head, his heart screaming for justice and for release, while his mind suddenly fought back and cleared. The image of Rohan's pride vanished and calm emptiness replaced it. The little voice spoke once more on his behalf. "Rhiannon is not my problem now."

Rohan's eyes widened with rage as he shot an incredulous glance at Lucian, who looked equally as taken aback. Liam never used her full name, and both of them knew it. Suspicion crept through both men like a dark, cagey spider.

They both looked to Stella then, who was standing calmly beside Liam. Her hand was resting on his shoulder in what should have been viewed as a sign of support. Instead both men felt it represented her complete control.

"Who are you?" Rohan demanded, fighting for understanding. The Liam his daughter had loved would have never dismissed her so coldly...

Stella's eyebrows rose innocently, and she looked back and forth at the two older men. "I'm just a girl from New Orleans. Nothing more."

"So it seems." Lucian frowned, crossing his arms over his chest to stifle the cold feeling haunting him. He shook his head as he eyed her, pain creeping into his heart. "I really hope that is all you are, dear."

With that, he whirled around and left the room, needing time to himself. Rohan watched him go, his earlier anger dwindled into embers amongst nothing but ash.

"My daughter suffers because of your cruelty," he said in a low, deadly voice as he turned, his eyes searching Liam's. "I cannot believe I ever trusted you with her."

Disgusted and defeated, he turned and left as well, shutting the door behind him with a loud bang.

Liam stared hollowly at the door, his mind empty of all thoughts even as his heart shriveled miserably into the shadows.

They wandered down into the courtyard, heading toward the oak tree in the meadow so Stella could go back to New Orleans. Liam had his hand in hers, and a sense of contentment in his mind. His eyes were glued to her face, as if he couldn't bear to look away.

She's so beautiful…so perfect…I think I love her.

"I love you." He spoke the words, his mind pleased and at ease but his heart shuddered, knowing it was a lie.

Stella smiled up at him, and her cornflower blue eyes honed in on his, drawing him in. "Good. That sounded very believable."

They continued to walk, and when Stella began to ask him questions, he answered without hesitation.

"So the older Earth and Fire Dryads don't get along?"

"Nope," he began, the words tumbling out of his mouth as his brain scanned through all the facts. He didn't even realize what he was saying, he only knew that there were fingers probing around in his mind, feeling around for all angles of the situation, so nothing would be left undisclosed. "It all started years ago when Brock was dating the Muse, Serendipity, and then she left him for Rohan, who was Brock's best friend at the time. Then, more recently, Serendipity had an affair with Brock, and now Rohan and she are separated. But neither Rohan nor Brock have ever forgiven each other for what happened."

"Interesting," Stella mused, tapping her lower lip with her fingertips. "And what's the story on Brock and your friend Blythe? Any tension there?"

"She thinks he doesn't spend enough time with her, and too much time with his ex-wife, her mother."

"And the Earth girl and her parents? Are there any conflicts there?"

"A lot." Liam had a flashing memory of Rohan's face, filled with vile hate, before it disappeared. "Since Rohan discovered that his wife was cheating on him, he's left her, leaving Rhiannon in the middle. Serendipity has been trying to get Rohan back, unsuccessfully. What's worse is that Serendipity arranged for Rhiannon to marry this guy, Michael, who was murdered. Serendipity blamed Rhiannon, and schemed with Michael's father to kill her."

"My, oh my." Stella smiled lushly as she digested all the information he'd given her. "What about the Air girl, is there any dirt on her that I should know?"

"Capri is marrying the Fury, Rian, in a few days," he said immediately, the words coming from the knowledge in his mind even as the suspicion in his heart flourished.

"Good, I'll be your date," Stella decided as they stopped in front of the oak tree. She turned to face him with a triumphant smile. "Until then."

She met his eyes and held them, unblinking, and he felt the misty fog inside his head thicken until he was nearly dizzy from it. Then she leaned up to kiss his cheek, and before she pulled away she whispered softly in his ear.

"You'll miss me, Liam. You won't think of anything but my face, my smile, my voice…my eyes. You love me and you don't care what anyone else thinks."

She stepped back and touched the tree, repeating the words he'd instructed her to use to get back to New Orleans. He stood there, numb from head to toe, lost inside himself as he watched her disappear in a flash of gold light.

And emblazoned in his mind was the image of her face, her blue eyes gleaming with ethereal power.

In the dark shadows of a Creole flavored dive bar buried deep in the French Quarter of New Orleans, they sat back with a glass of aged bourbon and toasted their success.

"To the loveliest southern belle ever to walk the Earth." Dante's lips curved as he eyed his companion, showing a glint of perfectly straight teeth in a smile that was as wicked as it was charming.

Stella held up her glass, her stunning blue eyes shining with victory and pure feminine mystery. "You were right, that boy was putty in my hands. And such a treasure trove of information…"

Tossing back his glass of bourbon, Dante let out a laugh and waved to the waiter for another. "I knew the moment I saw him that he was the key," he told her, his golden eyes glinting with the thrill of success as he reached for her hand, holding it in his own. "But you, darling, are invaluable."

Stella tilted her head and eyed him seductively, her tongue sliding along her upper lip in pure suggestion. "I feel we offer each other so much, Dante. I wouldn't be here if it wasn't for you, after all."

"No, my sweet. Without me you'd still be in Hell." Dante leaned in to capture her mouth with his, the hand that held hers clenching tight as his other hand came around to pull at her hair and hold her against him. She didn't mind the pain…in fact, she thrived on it.

"God, that boy's pathetic kisses compare nothing to yours," she groaned, her free hand raking nails down his chest as she bit his lip hard enough to nearly draw blood.

Dante chuckled, releasing her as their eyes met, enjoying the violent passion as much as she did. "Just a little bit longer, darling, and then we will have it all."

She smiled and downed the rest of the bourbon in her glass, the bite of it sending a pleasant shiver down her spine. She played with the empty glass in her hands, watching the light play over the crystal.

"Thea didn't even recognize me," she said, her eyes filled with glee. "I'll admit, I was a bit worried. But she said nothing."

"She is most likely suspicious," Dante reasoned, thanking the waitress who brought him a fresh drink. His brows furrowed as he took a sip. "But nothing about you is as you once were, not physically, at least."

"They're such fools." Stella laughed, loud and vibrant, the memory of their skepticism toward her darkly humorous. "They kept checking their stupid little devices to see if I was a demon. Damn fools."

Dante grinned. "Darling, they would never in their wildest dreams consider the possibility that you were one of them."

"As I said, damn fools." Stella rolled her eyes and sat back in her chair, bad memories haunting her mind. "But then again, it's been over one hundred years since I lived under Thea's burdensome rules. She never let me do things my way."

Bitterness clouded her eyes and she scowled at him when he laughed at her. "When you get your kicks waging wars between men simply by persuasion, of course peace loving Thea is going to banish you." He leaned in, reaching over to cup her face, desire and madness flickering with the greed in his eyes. "But I...I am like you. I live for violence, for bloodshed and tears. I want nothing more than to watch them all burn. And with you in my corner, darling, our power knows no bounds."

Stella's lips curved into a wicked smile. "In a fortnight, it all falls down. We'll make it burn, Dante. And then we'll dance in the flames."

Chapter Eight

"Don't be stupid, you're not walking with him,"
Blythe huffed, looking annoyed and restless as she
waited beside Rhiannon just inside the atrium doors.
In her hands was a bouquet of white cabbage roses.

Rhiannon smoothed out the skirt of her bridesmaid dress with her free hand, her own bouquet in her
other as anxiety and nerves raced up her spine. "You
are the maid of honor, and therefore you walk with
the best man. I'll be fine."

"Damnit, who cares?" Blythe asked in a loud whisper, not wanting anyone to hear them. "I'll walk with
Liam, and you can walk with Brogan. No one's even
gonna notice."

Rhiannon rolled her eyes. "It will mess up the
order at the altar, Blythe, how can you not see that?"

"So we make it work once we're up there, no big
deal." Blythe grabbed Rhiannon's shoulder with her
free hand and shook her, her fiery eyes intense with
emotion. "I know this is hard enough on you already,
and I'm honestly surprised you're still going through
with this, but I don't want you making yourself into
some kind of martyr when you don't have to."

"I'd do anything for Capri," Rhiannon murmured defensively, pushing Blythe away. "Just stop worrying about me, I'm fine."

Blythe rolled her shoulders restlessly and backed off, recognizing a brick wall when she'd hit one. "Whatever you want," she muttered under her breath, turning away so she wouldn't have to look at Rhiannon any longer.

She just didn't understand Rhiannon's reaction to Liam's betrayal, not one bit. She herself was furious and determined to fight for what she had considered a promising relationship between her brother and the Earth Dryad. But Rhiannon refused to fight, refused to do more than just accept and move on as if she had never loved him, and he had never loved her.

But Blythe knew better. She knew in her heart that Liam had loved Rhiannon....hell, he'd bought her an engagement ring. This bullshit about him being unhappy was a sham, and there was something going on with him that wasn't natural.

And coupled with her anger over Rhiannon's cold acceptance was her frustration over the lack of helpful information from all the research Rian and Jax had been doing. They were no closer to finding the secret to Liam's obsession with Stella than they had been the moment they'd found him in that night club in New Orleans.

But the days were slipping by, and Blythe was getting more and more worried that by the time they discovered what was happening to him, it would be too late. It was already the night of Capri's wedding, which Thea had insisted go on as planned, and she was still at such a loss with him.

There was a noise behind them and they turned to see Liam approaching. Brogan lingered behind him, his dark eyes shooting daggers into the Water Dryad's back. But Liam had his usual carefree smile in place, and he leaned in to kiss Blythe's cheek cordially.

"Nervous?" he asked, smiling over at Rhiannon as well even though she refused to look at him.

"Among other things." Blythe stared at him through narrowed eyes, as if trying to see what couldn't be seen. "You're going to be walking with Rhiannon. You might as well get into place. I think we're about to start."

Brogan stepped forward and stood beside Blythe, hooking his arm in hers. She glanced over her shoulder warily and saw Rhiannon do the same with Liam, her face void of all emotion. Liam's expression was oddly blank as well, but before Blythe could think about it, the music began and they were ushered out.

As planned, Blythe and Brogan walked out first down the cobblestone pathway covered in delicate pink rose petals, leading up to an altar several yards away made of a white archway decorated with climbing roses and lilies. A soft, lilting harp played over the cool air, and the smell of warm jasmine drifted throughout the courtyard.

Overhead, the morning sun shone beautifully warm through the trees, creating a golden glow throughout the gardens. Birds chirped cheerfully as they darted from tree to tree, and hundreds of tiny white butterflies floated on the breeze.

People were seated in pristine white chairs on either side of the walkway, and among them Blythe spotted Stella, wearing a blood red dress that obnoxiously hugged every curve. She wanted nothing more than to snap the bitch in half for having the gall to even be there.

Rhiannon and Liam walked steadily behind them, arm-in-arm but as distanced as two people in such a situation could be. Rhiannon purposely held her head high, and tried desperately not to smell the scent of his soap, one that she regretfully knew all too well.

Instead she focused on Rian, who stood at the altar, his lips curved in a satisfied smile and his hands clenched together behind his back. When he met her eyes, she attempted to smile at him, but wasn't sure how well she succeeded. By the concerned look he gave her as he nodded in return, she had a feeling she'd failed miserably.

She did her best to ignore Stella, who sat in the front row right next to where Liam would be standing. But unfortunately, when she reached the altar and took her place beside Blythe, she had an uninhibited view of the woman regardless.

Averting her eyes, she looked instead at Thea, who stood in the center of the altar, adorned in a dress the color of peacock feathers, her dark mass of curls wild and free over her shoulders. Her expression was filled with love and pride, and Rhiannon tried desperately to absorb some of the confidence Thea projected. She was going to need it to get through the ceremony.

Though he hadn't had any inclination to do so, something drew Liam's eyes to Rhiannon in that moment. And so he stared at her, his heart filling with this indescribable feeling. It yearned toward her, thudding hard in his chest and filled with needs and desires, so much so that his mind was shouting for him to ignore it but for some reason he just couldn't…his heart was winning the battle, it was shutting out the little voice…

Shaking his head slowly, he watched with stunned and wide eyes as Rhiannon glanced over at him, as if she could sense his urgency. And when she did, the look she saw in his eyes had her knees nearly giving out beneath her. Oh, God, that look…that old, familiar look…

"Rhia," he whispered the nickname, his eyes filled with desires and questions and pain. He watched as Rhiannon nearly crumbled to her knees, her face pale with shock. Blythe managed to catch her, righting her before anyone could notice what was happening.

"What the hell's going on?" she muttered, holding Rhiannon and glaring at Liam, only to see the devastation on his face. "What, you have a change of heart?"

But then she realized that he had uttered Rhiannon's nickname for the first time since returning from New Orleans, and her eyes widened with understanding as they shot to where

Stella was sitting. What she saw had a jolt of panic shooting down her spine.

Stella's eyes had hardened to a cold, icy blue, and her face was contorted into a kind of cruel and determined scowl. She paid no mind to Blythe's watching eyes, but instead was staring very intently at Liam, who had suddenly gone very still and very quiet.

Looking back to her brother, she noticed his face had cleared of all emotion, and his lips were curved in a kind, nonchalant smile. No one would have known he was, just moments before, crumbling under the weight of heavy emotion. He now looked as if nothing had happened.

"Goddamnit." Blythe turned to Rhiannon, who was still pale and shaking, recovering from what she had seen in his eyes. For a moment, he had been himself again… "Are you okay, honey? Can you stand?"

Rhiannon nodded, inhaling deeply to calm herself as she looked away from Liam, acknowledging that the moment was gone. "I'm fine."

"Good, because Capri's coming out. Hold in there for a little bit longer, and then we'll get to the bottom of this."

She released Rhiannon, who stood tall and ignored Rian's questioning glance. She hoped no one else had seen the exchange, brief as it had been. She didn't want to think about it, didn't want it to be real…

She saw a flash of white out of the corner of her eye and turned to see Capri emerging from the entrance doors of the castle with her father, who was beaming with pride and emotion. She let herself envy, let her heart fill with love for her young friend, and felt all thoughts of Liam fade. Today was a day only for Capri.

Liam beamed at Capri and Rian, enjoying the moment as they were joined by Thea as husband and wife. He was smiling, his eyes lit with joy and pleasure, and his stance was confident and sure.

But deep inside, he was weeping. He wanted out, wanted to be released from this prison, and yet he couldn't formulate the thoughts to understand what his heart was feeling. He was lost, swimming in nothingness, while the world went on around him.

Stella, Stella, Stella...

Her name repeated over and over again in his brain, a constant repetition that pounded into him until he became absorbed in it.

Stella, Stella, Stella...

And his heart turned over piteously and raged.

His eyes watched unseeingly as Brogan handed Rian the rings, as he and Capri recited vows that were nothing but words to him. He felt them land on the surface of his mind and then evaporate into nothing as if they hadn't existed.

But the second Rian slipped the ring onto Capri's finger and the diamond glittered beautifully in the light, the memory of the ring he'd chosen for Rhiannon jolted through him in a vivid flash, along with the memory of her face, smiling at him with those quietly serious jade eyes. He'd forgotten about the ring, and his intent to propose...

Stella would like the ring...she loves sapphires...

The voice echoed through the memory, slicing the vision of Rhiannon's face free so it flew swiftly away, leaving only the ring. His lips suddenly curved as the little voice encouraged him.

I should marry Stella...

But the yearning to see those jade eyes again had him glancing away from the ring and looking at the girl who stood across from him, dressed in dusty rose with silent tears in her eyes. She watched as Capri and Rian kissed, sealing their life together, and her hands came together to clap along with the entire crowd as the newlyweds turned to face their family and friends.

His heart forced his eyes to stay on Rhiannon, despite what was happening around them. Had he wanted to marry her? Why couldn't he remember?

She had always been the most beautiful creature he had ever laid eyes upon...

Stella is so much more beautiful. Those eyes, so blue...

His heart darkened under the clouds as the voice took over and the storm rolled in, filled with Stella's face and name, causing him to forget his thoughts about Rhiannon.

And when she briefly glanced up at him as they hooked arms to walk back up the aisle, he only smiled, not remembering the thoughts that moments before had shaken his very soul.

He held Stella close as they danced, a pleasant smile on his face while a war exploded inside him. But on the outside he looked like a man dancing with a beautiful woman and celebrating the union of two of his closest friends.

"I never understood the need to have it be morning all the time," Stella muttered, rolling her eyes as she glared around at the courtyard irritably. "It's so contrived."

"Mmm," Liam responded, not even hearing her comment. He was shrouded in the fog, encased in the cocoon of her control.

"Liam, I want you to tell your friends and family that you love me," she said, meeting his eyes intently. "We're on track now, but we have to keep pushing."

"Okay." He smiled, his mind flashing with her instructions even as he felt sick to his stomach. When he winced from the nausea, her eyes narrowed in annoyance.

"What is it?" she asked, reaching up to touch his cheek so he would look at her again.

The pain cleared from his face almost instantly, replaced by cool indifference. "Nothing."

"Good." She glanced over his shoulder and saw Blythe approaching, and it took all the control she had not to sneer. That brat was getting on her nerves, and fast.

Blythe tapped Liam's shoulder, causing him to turn around.

"Wanna dance?" she asked, even as her eyes narrowed in on Stella territorially. The message was clear, but Stella conceded, knowing it wouldn't do to cause too many waves.

One dance would be nice.

Nodding, Liam grinned. "Sure."

As Stella stepped away to take a seat within eyeshot at one of the nearby tables, Blythe let Liam pull her close and she made a point of meeting his eyes. She was determined to get to the bottom of what had happened during the ceremony between him and Rhiannon. There had been some kind of breakthrough, she was sure of it…but just what had caused it or allowed the true Liam to come through, she just couldn't be sure.

But damn it to hell, she was going to figure it out.

"The ceremony was nice," she began, watching his every facial expression with discriminating care. One wrong move that seemed out of place and she would notice.

Liam only grinned. "Very nice. They're good together." He nodded over her shoulder to where Capri and Rian were seated at one of the tables, faces close as they spoke quietly to one another, smiling and laughing. He felt a stab of envy at the sight, but the feeling was purposely ignored.

"Was it awkward for you to walk with Rhiannon?"

"Not at all," he assured her, smiling again. "She understands that I'm with Stella now. There's no hard feelings."

"Aren't there?" Blythe managed, saying the words before she'd even given them any thought, pain in her eyes. She'd seen the anguish on his face earlier, and the pale shock on Rhiannon's. She'd be damned if he'd try and say there were no feelings involved.

"No, Blythe, there aren't," he replied sternly, frowning at her. "It's time for you to let this go. Besides, I love Stella and I'm going to ask her to marry me."

Blythe cursed violently under her breath and felt instantly sick, unable to even look at him. "You can't mean that," she groaned, feeling her frustration and temper rise within, burning red hot. "Goddamnit."

She flung him off her, only to grab him by the shoulders and shake him violently.

"*What have you done with my brother?*" she shouted, her eyes filled with furious tears and her throat tightening with emotion. Damnit, this just wasn't Liam…around them, people began to stare, alarmed by the shouting.

Liam gaped at her, startled into sudden clarity by the look in her eyes and the sight of her tears. Abruptly, an image of her flashed in his mind, taking him back to the bridal store, where she had stood with both Capri and Rhiannon, all of them smiling happily at him. He saw their faces, clear as day, and the feeling it gave him filled his heart with a warm, liquid love that he had forgotten how to feel…

His eyes widened as he came back to reality and reached out to Blythe, cupping her face in his hands, suddenly mortally afraid.

"Help me," he whispered so softly she barely heard it. Blythe gripped his wrists and shuddered, the look in his eyes terrifying her.

"From what? What's happening to you?" She felt the hope rise within her, mixing with the adrenaline pumping through her veins.

But the look of terror in Liam's eyes began to fade and she saw a quiet calm replace it as his face went slack, devoid of any emotion. She shook him, begging him to come back to her, but the blank look in his eyes indicated he was already gone.

Stella was almost instantly at his side, and her hand slid possessively over his shoulder, resting there confidently as she stared Blythe down with a knowing smile.

"I'll have him back now, if you don't mind." Stella pulled Liam away, leaving Blythe standing in the middle of the dance floor, stunned into silent surrender. Around her, people began to murmur, unsure what was going on. She could care less about any of them.

Jax was watching her apprehensively from the edge of the dance floor, and she suddenly whirled around and went to him, grabbing his arm and dragging him away from the crowd, needing to share what had happened. Lucian immediately followed her, having witnessed the exchange.

When they were out of earshot of the party, which resumed as if nothing had happened, Blythe stared at both men, real fear in her eyes.

"He's being controlled by Stella. I don't know how, but he is," she began, her hands shaking from both panic and adrenaline.

"What happened out there?" Lucian asked, glancing briefly at where Liam was sitting at one of the tables, Stella beside him. He looked cheerful and carefree as always, as if the exchange with Blythe hadn't even occurred.

"I don't know what really happened, but it was like he suddenly came out of whatever stupor he's been in, and he begged me to help him." Blythe's voice hitched in her throat at the memory, the helplessness she felt destroying her inside. "And then it was like he vanished again…poof, gone."

She waved her hands in the air to demonstrate, her eyes wet with furious tears. She hadn't known what to do, hadn't been able to keep him there…

"Christ," Jax cursed, running a hand through his hair as a cold shudder ran through his body. It was worse than he thought.

"Then the bitch came and took him away," Blythe snarled, her hands clenching into fists. "I don't know how she's doing it, but it's her. Even during the ceremony, it was like he snapped out of it for a brief moment, and he said Rhiannon's nickname… he hasn't said it since he came back, but he said it while we were standing there."

"We need to tell Thea," Lucian decided, looking over Blythe's shoulder in search of Mother Earth. "She might know what it all means."

"We have to do something." Blythe crossed her arms over her chest, suddenly feeling cold. "Damnit, he needs me and I have no idea what to do."

Lucian hugged her, needing comfort himself. He only wanted his son back…

Jax watched Blythe silently cry, tears streaming down her cheeks as she grieved with Lucian, and he felt disgust and fury rise in him. Glaring over at Stella, his eyes narrowed with suspicion.

"I'll go talk to Thea," he said suddenly, meeting Blythe's eyes determinedly. "We'll get to the bottom of this."

Thea listened to Jax's explanation in the garden room with silent patience, her hands folded primly in her lap. They were seated side-by-side on one of her long sofas and they were alone. Outside in the courtyard, the wedding reception continued on without them.

She appreciated Jax's expertise, trusted his sharp mind and ability to figure all the angles of a problem. But she just wasn't sure if she could trust Blythe's interpretation of the events. The girl had been in an angry and emotional state of mind, and she had been looking for any sign to point to Liam not being himself. And while they had all noticed Liam behaving strangely, it did not necessarily mean anything other than a simple change of heart on his behalf. She had to look at everything under a broad scope, and take everything into consideration.

Though she had to admit, the idea of Liam being under Stella's control had merit, but unfortunately there was very little hard evidence to back up the claim. What Blythe had witnessed both during the ceremony and during their dance was alarming to say the least, but there was no way of knowing what it truly meant.

Blythe could have heard him wrong, could have read more into his words than what was intended. Or she could be right.

When Jax finished, Thea nodded and thought over the situation, weighing the options. They could interrogate Stella, force the truth out of the girl. But then it would be prudent to interrogate Liam as well, and that made them no better than Burke had been several weeks earlier. Thea had no intention of going down that path again. Trust was important to her and she wanted to trust those she cared about. Hadn't her lack of trust led her years before to banish Bristol and to banish Brock for a crime he hadn't even committed?

No…she was supposed to be opening herself to trusting more, and while her trust in Burke had proved faulty, she had to have faith that Liam wouldn't purposely put the family in danger. So really, there was only one answer…

"I want you to keep an eye on Stella, but I don't want you to do anything drastic just yet," Thea instructed softly. "We can't be sure what is happening. This could all be innocent, and if it is, we will only be unnecessarily hurting one of our own."

Jax stared at her in disbelief. "That's it? You don't want to do anything?"

"Except watch," Thea corrected, her dark eyes sharpening with conviction.

Jax rubbed his face in frustration. He had hoped Thea would take his side on this, but he had to follow her orders regardless of what he felt was the right action to take.

"Look, Rian and I have been researching and all that we've turned up is that there have been instances of demons inhabiting a human since birth and becoming so connected to that person's soul that they can no longer be distinguished from the human they inhabit. But that seems faulty because we know for certain that Liam is not possessed himself."

"But you feel something's off with Stella," Thea stated, nodding in agreement. "I've felt it too. There's something familiar about her...but Jax, this could also be us overreacting to the circumstances. We're all upset for Rhiannon, but it is not up to us to dictate what Liam does with his life."

Jax let out a huff of breath and rose to his feet, reaching for her hand to help her up as well. Face-to-face, he met her eyes with a firm and steady resolve.

"He's not acting on his own accord, Thea. I guarantee it."

He turned and left the room, leaving her hanging on his words. And as she stood there, lost in her own thoughts, something occurred to her that at first seemed so outlandish and ridiculous that she nearly laughed at herself.

But when she gave it a bit more credence, she realized that it was quite possibly the only answer that made sense.

If and only if Stella truly was controlling Liam and he was not acting of his own free will, then there was really only one likely explanation. And the fact that the girl seemed familiar only gave more credit to the assumption, coupled with her clearly not being under the influence of demons.

If Stella wasn't an innocent human, then she must be a Muse.

Chapter Nine

Blythe found her in the Greenhouse, fussing with one of the large, freestanding corkboards that held numerous charts and drawings. It was obvious she wanted to keep her mind off what had happened by diving into work that could have easily waited until morning, but Blythe didn't care for Rhiannon's bizarre defenses at the moment. She wanted to get a rise out of her. She wanted her to fight back, to at least show some concern for what was happening to Liam.

She kept her head high as she walked into the Greenhouse; backing down was not an option.

"We have to talk about this, Rhiannon," Blythe began, noting Rhiannon flinch at her words, though she didn't turn around.

"I'd rather not," she answered simply, continuing her organization of the charts and drawings, wishing Blythe would just leave her alone. She was not in the mood for one of her tirades.

"Don't you remember when Capri told us she was getting married, the four of us made a deal to not let anything come between us ever again?" Blythe charged, edging closer, determined not to let Rhiannon slink out of this.

Rhiannon closed her eyes and sucked in a deep breath, the memory of that day painful for her. It was one of those moments that she was fighting to convince herself had never happened...

"Nothing has come between the four of us, Blythe," Rhiannon said, her eyes opening as she turned and stared at the Fire Dryad. "What has happened between Liam and me does not concern you and Capri. I hope I can speak for him as well as for myself when I say that I don't want this to undermine the unity we have now as Dryads."

Blythe scowled, crossing her arms and letting out an impatient huff of breath. "You're such a damn adult sometimes. Can't you just admit that you're pissed off about this, that it is a big deal, and that you want him back?"

"No." Rhiannon stood tall and unyielding, just as stubborn as Blythe was. "He can do whatever he wants with his life. I'm not going to stand in his way."

"So you're going to stand here and lie to my face about what happened to you earlier? I saw you damn near collapse when he said that stupid name he always called you. And you and I both saw the look on his face." She stepped forward, fighting back the urge to shake Rhiannon out of her defiant indifference. "He was himself again...don't you understand?"

Rhiannon's throat clenched painfully at the grief in Blythe's voice. Of course she had seen it...he'd looked at her like he always used to, in a way that he hadn't since he'd come back from New Orleans.

But she couldn't let it change things...she couldn't give in to some wild hope that this wasn't reality.

"Even if he tried to reconcile with me now, I don't think I could forgive him," Rhiannon murmured, her heart shivering with ice. "I won't let this happen to me again."

"And what if you found out that he was being controlled by that bitch? That she had somehow gotten into his head and was manipulating him?" Blythe argued, fisting her hands on her hips angrily.

"That's absurd." Rhiannon shook her head, her eyes hard and cold.

Blythe had to beat back the urge to scream and shout and rage, whatever it would take to make Rhiannon react. But she'd yet again hit a brick wall and all the screaming in the world wouldn't break through it.

"When I figure out what's going on and he comes out of whatever this is, I'm going to tell him that you abandoned him," she said, sneering at Rhiannon with disgust in her eyes. "He'll know just how easily you gave up."

"I'm giving him freedom," Rhiannon pointed out, though Blythe's words had hit a chord with her.

Blythe chuckled, though there was no humor in the sound nor in her expression. "You're a damn fool, Rhiannon."

If she had shouted the words they would have had no greater impact. Rhiannon watched wearily as Blythe left the Greenhouse, shutting the door forcefully behind her.

A group of them crowded around the giant oak tree in the meadow while Thea transitioned the sky from day to night, closing out what had been, for the majority of the guests, a spectacular wedding and reception.

Rhiannon pulled Capri to the side, wanting to say her goodbyes in private before the newlyweds left for their honeymoon.

"Did you remember to pack extra film for your camera? And the maps I gave you? Oh, and the small pill box with your vitamins and aspirin?"

Capri smiled, laughter in her eyes. "Of course, Rhiannon. I got everything on your list, I promise."

Rhiannon let out a quick sigh, biting back the rest of her worries over the three day trip to Maine. A tiny bed and break-fast tucked into a quiet seaboard town sounded safe, but she still worried.

"Promise me you'll be careful," she told Capri, giving her a hug.

"I promise. Rian is bringing half his artillery with us it seems." Capri giggled and rolled her eyes affectionately as she pulled away. "I'm more worried about you, really."

Rhiannon brushed her friend's concerns away. "I'm perfectly fine. Now go on and have a good trip."

"Alright." Tears filled Capri's eyes as she hugged Rhiannon one last time, fighting back her own concerns. "Goodbye."

Rhiannon watched her say goodbye to the others, and as she did, she realized what she had to do. Perhaps Blythe was right and she was a fool, but she was determined to preserve her own sanity. And unfortunately, staying where she was and continuing on while trying to maintain a blind eye was not working.

She was having a harder time than she wanted to admit to herself watching Liam with that woman, with her gorgeous blonde hair, stunning, perfect blue eyes and amazing body. How could she fault Liam for wanting Stella over her?

But she was still a practical woman and she knew her worth. She could move on and she would survive. But she would never, ever let herself love again. It was much too dangerous.

Even now, the temptation to look at him, to search his eyes for that old familiar look sang through to her very bones. But she was terrified that she wouldn't see it, that it just didn't exist any longer.

So perhaps it was time for her to escape, at least until her system settled down and she could confidently say she was back to normal. It would help, she knew, to distance herself geographically from him for awhile. It would give them both time to resume life as it had been…before.

She felt her father come up behind her and place a soothing hand on her shoulder. She leaned into him, oddly content for the first time in days, and watched as Capri and Rian waved goodbye to everyone before disappearing in a flash of golden light.

Liam watched Rhiannon with her father, a symbol of quiet strength, and suddenly it hit him that he had always loved that about her…she was so unbelievably strong, no matter what happened. And she used to never cry, but he'd opened her heart and freed her…he loved her, more than anything in the entire world.

The sudden pain that struck him was as fast and violent as a bolt of lightning. His knees gave out as he fell to the ground, clutching his chest, his heart thundering loud and clear. It was war, plain and simple, and his heart wanted to win.

Stella knelt beside him and smiled reassuringly at those few who turned curiously to stare. She pressed her hand over the back of his neck and, at the same time he felt her fingers touch his skin, the little voice resounded loudly in his mind.

The pain is nothing. Go with Stella, show everyone how much you love her.

"No…" he groaned, fighting back against the voice. He reached up to clutch his head now, his heart a trapped bird scenting freedom. If he could just beat back the voice…if he could keep his own thoughts…

There's no point in fighting. It's easier to give in.

She squeezed her hand and with a flashing white wave he felt his mind go blank and his body go numb, the fog settling in. She coaxed him back to her slowly, cursing herself for letting him get even that close to breaking her hold over him. He had a stronger heart than she'd given him credit for…

"Come along, handsome, let's go get another glass of champagne," Stella told him, casually pulling him to his feet and smiling at those around them.

Liam saw nothing but her face and heard nothing but the echoing of her name as he followed her blindly.

It was nearly midnight and Rhiannon walked through the dark, empty corridor in silence. In one hand she clutched her suitcase, filled with the essentials she would need for her time away. In the other hand, she held the notes she intended to leave for both her father and for Thea, explaining her absence and apologizing for any inconvenience it may cause them.

In the note, she'd neglected to leave a hint as to when she would be returning, since even she herself didn't know. She'd only said that she would not be too long and that they were not to worry about her. This was a necessary step and a much needed break from the strain of maintaining nonchalance in the light of what had been happening. She knew, well she hoped, that all of them would understand.

In her efficient way, she went first to the Greenhouse and neatly pinned her note addressed to her father to the wooden door. She pressed her fingers gently to her lips, and then touched the note affectionately, sorry that this was going to cause him grief. But he would have to make do, as she had already made up her mind.

Next she went to the garden room and pinned Thea's note to the door as well. She stepped back and stared at the door a moment, knowing Thea would understand. That had made her decision easier in a way, though she hadn't needed anyone's approval.

She didn't want anyone to know where she was going. Well, she was practical enough to tell one person, just in case there was some kind of an emergency. But she knew the information would not be shared and therefore they would be forced to leave her alone.

Tilting her head up confidently, Rhiannon strolled out of the castle and through the courtyard, down into the meadow and to the oak tree.

No one was awake to see the light of her departure.

When Rohan found the note, he almost didn't believe it. Rhiannon take off spontaneously on a whim? That wasn't like her...

But the note said it all, and he knew his daughter's neat, pristine handwriting better than anyone.

Father,

In light of everything that has happened, I have decided to take some time away in order to recharge and reflect. I hope this does not cause you much inconvenience and I promise that I will work extra hard to make up the time when I return.

I'm sorry to leave this way, so suddenly and without much explanation, but I hope you will understand that this is vitally important for my wellbeing.

I'm not going to disclose the location of where I will be staying because I do not want you or the others to try and find me. I need to be alone, plain and simple.

I do not know when I will return, but I promise it will not be too long. I just need a little bit of time to myself and once I have that I will be fully at your disposal again.

Please don't worry about me. I love you.

Rhiannon

His hands were shaking as he went straight to the garden room, needing Thea. Fury began to mix with the concern and grief in his gut as he headed through the corridor, the note clutched tightly in his hands.

The door to the garden room was open so he didn't bother knocking as he went inside, his eyes landing on Thea who was seated on one of her lounge chairs.

Before he could speak, he saw a note in her hands as well, and steady tears in her eyes as she stared at him.

They both were silent, each knowing exactly what the other had just discovered. Rohan numbly took a seat beside Thea.

He handed her the note, then buried his face in his hands and wept.

She rubbed his back consolingly as she read it, pain resounding deep in her heart. She should have been expecting something like this, but the truth was that she hadn't. Rhiannon had seemed to be taking everything so well, with that spine of steel Thea had always known the girl possessed. But something like this…it was so drastic, so unlike her. And yet, how could Thea blame Rhiannon for wanting to get away? It really was the best solution. Her only worry now was whether or not Dante would somehow locate her…she would be so vulnerable.

But there wasn't anything that could be done. Rhiannon didn't want them to be able to find her. If something were to happen to her…but no, Thea shoved the thought away, knowing she couldn't dwell on the what ifs. Rohan had come to her because he clearly needed comfort and guidance, and it was her duty to provide him with it.

"Your daughter is strong and capable, Rohan, you mustn't worry about her," Thea said soothingly, continuing to rub his back while he sobbed. "She is smart enough to stay out of trouble and in a safe location, and before you know it she'll be back, refreshed and happy again."

"This is his fault," he managed, raising his head to look at Thea, rage now filling his eyes. "That boy took advantage of her, and she tried to convince me she was fine with it but this proves how badly he hurt her."

"Rohan, this is for the best," Thea said assuredly, unnerved by the violence in his eyes. "It will be good for Rhiannon to get away for awhile."

"What's this?" Sebastian questioned as he strolled into the room, his warm gray eyes assessing the situation. He could all but feel the tension and the anger in the air, and saw from the look on Rohan's face that he was projecting the bulk of it. "Rhiannon is gone?"

"She left us notes explaining that she is taking a vacation for awhile. That is all," Thea told him, handing him her note as he approached and took the seat across from her.

"That's strange…" he murmured as his eyes scanned the note, reading Rhiannon's lovely handwriting.

Thea,

I know this is sudden, but I have decided to take a brief vacation in light of what has happened. I feel it is best that I get away for awhile and take some time for me. I have been regrettably distracted as of late, and some time away will help me recharge and reflect.

I apologize in advance for abandoning my duties for this currently unknown period of time, but I promise I will make it up to you tenfold.

I hope that you will not think less of me for leaving on such short notice and I really hope you do not feel I am being weak. Perhaps I am, in a way, but I see no other option than to distance myself from Liam for the time being.

Please tell the others not to worry, I won't be gone long. Do not attempt to find me, as I do not wish to be found.

Rhiannon

Sebastian let out a long sigh as he handed the letter back to Thea. He settled back against the sofa, thinking about what he had read.

"This is in her best interest, Rohan," Sebastian said, meeting eyes with the Earth Dryad, knowing it wasn't what he wanted to hear. But it needed to be said. "Liam traipsing around the castle with the blonde has not helped things."

Rohan's teeth clenched as he scowled. "I can't believe I was so wrong about him."

"We are all surprised by his behavior," Thea began, looking at Sebastian worriedly. "But these things tend to work themselves out. Rhiannon is an incredibly strong girl. I do not see her suffering from this for very long."

"No, but he is not suffering at all," Rohan spat, his eyes now dry. In place of his earlier misery was resentment and fury. "It's not right."

"Perhaps not, but his actions are not within our control. All we can do is support Rhiannon as best as we can." Thea placed a gentle hand on his knee, hoping to ease his anger. "Go back to work, Rohan, and forget about this for the time being. Your daughter will be fine."

He nodded, sensing the dismissal in her voice. Rising to his feet, he left the room without looking at her or Sebastian. He wasn't going to stop thinking about it, how could he when his daughter was missing? It was all Liam's fault...

He nearly ran into Serendipity as he swept into the corridor, and the sight of her startled him. She stared up at him, a bit shaken herself.

"Good morning, Rohan," she greeted politely, attempting a small smile. It hurt her to see him, especially since he had, for weeks now, refused to touch her or even look at her. He still had yet to forgive what she had done, and none of her attempts to reconcile had been successful. But there was something in his eyes now, some kind of desperation that she latched onto with the hopes of being able to break through his shield. "What's wrong? Are you alright?"

Rohan debated just walking away since the sight of her still caused an ache deep within his chest. He still loved her and he knew he always would…but he definitely did not trust her.

However, Rhiannon was her daughter as well, and she had a right to know what was happening.

"Rhiannon is gone. She left Thea and me both a note this morning saying that she is taking some time away from Euphora. We don't know where she is or when she'll return," he said, crossing his arms to squash the urge to seek comfort from her.

"Dear God." Serendipity's hand flew up to cover her mouth, alarmed by the news. And immediately following the alarm came the guilt. "Did she say what upset her?"

"Isn't it obvious, Serendipity?" Rohan demanded, throwing his hands up in the air bitterly. "That low life son of a bitch and his new girlfriend have driven our daughter away from her own home."

"I see…" she murmured, despising herself for being grateful that he hadn't said it was because of her own wretched misdeeds. "Was Rhiannon really hurt by what happened? I haven't had much time to really speak with her…"

"Damnit, of course she is hurt, she loved him!" Rohan shook his head, fighting to keep his temper under control. His entire life he had known how to do it so well, but lately he'd been like a powder keg, fuse lit to burst at every opportunity. "I guess you wouldn't really understand love, though, would you?"

Hurt, Serendipity stared up at him miserably. "I know I've done so much wrong, Rohan, but if you give me the chance to make it right, I promise I'll do my best…"

"Your best does not mean much, Serendipity. I expected your best from the start," he said flatly, straightening in an attempt to ignore the obvious despair in her eyes. He wasn't ready to accept her back into his life, not yet. "I have to get back to work."

He pushed past her and left her standing in limbo, wondering if he was ever going to forgive her.

Chapter Ten

Liam didn't care that Rhiannon was gone. The news slid into his brain, processed, then slid right back out again with a shrug of indifference. So she was out of the way. That was fine. It made things easier. He could spend more of his time focusing on Stella. Why should he care if Rhiannon wanted to take a little vacation? She didn't mean anything to him.

While the news had done little to stir his mind, it had quite the opposite effect on his heart.

But because the little voice would not let him understand what the ache in his chest truly meant, he had no idea just how anguished he actually was. The part of him that was buried deep inside was writhing with worry and fear, but he couldn't reach the emotion through the haze of fog. And so it was his burden to brush off the issue without a care in the world, despite the accusing stares he was receiving from nearly everyone on Euphora.

The only person who seemed as unperturbed as he, was Stella. And together, the two of them resumed as if nothing out of the ordinary had occurred at all.

"So tell me about your parents, Liam," Stella asked, feeding him a grape as they lounged beneath one of the large trees in the courtyard. Liam's head was nestled comfortably in her lap while she pressed him for information.

"Their marriage was arranged," he began, swallowing the grape and smiling pleasantly. "He loved her, but she didn't love him, but they decided to get married out of obligation. They both needed to produce an heir, and so they decided to come together and use one another. I never knew any of this until recently when I overheard them arguing with each other. My dad can't understand why my mom supports Serendipity, while he supports Rohan. The issue has divided them."

"Very interesting…" Stella mused, feeding him another grape as she absorbed the information, filing it away for later. "So your father and Rohan get along?"

"Usually. But sometimes their differences get in the way."

"How so?" she pressed, wanting more.

"My dad doesn't like Serendipity, never has. It's been a touchy topic between them for years."

"Because Rohan loves her, despite your father's disapproval?"

"Yes. And he used to always defend her, until she wronged him and Rhiannon so badly that he's now separated from her. But I don't think he's ever stopped loving her, despite everything."

"Pathetic." Stella chuckled, enormously pleased by how much drama there was to choose from. "Tell me, Liam, what is Thea's greatest fear?"

"Losing one of us, or all of us," he casually replied, smiling up at her. "She's scared of death, even though she cannot die."

"No, but all of you can." Stella smiled wickedly, stroking her fingers affectionately through his dark hair. "I wonder what would become of her and Sebastian if all of you perished, and if this place was reduced to nothing but rubble and ash…"

"They'd rebuild," he said automatically, causing her to scowl down at him.

"Then we would destroy everything again and again, until she hadn't the strength to bother trying. We would drive her from this Earth and then we would rule." Stella's hands clenched excitedly in Liam's hair, causing him to wince from the pain. Sensing him suddenly slipping from her control, she swiftly guided him back to her, encasing him in her thick cocoon. "Liam…you're mine now, don't forget. My little puppet, my little mind to probe and use to my heart's desire. Don't you dare think of fighting back, because you won't win…"

Out of the corner of her eye, she spotted Clarity and Serendipity approaching, looking apprehensive and concerned. Forcing the greedy vengeance from her face, Stella smiled up at the two women and encouraged Liam to do the same.

"Hello there," she said cheerfully.

"Ladies," Liam greeted, grinning at his mother.

Clarity wrung her hands in front of her, her pretty face contorted with anxiety.

"Liam, can we speak with you, alone?" she requested, her eyes darting to Stella uneasily. Stella had to bite back the urge to roll her eyes and instead instructed Liam on what to say.

"Does Stella have to go? Whatever you have to say to me, you can say in front of her."

"It's important that we speak alone, Liam," Serendipity added.

Knowing it would look too suspicious if he refused again, Stella spoke for him.

"Go ahead, handsome. I'll wait right here." She smiled down at him and winked, knowing she was putting on a show. He grinned in return and sat up, kissing her before climbing to his feet.

"I'm all yours," he announced, following the Muses as they led him several yards away where they would not be overheard.

Serendipity spoke first, her agitation clear. "I have to ask, Liam, because I am concerned for my daughter. Why have you done this to her? She's distraught enough that she's left her home and you don't seem to care."

His responses were ingrained in his mind like a speech to be recited on cue. "To be honest, I don't care. If this is what will bring her peace of mind, then it's fine with me."

Clarity frowned, unsure why her normally caring son should be so callous. "Aren't you worried about her, even a little? She's out there somewhere, alone, because she's hurting over you."

He shrugged, tucking his hands into his pockets and grinning. "Not really my problem."

Startled, Clarity and Serendipity stared at each other and gaped, not believing what they had just heard.

"How can you love someone one minute and then not even care at all about them the next?" Clarity asked, confusion in her eyes as she stared at her son as if he were a stranger.

He turned to her, and something dark flashed over his face even as he continued to smile. "I don't know. How could you marry dad without any intention of ever returning his love for you? You used him all these years and have never given back what you've taken from him."

"What?" Clarity stammered, her hands flying up to clutch her chest in shock. Beside her, Serendipity looked irate.

"That is none of your business," she declared, scowling at him.

Perhaps she should have seen it coming when he turned on her next. "You're even worse. You broke one man's heart to marry another, never truly loving either of them. Then for years you pranced around criticizing everyone else while you have been the worst of all. You cheated on your husband and hurt him, then you accused your daughter of murder and hurt her, and now you have nothing. You are the definition of a disgrace."

"Liam!" Clarity managed, turning to Serendipity apologetically. "I don't know what's gotten into him, he's not normally like this."

"Don't apologize, Clarity," Serendipity said sharply, the wound he'd ripped open in her heart pulsating painfully. "It isn't your fault your son is cruel." She jabbed a finger into his chest, her eyes hard and cold as ice. "I warned Rhiannon that you were good for nothing and for awhile I thought I was wrong. But now I see that I was indeed correct. You disgust me; you disgust all of us."

She grabbed Clarity's arm and whirled around, dragging her away. Liam watched them go, scratching his head curiously at the sight. Had he upset them?

But before he could give it much thought, the little voice came into his mind again and urged him to go back to Stella.

It didn't take long for the Muses to relate to their husbands what Liam had said. And it took even less time for both Lucian and Rohan to head out into the courtyard to demand he explain himself. Neither of them could believe that Liam would be so insensitive to his own mother and another woman, but if the Muses were being honest, then he had definitely crossed the line.

They walked together, side-by-side, both fueled by anger and frustration. Lucian's anger was more miserable and helpless, and Rohan's was red hot. But both men could agree that they were at their wits end with Liam.

"What did you say to my wife?" Rohan snarled, approaching where Liam lay in the grass with Stella. Lucian stopped beside Rohan, crossing his arms and staring down uncertainly at his son.

Liam glanced up at both men, and for a brief second felt fear and confusion race through him. But when Stella ran her fingers through his hair, caressing him soothingly, the feelings subsided and were replaced by cool indifference.

"I just told them the truth." Liam smiled as he sat up, eyeing both men. "What's the big deal?"

"What you said was uncalled for and insensitive," Lucian charged, shaking his head disbelievingly. "It's not your business to get involved in the details of my marriage, Liam. Do you hear me?"

Liam chuckled, rolling his eyes. "So she was offended. Big deal. She needed to be put in her place."

Lucian's eyes widened in shock as he glanced over at Rohan, who was barely constraining his fury.

"I've been waiting for any excuse to punish you for what you did to Rhiannon," Rohan began, clenching and unclenching his fists as his lips curled into a sneer. "I'd say you causing my wife distress is a good enough reason."

He lunged forward, only to have Lucian grab him and hold him back.

"*No!*" Lucian shouted, shoving Rohan and standing defensively between the Earth Dryad and his son. "I will not stand by and watch you beat my son to death, Rohan."

Rohan looked at his old friend, his eyes filled with bitterness and rage. "I've given him plenty of grievance over this, Lucian, and you know it. But I can't put up with it any longer."

"Taking your anger out on him physically is not going to accomplish anything," Lucian reasoned. "Whatever he may have done, he is still my son."

"And what about my daughter?" Rohan snarled. "Your son was supposed to love her, he was supposed to protect her. And instead he broke her heart and left her to bleed on the damn floor."

"You don't know that," Lucian said darkly, his hands shaking as the adrenaline pumped through him.

Rohan paused for a moment as he interpreted Lucian's words, his eyes trailing down to look at Liam and Stella, who were still sitting in the grass silently. He felt a sudden disbelieving laugh bubble in his throat, and he let it out gleefully.

"I know what I see with my eyes, Lucian." Rohan smirked cruelly. "And I see your selfish son ruining his life. Serendipity was right; he is worthless."

"*Damn you!*" Lucian launched himself at Rohan, fists flying, his vision hazed with red. Rohan fought back, and the two men swung at each other and tangled together, clawing and pounding, intending to destroy.

Brock cursed loudly as he and Clynn appeared suddenly from the castle, racing down the cobblestone walkway, both fighting back the initial shock at seeing their two friends brawling.

Brock grabbed Rohan and forcefully yanked him off Lucian, which wasn't hard since he was by far stronger. But Rohan swung out and clipped him hard in the jaw, causing him to howl in pain. His own temper burst and he would have struck back had Clynn not shouted at the top of his lungs, halting the fighting.

"*Stop this, now!*" Clynn yelled, one hand on Lucian's chest and the other gripping Brock's shirt, his face contorted with fear and anxiety. "We mustn't fight, please," he managed, his breath ragged and his heart racing.

Brock stepped back from Rohan, hands raised in the air and shutting his eyes to calm himself. He had come out here to stop the fight, not to get involved...

Rohan wiped at the blood that was dripping from his split lip, his eyes dark and dangerous as he glared at Lucian. But seeing the hurt on Clynn's face had guilt creeping into his system.

Lucian pressed the palm of his hand to his right eye, where he was certain he'd have a shiner. His biggest fear at the moment was how they were going to explain to Thea why they had fought.

Taking a deep breath to steady himself and sensing the worst of the anger had passed, Clynn backed off Lucian and stared accusingly at all three men.

"Look at what's become of us," he declared, shaking his head, misery in his eyes. "We used to be like brothers, the four of us. Why are we doing this to ourselves?"

Blythe, having seen the scuffle from her window upstairs, had raced down as quickly as she could and was now running toward them at full speed.

"What the hell is going on?" she cried, reaching Brock first and hugging him. Immediately she pulled away, examining his body for injuries. The only clear one was a bruise already blooming on his jaw. "Christ, dad," she whispered, at a loss for words as she reached up to tenderly touch the bruise, frightened and furious tears in her eyes.

"I'm alright, babydoll." Brock tried to smile, but winced from the sharp pain.

"Goddamnit, explain yourselves!" she shouted, rounding on the other three older men. She had to bite back a gasp at the sight of Lucian and Rohan, bleeding and bruised, both panting from the fight. "Did it start with you two?"

Lucian nodded, feeling ashamed. He shot a glance down at Liam, who was sitting there, his face oddly calm and blank. Stella's eyes gleamed with excitement, but he was too weary to pay much attention to it.

"I'm afraid Rohan and I let our tempers get the better of us," he explained, reaching out to Blythe, deeply embarrassed. "But it's over now and I think we both feel better, at least emotionally. Right?" He glanced over to Rohan, who was taking deep, steady breaths in an attempt to calm himself. He met Lucian's eyes as he nodded.

"I'm sorry, Lucian. Please forgive me," he apologized, though there was no emotion in his voice.

Blythe found herself feeling oddly sorry for him. He was obviously on edge since Rhiannon had taken off and she supposed she couldn't blame him. "Clynn, can you take them inside so they can get cleaned up? Then maybe you can explain to Thea what happened, smooth things over before she has to see the damage."

Clynn nodded. "Certainly. You heard the girl, let's go inside before Thea catches wind of this."

The four men headed inside, and it pleased Blythe to see Lucian pat Rohan on the back, and Rohan turn and smile at him. She had learned that with men, it seemed arguments were sometimes best settled with fists, not words.

With a heavy sigh, she turned to Liam and Stella. As calmly as she could, she asked her first and most important question.

"Did you encourage them to fight?"

Her question was directed at Stella, but it was Liam who responded. "No, of course not."

"I didn't ask you," Blythe said, her voice level despite the quick flare of temper. "Stella, did you encourage this fight?"

Stella smiled innocently. "I just don't know what you mean by that, honey. How could I get two grown men to bicker with one another?"

"You know damn well how, bitch," Blythe spat, her eyes hard as steel. "I know you are somehow controlling my brother. So tell me, did you cast some kind of voodoo magic over Lucian and Rohan?"

"Voodoo's for sinners, hun. I don't play around with that stuff." Stella batted her eyes and turned to Liam, brushing his hair away from his face affectionately. "Tell her what a good girl I am, Liam."

Liam's lips curved into a slow smile as he met Blythe's eyes. "Stella and I only watched, Blythe, we didn't do anything. She wouldn't hurt a fly, much less start a fight."

"But something did," Blythe concluded, shaking her head at him. "They never so much as argue."

Liam shrugged nonchalantly and grinned. "It's over now."

"Yeah, I guess." Feeling strange and disillusioned, Blythe wrapped her arms around herself and turned away, unsure just what was happening to her family. She didn't even glance back when she heard Stella and Liam laughing, as if they hadn't a care in the world.

That night, Liam lay alone in his bed, moonlight washing over him in pale blue rays, sleep successfully evading him.

Her name and face flashed constantly in his mind like neon signs, vivid and glowing.

Stella, Stella, Stella…

And yet his heart felt heavy in his chest, aching from some long forgotten pain. But he couldn't shake the image of her blue eyes, glittering hauntingly at him, drawing him in possessively…

The memory of his father arguing with Rohan and literally going to blows with each other flickered in his mind, and he was uncertain why he felt upset about it. Stella told him it hadn't mattered and his mind had seemed to agree. Their argument had nothing to do with him just like Rhiannon's disappearance had nothing to do with him.

There was that damn pain again…he thought angrily, his mind fighting to push it away.

I don't even feel it, it's not important. Think of Stella, lovely Stella…

But he didn't want to ignore it; he wanted to know where it came from and why. It had been plaguing him for some time, getting worse at the mention of Rhiannon's name or when he saw her face…but he was almost positive that he didn't care about her so why did it hurt?

He loved Stella. He wanted to marry Stella.

Right?

He stared up at his ceiling, his blue eyes sharpening suddenly as the memory of Rhiannon's face flashed in his mind, her smile a bit shy, a bit uncertain, but the surrender clear in her eyes. So beautiful…

And then the vision of her rising over him, ivory skin glowing white in the moonlight as her body cruised over his. Her dark length of hair slipping from her shoulders, draping down to his chest as she leaned in to cover his lips with hers, her eyes glittering like emeralds in the dark.

Those hands, practical but delicately feminine, sliding over him, his body reacting to her touch. He could almost feel her, warm and close against him, as he pulled her into his arms and loved her.

His heart filled with it, this love for her, and he felt hot tears spring into his eyes as the pain mixed beautifully with this warmth and desire. She was Earth...he was Water...the two elements that best suited each other, so perfectly. She needed him, and he had saved her...

No! Stella! I love Stella!

I don't think so...

Rhiannon means nothing, she's worthless to me. I love Stella, only Stella.

He saw as clear as day Rhiannon arching beneath him, her lips parted as she said his name...

Where is she?

It doesn't matter. Who cares? She's history.

But this hurts...this pain, God, it hurts...

Ignore it.

I can't.

Yes, I can. Stella, Stella, Stella...

And then the memory of her voice, Rhiannon's voice, saying the words he'd waited all his life to hear...as long as you want me, I'm yours.

Of course I want her. I love her.

No.

Yes. God, yes, I've always loved her...

NO!

YES!

He shot up into a sitting position, clutching his violently beating heart and gasping wildly for air, his eyes wide with stunned clarity. The fog vanished from his mind as he stared around him, for the first time in days actually feeling his hands, feeling his face and his heart thudding in his chest. It was like waking up from a nightmare...cold sweat dripping down his back, painful aches still resonating in his chest, echoes of the dream still pulsing through his mind.

Stella. Who the hell was she?

And what had happened to him? Had he fallen asleep?

He tried to get to his feet, but felt dizzy and had to imme-diately sit back down, his mind still swimming with random images that seemed to make no sense...

This blonde woman, kissing him in the courtyard. His father and Rohan, shoving at each other and shouting. Blythe's angry tears and frustrated cries. Thea slapping him hard across the face, her dark eyes filled with disgust. Capri and Rian sharing a kiss at the altar. Rhiannon's pale and stunned expression as she collapsed against Blythe.

God, where had all of that come from? He pressed his palms into his eyes, willing the images away. That must have been one hell of a dream...

Taking a deep breath, he opened his eyes and fought to clear the wave of dizziness from his mind. When he felt slightly more stable, he got to his feet and slowly wandered into his bathroom, switching on the light.

He stared at his face in the mirror, examining himself. He frowned at how pale he was, at the dark shadows under his eyes and the sweat that was still dripping down his face. But it wasn't until he caught his own eyes in the mirror that he remembered.

New Orleans.

How had he gotten home? The last thing he remembered was a woman...a blonde woman.

Shaking his head, he flipped on the faucet and splashed cold water on his face, letting it soothe his skin. He realized his hands were trembling and he groaned, his head feeling hollow and wounded.

It was like something had been inside his mind and now it was gone. But that didn't make sense...

It was probably just something from the dream, he decided, drying his face and heading back into the bedroom.

And then he spotted the sapphire engagement ring, resting on the surface of his dresser, the stone glinting in the moonlight.

His eyes widened as the memory came back to him of Rhiannon, sitting on the stone steps of the back gardens, listening to him explain to her that he didn't want to be with her anymore, that things weren't working out.

We can still be friends.

Good God. That had happened, he was sure of it. What in the world had caused him to say those things to her? The last thing he wanted was to break up with her, especially after all the years he'd waited for her to love him in return.

Damnit, whatever the reason, he had to set it straight.

Grabbing the ring, he threw on a pair of jeans and left his room as quickly as he could, his heart thudding with panic and uncertainty.

He would never forgive himself if he had somehow screwed this up.

Chapter Eleven

The moment she lost it, she screamed.

"What the hell is it?" Dante demanded, looking more irritated than worried.

Stella clutched her head and rocked back and forth, trembling. "He broke the connection...I've lost him..."

"Shit!" His mood severely soured, Dante got to his feet and violently upended the chess board they'd been playing with, scattering marble pieces everywhere. Those nearby in the hotel lounge eyed him warily, but he ignored them. Leaning over Stella, he gripped her shoulders tightly and forced her to look at him, his eyes darkly dangerous. "Try and reestablish the connection. *Do it!*"

"I can't," she murmured, her eyes glassy and unseeing, her face suddenly pale. "He's gone."

"Useless bitch." Dante shoved her back and stepped away, trying to figure out what to do about this unfortunate turn of events. There was still more information he wanted Liam to unearth for them and he needed Stella on Euphora to continue to weaken the relationships.

But…a lot had already been accomplished, especially in regards to his foolish brother. Perhaps it would be enough.

"Get up," he ordered, roughly grabbing Stella's arm and dragging her to her feet. "We're going back to the room. I think I might have another idea."

"Okay," she stammered, stumbling along as he dragged her. He found it pathetically amusing that the humans looked so concerned for the woman. He wasn't going to hurt her. No, he still had use for her yet.

He punched his fist into the up button for the elevator, just because he felt like it. In fact, he wasn't really all that angry anymore. Instead, he was feeling rather excited.

When the mirrored doors opened, he pulled Stella in with him and then patiently waited for the doors to close again.

As they did, he punched the button for the sixth floor and pushed Stella into the corner so she would be forced to look at him.

"You said that the Earth Dryad took a little vacation, right?" He cupped her chin roughly in his hand, his fingers digging into the flesh of her face.

She nodded, fear in her eyes.

"Good. Did they say where she went?"

She shook her head and he scowled. "Then I want you to do whatever voodoo hoodoo thing you did to find the boy and find her." His lips curled into an eerie grin, madness flashing in his eyes. "Oh, how they'll come running the second they know we have her. Things will work out, my sweet. You just wait and see."

He went to her bedroom door, finding it closed. Unsure if barging in on her was really appropriate given that he wasn't even sure just what was going on between them, he swallowed his urgency and knocked.

He waited a few seconds, hearing no sounds inside. Knocking again, he pressed his ear against the door, imagining her lying in bed, ignoring him.

Frustration overriding any hesitation he had felt, Liam pushed open the door and swept into the room, a smile already spreading over his lips just at the thought of seeing her.

The empty room had him stopping short, confusion hazing his brain as he stared around. Maybe she was down in the kitchens…

He didn't even notice that many of her things were missing or that the room was cold, the scent of her faded and gone.

Instead he swung around, adrenaline pumping as he left the room, slamming the door shut in his hurry to get to her, wherever she was.

Blythe suddenly appeared out of her room across the hall, rubbing her eyes sleepily, having heard the noises.

"What are you doing?" she asked, yawning hugely and stretching her arms over her head.

Then she saw the brightness in his eyes and felt his urgency. Blinking back the sleep from her vision, she stepped toward him and reached out to grip his arms, holding him in front of her even as he started to go.

"Liam?" she asked, staring into his eyes, unsure whether she was really seeing him. "Is it you?"

He laughed at her, wondering what game she was playing with him. "Dork, of course it's me."

He reached out to playfully ruffle her hair, grinning. "I was just trying to find Rhia. Do you know if she's downstairs?"

Blythe faltered, her breath hitching in her throat as tears sprang almost instantly into her eyes. Her hands came up to cover her mouth, stifling a sob.

"Thank God," she whispered, suddenly throwing herself on him. He stumbled back from the force of her as he caught her in his arms, still confused by what was going on.

When Jax emerged from Blythe's room, caution in his eyes, Liam shook his head and tried to smile.

"What's wrong with her?" Liam nodded down at Blythe. "I just told her I was looking for Rhia, and she started crying."

Understanding flashed over Jax's face as his eyes narrowed in on his girlfriend. But Blythe suddenly pushed back from Liam and started beating her fists against his chest frantically, furious tears streaming down her cheeks.

"Damnit, what the hell has been going on with you?" she cried, anger and frustration exploding out of her. She was so mad at him for everything that had happened, even though the reasonable part of her that cowered in the back of her mind reminded her that it probably wasn't his fault at all...

Liam gawked at her and tried to block her blows, alarmed more than hurt by her attempts to take out her anger on him.

"Blythe, stop it," he grunted when she landed a punch straight into his gut. "I don't want to have to hit you back, but damnit, I will if you don't stop."

Jax grabbed her and pulled her away, pinning her against him until she stopped fighting back. Her breath was heaving out of her chest and her mass of fiery curls fell over her face.

"Calm down, darlin'," he murmured, rubbing her back to relax her while she fought back the beast that had burst from within.

"I'm fine," she muttered, stepping back from him and brushing her hair out of her face, taking deep and calming breaths.

Sensing she had regained control of herself, Jax looked at Liam. He crossed his arms over his chest and leaned casually against the doorframe, firmly eyeing the other man.

"Rhiannon is gone," he said flatly, noting Liam's instant denial and confusion.

"What? Where is she?" he asked, looking down at Blythe. She met his eyes and slowly shook her head.

"You don't remember?" she asked, a bit wearily, unsure how to even break the news to him. "Liam, you broke her heart. So she left."

"I don't understand." He glanced back at Jax, as if he would come out at any moment and confess it had all been some kind of joke. But from the stern look in Jax's eyes, this was far from a joke. "I remember saying something about us just being friends, but I didn't mean it. I just need to talk to her."

"Damnit, Liam," Blythe cursed, battling back the rage and emotion again as she turned away, unable to look at him. She stared dully at the stone wall in the hallway, knowing her next words would utterly destroy him. But he had to know, now that he was free from whatever had been controlling him. He had to know what he had done…

"What happened to me?" Liam ran a restless hand through his hair, panic beginning to set in. He didn't like the look in Jax's eyes, nor did he like the anguish in Blythe's. God, what else had he done?

"I can't believe you don't remember any of it…" Blythe managed, leaning against the cool stone of the wall and resting her forehead against it, fighting to breathe. "You went to New Orleans when there was that oil spill, and you were gone for several hours. We were panicking, thinking you had gotten lost or hurt or worse…and so we came looking for you. We found you in some night club in the French Quarter, cozying up with some blonde…"

"No." Anger sprang into Liam's eyes then as he rounded on Blythe, not believing her. "You're making that up."

Blythe laughed, though the humor didn't reach her eyes. "Honey, I couldn't make this up even if I tried."

"She's telling the truth, Liam," Jax added, continuing to lean against the doorframe, carefully removed from the vibrant emotions stirring the air around them. "I was there. We saw you sitting with the girl, your arms wrapped around her. You kissed her. We didn't want to believe it, either, but the fact is it happened. And when we questioned you about her, you said that you had met her on the beach and that you weren't happy with Rhiannon."

Liam's brows creased painfully as he fought to control the indignation building in his chest. "I don't understand. I don't remember any of this."

"That's probably because that bitch was controlling you somehow," Blythe spat, shaking her head bitterly. "I knew you weren't being yourself this whole time."

"What else happened?" Liam managed, staring up at Jax when Blythe was silent.

"We brought you home and you broke it off with Rhiannon. Then you brought the girl to Euphora, and you paraded her around. You told all of us that you loved her. Shit, son, even at Capri and Rian's wedding, you told Blythe you wanted to marry the girl. It'd only been a week since you'd met her."

"Stella," Liam said then, the name flashing in his mind once again, his eyes widening as he looked at both of them. "That was her name, wasn't it?"

They both nodded, and he rubbed his face with his hands, scattered memories and clips of events flashing through his mind in quick succession.

Rohan's angry face, accusing Liam of hurting his daughter. Dancing with Blythe, telling her about wanting to marry Stella. Watching Rhiannon while Capri and Rian waved goodbye in the meadow, thinking about how he loved her.

But the memories seemed so vague, so cloudy and distant, as if they hadn't really happened. But they must have...

"I have to talk to Rhia," he said then, his mind made up. Somehow he was going to have to explain to her that he wasn't himself, and he could only hope it wasn't too late...

"We don't know where she is, she left without telling anyone," Jax told him, ignoring the violent oath Liam cursed at him. "She doesn't want to be found right now, but she'll come back eventually."

"Yeah, there's nothing we can do about her right now." Blythe decided, nodding at Liam. "Look, we need to figure out who the hell this Stella bitch is and how she was controlling you. We have to go to Thea."

For a moment, Liam was silent, weighing all this new information in his head. Somehow, he'd been under someone else's control for the last several days, and because of it he'd broken off his relationship with Rhiannon, causing her to leave Euphora for God knows how long. And who knew who else he hurt in one way or another. For all he knew, he could have killed someone and he would have no idea.

"God." He rubbed his face in his hands, remorse and anger aching painfully in his chest. "I can't believe this."

Feeling horrible for him, Blythe reached out to pull him into a hug. "We'll get everything straightened out, Liam. Don't worry. Then things will go back to the way they should be."

"She might not take me back," he said then, his voice dark and miserable as he pulled away to stare at her.

She glared up at him, needing him to stay positive. "She will, Liam, because she loves you." She started to pull away, to drag him down to wake up Thea, before turning back with one final thought. "And if she doesn't take you back, then she'll have to deal with me. And I promise you, I won't be nice."

Within the hour, they were gathered in the garden room, and for the first time in days Lucian had a genuine smile on his face.

"I knew it, boyo, I just knew it," he managed, hugging his son tightly and shutting his eyes against the tears that had suddenly sprung in them.

"I'm sorry, dad," Liam said as he pulled away, sincere regret in his eyes. "God, I don't even remember…"

"Sit down, Liam," Thea said, pointing to the armchair at his right. "Tell us what you do remember and we'll start from there."

He did as he was told, facing the others, feeling singled out. But, then again, there were a lot of unanswered questions and he was at the heart of them.

Jax, Blythe, Lucian, Sebastian and Thea all quietly watched him as he launched into his best account of what happened.

"I remember going down to the Gulf and standing on the shoreline. I tested the water, made some adjustments, and when I was about to leave there was this woman, standing in the sand, watching me. I remember smiling at her and she came up to talk to me. I thought that she was flirting with me so I tried to figure out how to get away so I could head home. But something stopped me, held me there..." He closed his eyes tight and rubbed his face, trying to remember. "I think it was her eyes. I looked her in the eyes and it was like I fell asleep or something."

"You're certain she used her eyes?" Thea asked, glancing at Sebastian uncomfortably before looking back at Liam.

"Yeah. God, I still have the image of her eyes in my head, it won't go away..." He frowned, rubbing his forehead restlessly. "So what does that mean?"

"Liam, your friends have been doing research to try and figure out what has been happening to you, but unfortunately they weren't able to turn up much," Thea began, taking a steadying breath. "But I've given this some thought myself and with what you have just told me, I fear that my suspicion may have been the correct one."

"And what's that?" Liam asked nervously. "Was she some kind of demon or something?"

"No...that was our first thought, of course. But neither of you were possessed, so we had to rule it out." Thea shot a quick look to Sebastian, who nodded encouragingly to her, urging her to continue. "I think Stella may be a Muse."

Liam blinked as he and the others were stunned to silence. Thea let the weight of her words sink in as she sat back against the sofa, knowing that what they discussed next could drastically change everything.

"But..." Liam stammered, shaking his head. "I don't understand. She's so young...if she is a Muse, why isn't she here, on Euphora?"

"That is what we need to determine," Thea told him, looking around at the others. "I had discussed with Jax just yesterday about how I had felt there was something familiar about Stella, something I couldn't quite place. And then with you saying that she used her eyes to get inside your mind...it's one method the Muses sometimes use to influence and inspire others, though they find the touch of their hands equally effective."

"So if she is a Muse, why did she do all of this to me?" Liam demanded to know, feeling frustrated. "I never did anything to her, I don't think."

"I don't know what her motives were or even who she is. But we cannot rule out the possibility that she's working with Dante." Thea's eyes flashed with righteous anger at the name, even as they focused on Liam and held, regret pushing aside the fury. "I owe you an apology, Liam. I was one of the few who believed, even though it was only with half my heart that your actions were your own. Perhaps I do not know you as well as your friends." She nodded to Blythe, Jax and Lucian.

"It's done now, Thea." Liam let out a huff of breath, still in an odd state of shock. "I really just want to find out who this Stella girl is."

"Thea, if I may..." Sebastian said suddenly, leaning forward slightly to clasp her hands in his own as he met her eyes. "Don't you find it odd that this girl, if she is a Muse, was able to fully control Liam's mind? That is not possible, even for the best and brightest of the Muses. They can influence, but they cannot control. I fear that we might be dealing with a Muse whose abilities have been altered or enhanced."

Thea nodded, acknowledging his point. "That is surely possible. And…" she paused, a dark shadow passing over her face as her eyes widened with sudden understanding. She looked at Sebastian, not sure if it was even possible. But who else could it be… "Vivica."

"Good Lord," Sebastian murmured, the magnitude of the situation suddenly much darker than he could have imagined. "Could it be?"

"Who's Vivica?" Blythe asked, nervously staring at both Sebastian and Thea. "Was she a Muse?"

"A long time ago," Thea said evenly, regaining her composure and turning to face the others. At the confusion in their eyes, she elaborated. "A hundred or so years ago, Vivica was one of my three Muses. But as she grew older, she developed terrible habits that she refused to stop. She was inspiring war, fear and hatred amongst the humans, causing widespread devastation all across the globe. She created a World War and inspired good men to turn on each other. I have never before or since seen a Muse do such terrible things and I had hoped that after banishing her it would be done."

"After all this time, surely she must be dead?" Lucian put in, not sure he understood their apprehension. "No one lives that long, except you two of course."

"After I banished her, I had the Enforcers keep an eye on her, just to be sure she didn't use her powers. And it seemed she was living amongst the humans peacefully without incident. Then we discovered that she had been violently killed in Mississippi, near the coastal border of Louisiana. I never did find out what had really happened, but the Enforcers who had been watching her had routinely mentioned her obsession with voodoo, which is an ancient kind of magic with humans in the region. It's quite possible that she was killed during some kind of ritual, but not before opening herself up to something sinister. Possession is a common occurrence in voodoo ceremonies… it's possible a demon came through and possessed her, frightening the other participants in the ceremony. They tried to destroy her, and when they did the demon simply took her back with him to the Underworld."

"But then how did she come back?" Liam asked, dread sweeping over him.

"Someone may have released her, brought her back. But the key is what happened to her while she was down there. There is evil there that may have taken what was left of her and made her into something much more, in the hopes that one day she'd make it back to the surface."

"Christ," Jax cursed under his breath, covering his face in his hands. Just when he thought things couldn't get much worse… "A hundred bucks says it was Dante who released her."

"Why? So he could use her to use Liam to hurt Rhiannon's feelings? Or so he could try and spy on all of us?" Blythe huffed, eyebrows raised skeptically.

Jax looked at her darkly. "I'd say that's exactly what he wanted to do."

Blythe gave his words more thought. "Okay, so he tells Stella, also known as Vivica, to control Liam so that she can get onto Euphora. Why doesn't she do something once she's here? We were suspicious, but we weren't expecting her to attack us in our sleep. We could have all been dead."

"Because she wasn't sent here to kill us." Jax's eyes left hers and focused on Liam, who was watching him warily. "She was supposed to tear us apart. Until she showed up, we were all getting along pretty well, weren't we? And now look at us."

"He wanted her to use me to hurt Rhiannon," Liam realized, pain clouding his eyes. "And by me doing so, my actions divided all of you. Dad…you and Rohan fought, didn't you?"

Lucian self-consciously reached up to touch the bruises on his right eye, but he nodded solemnly. "We were understandably on two different sides. He wanted revenge for what you had done to Rhiannon and I had to protect you."

"And Thea, you slapped me," Liam suddenly remembered, his eyes shooting to Mother Earth, who flushed with shame.

"I was angry with you, Liam," she explained, feeling terrible. "But that didn't make it right."

"The point is that you and I never argue, but Stella's influence over me caused us to."

"And a lot of us were pissed off at how Rhiannon was handling it, which didn't help," Blythe added, earning a fierce look from Liam. She held up her hands to stop him from arguing with her before she had a chance to explain. "Look, she was getting on my nerves because she acted like it didn't matter that you broke up with her. She was pretending to be fine with it, saying that it was your choice, that if you hadn't been happy with her then she understood. I never even saw her cry about it, Liam, it was pathetic. She just bottled it all inside and acted like none of it mattered." Rolling her eyes, she continued. "The point is, whatever friendliness we'd shown to each other pretty much evaporated over this. It wasn't until she left that I actually knew that she was hurting over you."

Liam scowled, feeling miserable and anxious and furious all at once. "Well, if Dante really is behind all of this, he's certainly gotten his wish. Everything's pretty well screwed up."

"She'll understand once we explain this to her, Liam," Lucian began, attempting a half smile to showcase some kind of optimism. "When she returns, we'll–"

"God…" Liam interrupted suddenly, panic in his eyes as he felt his heart drop like a rock. "Stella knows that Rhia is gone, doesn't she?"

"She would have no way of knowing where to find Rhiannon, Liam," Thea reasoned, fighting back a sudden wave of fear that rushed over her. "We don't even know where she is."

"She found me, didn't she?" Liam demanded heatedly, jumping to his feet as he turned to face all of them. "And when I broke the connection I had with her, she must have felt it. For all we know, she and Dante could be on the hunt for Rhiannon right now."

"Yeah, but what good will getting to her do? We already know what Stella is, so if she attempts to control Rhiannon and return her to Euphora, we'll be one step ahead of them." Blythe looked to her brother, not seeing the sense in it.

He met her eyes and the darkness in them frightened her.

"If they get to Rhia, then they have control over all of us, Blythe. Dante is smart enough to know just what lengths we would go to in order to get her back."

Blythe paled, glancing over at Jax, who nodded gravely, his eyes hardening. "He's right. Our only option is to get to her before they do."

Chapter Twelve

She curled her legs beneath her on the oversized, over-cushioned arm chair, lifting a glass of crisp chardonnay to her lips. The window before her was open wide to the fresh outdoors, where she watched the sun set slowly over the sloping hills in the distance. Twilight set in and the first few stars began to awaken as the cool evening air drifted in to caress her face.

Rhiannon smiled, feeling content in this place, surrounded by the fields of golden barley and the dark shadows of trees lining the horizon. She'd always come here when she needed to center herself, and now she needed it more than ever.

The little bed and breakfast had been a convenient choice and she couldn't have asked for more comfortable surroundings. She had her own quaint bathroom with a claw foot tub, a large four poster bed with fresh white linens, and a room decorated with cheerful knick knacks and floral wallpaper, all in shades of warm rose.

The wine had been an impulse buy when she'd ventured to the local market for something to eat, but she applauded herself for her choice. It was refreshing and crisp, and soothing to her heart and mind.

Here, in this space that was her own and away from the prying eyes of her family, she let herself mourn. Hours ago she'd cried herself dry, until there was nothing left but an aching throat and a decimated heart.

Then she had set out repairing it, bit by bit, building her defenses once more to bury deep the heart that Liam had freed. Now that it was done, she had no intention of ever releasing it again.

She did truly want him to be happy, but she wanted her own happiness as well. And the only thing she had left that made her happy was her work.

She missed it already, since neglecting her duties was difficult for her. The thought of all the responsibilities she was piling onto her father distressed her, but there just hadn't been any other option. Besides, she vowed to make it up to him once she returned, whole and new. Then her life could continue on, as if the last few months with Liam had never happened.

Taking another sip of wine, she purposely focused on his face in her mind, telling herself not to feel any anger, doubt or misery. She was only to feel neutral toward him, and it was important for her to ensure she could do so without faltering before she returned.

But when the image of Liam kissing the blonde intruded into her thoughts, she felt her heart clench pitifully, the pain resonating through her body. Annoyed with herself, she pushed aside the feelings and the image and tried again.

His face, one she'd known all her life. There, that wasn't so hard. No pain, no sorrow. Just neutral indifference. He meant nothing to her. He was only an acquaintance.

But when the image in her head smiled that goofy grin at her, and his eyes honed in on her with that look mixed with charm and a deep, barely restrained desire, she felt her throat tighten and a sob build within her chest.

No…no, that doesn't exist any longer. Do not cry over what does not exist, it's foolish.

But because she had a harder time shaking the memory, she gave up for the time being and poured herself more wine.

I just need more time, she thought as she lifted the glass to her lips once more and took a long sip. Outside the window, the moon began to rise in the slowly darkening sky.

She realized that she was sitting in near darkness, since she had yet to turn on the table lamp beside her. As she reached over to flip it on, there was a brisk knocking at her door.

Fear raced through her first, before she scolded herself and pushed it aside. There was nothing to be afraid of, no one knew where she was. And the humans who owned the inn had been very nice and hospitable. It was probably just one of them, knocking to offer her room service.

Rising to her feet, she set her wine glass on the windowsill and went to the door, unlocking it and pulling it open slowly.

Behind it she saw the elderly husband and wife who owned the house, and she smiled at them.

"Yes?" Rhiannon asked, feeling foolish for having expected anything else.

"Dear, I just wanted to see if you like your room," the wife asked, her voice warm and kind.

"It's important to us that you're comfortable," the old man put in, wrapping an arm around his wife and beaming up at Rhiannon.

"It's lovely, thank you," she assured them, glancing over her shoulder and motioning to the window. "I was just enjoying the evening. It's beautiful here."

"Yes." The woman agreed. "A beautiful room, for a beautiful girl."

"Very beautiful." Her husband smiled down at her, then stared back up at Rhiannon. "I think she may be running from something, don't you agree, dear?"

"Indeed," the woman replied, her eyes glittering with something odd that Rhiannon couldn't quite place.

"I told you both earlier, I'm here on vacation," Rhiannon reminded them, the urge to close the door and shut them out sweeping over her. But her carefully ingrained manners prevented her from doing so.

"What a boring vacation for a young lady," the man chimed, eyeing her with a strange smile. "I'd say she could use a little action."

"Excuse me?" Rhiannon asked, her brows drawing together in confusion.

"Action, dear," the woman said excitedly, nodding her head and smiling. "Watch this."

When Rhiannon saw the old woman began to tremble and shake, dark smoke seeping from her mouth, nose and eyes, she first thought that she was dreaming. Surely this wasn't happening, not really…

But when the initial shock and disbelief wore off, real terror gripped her heart.

The smoke formed a serpent on the floor at her feet, the old woman crumbling lifelessly into the hallway. Rhiannon's eyes shot to the old man, who looked completely unperturbed, as if this happened every day.

And when the serpent shifted and formed a man, Rhiannon jerked back in revulsion, her heart leaping into her throat to flutter like a trapped bird.

"Hello, darling," Dante grinned wickedly, adjusting his black leather jacket to showcase the pistol holstered to his belt. "Don't move or I'll have to shoot you."

She remained frozen in place, her eyes jolting to the elderly man, who was still standing in the doorway, calm as day. That was when she noticed a blonde woman step into the room and her eyes widened when she saw her face. Stella smiled and waved cheerfully.

"You," Rhiannon murmured, trembling down to her toes as her eyes shot back to Dante, who had begun to laugh.

"Aren't you impressed? You should be," he told her, sauntering forward, his golden eyes glittering with madness. "Rhiannon, darling, this is Vivica, my own personal Muse."

He reached out and wrapped an arm possessively around the blonde when she came up beside him, pulling her close. She smiled darkly at Rhiannon before tilting her head up for a kiss from him, her tongue erotically sliding along his lips.

Revulsion mixed with bewilderment as Rhiannon stared at the woman. So Stella had been with Dante all along? That meant that Liam had been tricked. He had fallen for her without even knowing where her true allegiances lay.

Knowing he had been played like a fool only made the whole situation considerably worse…but just what purpose had been served by having Stella, or Vivica, as Dante called her, manipulate her way into Liam's life and onto Euphora? And why were they here now, quite possibly to kidnap her, or even kill her?

Regardless, she wasn't prepared to stick around and find out. She had to get away, somehow…

She inched further back, wondering if she could make it to the window and escape. She'd only have a split second before he pulled his gun on her…

"I'm sure you're wondering what all of this means," Dante began, kissing Vivica's hand lushly, his eyes on Rhiannon. "The details are all very interesting, but I just don't have time to tell the story right now. Time is of the essence."

When he grinned at Stella, Rhiannon whirled around and flung herself toward the open window, frantically crawling over the armchair she had just been sitting in. Her hands grasped the windowsill the second his latched onto her waist and threw her back inside. She fell to the floor, crashing against the armoire beside the door, panting and groaning in pain.

He hovered over her, his booted foot pressing into her chest as she gasped for air. There was a dark and sinister evil in his eyes as he grinned.

"Nice try. Trash the room, darling," he said to Vivica, even as his eyes held Rhiannon's. "I want them to suffer with guilt and terror when they realize we found her first. In fact…"

He swiftly pulled a switch blade from his boot and, flicking it open, grabbed Rhiannon's hand, slicing her palm open. Hauling her to her feet, he squeezed her hand so blood droplets fell onto the beige carpet, staining dark red. For good measure, he smeared her blood on the dresser, on the chair, on the walls. He wanted to strike as much fear into them as possible, and picturing the boy's anguish gave him a tremendous amount of giddy pleasure.

Rhiannon winced against the horrible, pulsating pain, the sight of her own blood causing her stomach to roll pitifully as she shuddered. Vivica was cheerfully shattering ceramic figurines and toppling furniture as Dante threw Rhiannon painfully against the wall.

He pressed against her, his face mere inches from her own. His eyes, filled with madness and triumph, stared into hers.

"Imagine the boy's face when he comes into this room," he began, chuckling at the horror that flashed into her eyes. "Priceless."

"Why are you doing this?" she asked, her voice shaky but her eyes hard on his as anger pulsed through her.

Dante chuckled, his lips curving as he leaned in to whisper in her ear, his voice low and seductively sinister.

"Because I can."

It grated on him that he had no clue where she would have gone. He'd known the girl for his entire life, and had loved her all those years, and yet he couldn't for the life of him come up with any ideas on where she could be.

Liam scoured his mind for any memory of her mentioning a favorite park, or a city she really enjoyed, anything. But Rhiannon rarely ever talked about herself and the realization that he didn't know her nearly as well as he thought irritated and upset him.

She must have counted on that, knowing he would have no clue. The last thing she probably wanted was him showing up on her doorstep, brandishing flowers with a poetic declaration of love. But this was an emergency, damnit, and it was so unlike her to not prepare for the possibility that she may need to be contacted.

The others were looking to him for the answer, thinking he would be the key. But, even as he paced back and forth in the garden room before them, he knew he wasn't any closer to knowing her whereabouts than they were.

Running both hands restlessly through his hair, he shot Blythe an irritated look, simply because she was there.

"What?" she asked, on edge and temperamental. "Don't look at me that way."

"Someone has to have some clue of where she could be!" Liam shouted, his temper consuming him. "This is pathetic."

"Yeah, well if you don't know, then don't expect us to know. You knew her the best," Blythe charged, glaring at him.

"Stop arguing, that isn't helping," Lucian scolded them both, anxiety sharpening his eyes. "Perhaps we should try and reach Capri and Rian in Maine. She might have gone there to visit them."

"She wouldn't want to intrude," Liam argued, shaking his head. "Plus Capri would just worry over her and she hates that."

Thea suddenly rose to her feet, an idea occurring to her. She excused herself and swept from the room, leaving the others behind to continue to brainstorm in frustrated silence.

When Thea returned moments later with Brogan at her side, everyone turned to look at them anxiously.

Brogan only had eyes for Liam and the loathing in them was apparent. "So is it true? You were under that woman's control?" he asked, his dark, poetic eyes narrowing suspiciously.

Liam scented the challenge and returned the glare with equal hostility. "Yes. But I'm free of her now and I'm worried for Rhia's safety."

"How do I know you're not making this whole thing up?" Brogan frowned, his voice cold and accusing.

"Why the hell would I lie about this?" Liam growled, his hands clenching at his sides. "I love her."

Brogan sneered, shaking his head. "You destroyed her. You led her on and convinced her to open up to you and then you betrayed her. I watched her suffer over you and I could do nothing to help, except promise her that I wouldn't let you try and weasel your way back into her life."

"What, so you could slide cozily into my place? I know you've always wanted her." Liam's eyes narrowed to slits, jealousy and resentment a hot flash in his gut. "But regardless of what's happened, she's mine and I intend on getting her back, and I won't let you stand in my way."

"Rhiannon belongs to no one but herself," Brogan asserted, angling his face so he could stare down at Liam in disgust. "Unlike you, I won't betray her trust."

"So you know where she is?" Liam started forward, his hands reaching out to grip the other man's shirt angrily. "Tell me, damnit."

Brogan shoved Liam away with surprising force, causing Liam to launch himself back at the Fury in retaliation. Fists were flying as they collided, both fueled by jealousy, bitterness, and rage.

Those around them jumped to their feet, eyes wide at the sudden outbreak of a fight. Thea started to move forward to break them up, but Sebastian held her back, fearing for her safety.

Instead, Jax and Blythe stepped in, grabbing both men and tearing them off each other.

"Stop fighting!" Blythe shouted, pinning Liam's arms behind his back while he struggled to get free. She managed to hold on, kicking the back of one of his knees for good measure.

"Ouch! Jesus, fine, let go," Liam grunted, falling to his knees as Blythe released him, panting.

"This is ridiculous!" Thea glared at both Brogan and Liam with wide eyes. "First the Dryads, and now you two? The fighting needs to stop!"

Jax released Brogan, who rubbed his arms bitterly and stared at Thea, his face flushing with shame. "I apologize, Thea."

"Yeah. Sorry," Liam said flatly as he looked up at Brogan, heat still in his eyes. "Look, I know you think I hurt Rhia on purpose, but I didn't, okay? And now we think Dante might be going after her so we need to get her before he finds her."

Brogan scowled as he looked questioningly at Thea. "Is this true?"

She nodded, feeling an intense headache pulsing in her right temple. "Did she tell you where she was going?"

For a moment Brogan said nothing, he only stared into Thea's eyes, clearly pondering his response. His silence was answer enough for Liam.

"Damnit, answer her!" he shouted, getting to his feet, frustration painfully clear upon his face. "Don't you get it? Rhia could be dead if we don't go to her."

Brogan turned to Liam, eyeing him thoughtfully before he spoke.

"She's in Idaho, at a small bed and breakfast overlooking the barley fields," he revealed, hoping to God he hadn't just betrayed her trust for nothing.

"Give Liam and Blythe the address, and the two of them will go," Thea decided, nodding to Blythe. "We can't waste any more time."

They transported into the middle of a group of dark trees amidst a cool Idahoan night. The cloudless sky above them glittered with stars in the way only country skies ever could.

Liam spotted the little town up the road, seeing only a single street lamp and very few lights on in the houses. But he had to trust that this was the right place, since it matched the location Brogan had given them…

"Geez, this place is quiet," Blythe muttered, cautiously staring around her as if she expected something to burst out of the barley fields and attack them. "I can see why she'd want to come here, but God, even El Paso isn't this quiet."

"He said the place is called *Le Petit Chateau*," Liam told her as they walked through the barley toward the town.

Blythe snorted out a laugh, shaking her head. "Sounds just like something she'd pick. Prissy and refined."

"Shut up." Liam punched her playfully in the shoulder, grinning as they reached the street. He spotted the sign declaring the inn a few houses down, and seeing it lifted his spirits. Almost… they were almost there.

Crickets could be heard amongst the night sounds, coupled with the occasional screech of an owl or the murmured voices coming from an open window across the street. Liam's heart rate began to quicken as they got closer, his eagerness to get inside overwhelming.

When they reached the door of the quaint brick building, a straw mat at their feet cheerfully displayed the words *The Friendliest Place in Town!* scripted in black letters. He knocked on the door, which was almost immediately answered by an elderly woman with a kind smile.

"Good evening," she greeted, stepping aside so they could step in. "Welcome to *Le Petit Chateau!*"

"Thank you." Liam glanced around at the tidy parlor, equipped with a check-in desk with phone and computer, a couple of worn and comfortable looking loveseats grouped together around a mahogany coffee table, and a wicker bookcase filled with hundreds of ancient looking books. The wallpaper was patterned with French pastoral scenes in warm pinks and blues, and cheered him enormously for reasons he couldn't really explain.

"Are you two in need of a room?" The elderly woman asked, clasping her hands together, clearly thinking them to be a couple.

Blythe would have laughed but she knew it might offend the woman. "No, our friend Rhiannon is staying here. There's been an emergency and we need to speak with her."

"Oh my." The woman gasped, her hands jolting up to cover her mouth as the humor died out of her eyes. "Yes, she's just down the hall. In the Tranquille room."

"Thanks." Liam led the way down the hall, reading the names on the doors as he passed. He glanced back over his shoulder, and saw that the elderly woman had taken a seat on one of the loveseats and resumed reading her book. Smiling to himself, he found the door that the woman had indicated was Rhiannon's room, and he knocked politely.

Blythe came to a stop beside him, chewing her bottom lip nervously. There was some kind of bad juju in the air, she was certain of it. Something was off, either about that woman, or about this place. It didn't feel right and the nerves were skittering up her spine and annoying the hell out of her. The place looked normal, after all. What could possibly be wrong?

When no one answered the knock, Liam called out her name. "Rhia? Rhia, it's me. Please open up, I have to talk to you."

Again, nothing. He frowned as he shot an annoyed glance at Blythe, who had crossed her arms tightly over her chest and was looking extremely agitated. "I should have known she'd ignore me," he told her, his eyes narrowing. "What's wrong?"

"I don't know," Blythe faltered, sweat beading on her forehead. "Something's wrong, Liam. Someone's been here, someone bad. I don't know how I know, but I do."

"You can't be serious." He tried to smile, thinking maybe she was just joking with him. But the terrified look in her eyes alarmed him enough to have him second guessing the situation. "Alright, stand back, I'm going to kick in the door."

"Okay." Blythe nodded, moving back to give him room. He sucked in a sharp breath and shoved his foot forward, shattering the little lock that had held the door closed. Down the hall, the elderly woman rose to her feet and gaped at them, startled.

Liam shoved open the door and stepped inside, and what he saw froze his heart to ice.

The four poster bed was in shambles, with pillows ripped to shreds and blankets torn and tossed onto the floor. Almost every piece of furniture had been upended and destroyed, with shards of wood scattered across the carpet. Clothes and pieces of porcelain and ceramic littered the floor amongst the wood and feathers from the pillows. A single table lamp lay on the floor, the bulb glowing brightly up at the ceiling, its lampshade smashed in upon itself.

And then he saw the blood.

Rushing forward, he pressed his hand to a smear of blood that streaked across a section of the cheerfully floral patterned wall, feeling sick to his stomach. The blood was still slightly wet, and stained his fingertips a rich and awful red.

The only window in the room was wide open to the night and a cold breeze hauntingly fluttered the drapes. Outside, the world was disturbingly quiet.

Blythe stood in the middle of the room, examining the destruction, her hands fisted in her hair as she fought back the urge to scream.

Turning to look at Liam, she met his eyes and saw the staggering grief in them. For a moment they said nothing, both reveling in shock and disbelief.

He felt his legs give out as he suddenly stumbled toward her and crumbled to his knees at her feet, amidst the shards of porcelain, wood, and drops of dark red blood that he knew was Rhiannon's.

Dante had made her bleed. He had caused her harm. And then he had taken her.

He clutched his head as the pain and denial tore through him, the helplessness and the regret. His body shook with aching sobs as the agony of it all quite simply destroyed him.

When he let out an anguished, almost inhuman cry of pain, it shook Blythe to the very core, shuddering through her violently as she knelt down shakily to hold him while he wept.

They were too late.

Chapter Thirteen

While Blythe spoke with the elderly couple that owned the inn and the police were contacted, Liam stood in the little room beside the open window, his eyes glassy with pain and shock. He reached out to lightly touch the half empty wine glass that was perched on the window sill, picturing her sitting in the armchair, sipping wine and enjoying the night. That is, until *they* came.

He had heard the elderly woman mention that the last thing she remembered was a dark haired man and a blonde woman coming to the door. Then the next thing she experienced was waking up beside her husband on the loveseat in the parlor, unscathed. She'd thought she had just fallen asleep and dreamed up the strange couple. But by the destruction in the room Rhiannon had occupied, it had been no dream.

So Dante and Stella had possessed and controlled their way into the building, most likely fooling Rhiannon and toying with her before making themselves known. And then they had terrorized her and taken her, fleeing out the open window and going God knows where.

And since the sensor Blythe had brought with her had informed them that not only had a demon been present, but a Muse as well, there was now no doubt in their minds just what Stella was.

He stared out at the starry night sky and wondered desperately where Rhiannon was now. Did she think he would be trying to find her? Or was she still convinced that he had truly wanted Stella over her?

Who knew how much of the plan Dante would fill Rhiannon in on while he held her captive. He might be filling her head with more poisonous lies that very moment.

Frustrated and emotional, he tore his eyes away from the sky and whirled around to search the room. Maybe they had left something, anything, giving a hint as to where they were going with her.

He saw her practical black suitcase lying beside the bed, torn to pieces, her clothes and toiletries scattered. Inside, he saw a copy of Jane Austen's *Emma*, and his eyes filled miserably.

Some part of her hadn't wanted to forget him, not completely…

"The police are here, so we're gonna have to give statements," Blythe said as she came into the room, stepping gingerly over the shards of porcelain on the carpet. "But I was thinking we should just book it, because we really don't have time to deal with all of this. Not like we can tell them the truth, anyhow. They'd lock us up like crazy people."

Liam looked over at her, shaking his head. "Get Thea on the phone, Blythe. Tell her what's happening. I'll go feed some kind of story to the cops. We really shouldn't leave that older couple hanging."

Blythe nodded and turned away, digging the cell phone out of her pocket. Liam started to leave the room, when something resting on the nightstand caught his eye.

He stepped over Rhiannon's destroyed suitcase and grabbed the envelope, his chest tightening at the sight of his name scrawled across it. Tearing it open, he unfolded the letter and frantically began reading it.

To Liam and the people of Euphora,

If you are reading this, then you are aware that we have the girl and that you are too late. If I were a kinder, more honest man, perhaps I'd guarantee her safety and demand a ransom for her head, but...that's not much fun, is it? So I'll say this instead. I may or may not hurt her. I may or may not kill her. But I know that you want her, so therefore I'm going to give you one chance, and one chance only, to get her back.

I want all of you to come to Times Square in New York City tomorrow night at eight o'clock sharp. Perhaps I will be there, if I feel like it. And if I am, then we can chat, and maybe, just maybe, I'll give her back to you.

She is rather pretty, I might just keep her. Though she isn't my first choice...besides, I have loftier goals than keeping a woman. Come to Times Square, and perhaps I will share with you what those goals are...

Danie

P.S. - Vivica sends her warmest regards to Thea and Sebastian. She's rather offended that they did not recognize her, but then again, her disguise is rather good.

"Blythe," Liam stammered, whirling around while his sister spoke in muted tones to Thea, describing what they had found. He stumbled over the suitcase and tripped over a crumbled chair, but managed to get to her and whirl her around. "Give me the phone."

"Hold on, Thea, Liam wants to say something." Blythe handed him the cell phone, confused and irritated until she spotted the letter he held in his hands, at which point hope and adrenaline began to pump through her.

"Thea?" Liam's eyes met Blythe's with a sudden stone cold resolve. "He left a letter for us. He wants us all to meet him in New York City tomorrow evening."

Blythe's eyes widened as Liam read the note to Thea, and she rubbed her face in her hands as the weight of what all of this meant hit her. Dante was using Rhiannon to lure all of them from the safety of Euphora and out into the open, where they would surely be vulnerable...

"Blythe and I will catch a flight out to New York right now, and I want the rest of you to meet us there tomorrow at six o'clock in the evening." He paused, listening to Thea question whether it was wise for all of them to fall in line with what was obviously a trap. "Damnit, Thea, this is the goddamn battle, okay? This is the war we've been waiting for."

"And what other option do we have?" Blythe put in, shrugging.

Liam nodded at her, fierce determination in his eyes. "Dante and Vivica have Rhiannon, Thea. Period. I'm not going to lose her, not again, not like this."

"I really hate airports," Blythe grumbled, wading her way through the crowded terminal, Liam at her side.

He frowned at her, nearly running into a man who suddenly stopped in front of him to tie his shoe. Dodging the man, he rolled his eyes and growled. "I was going to ask you why, but never mind. I think I know."

"Too many stupid people, it's like a zoo." Blythe shoved her hands into the pockets of her bright blue hoodie, glaring around for examples. "Like that guy over there, with the kids? He's stuffing his face with a hotdog while his two brat kids play right in the middle of the walkway, forcing everyone to walk around. No consideration for other people whatsoever."

"Some people just shouldn't procreate," Liam suggested, finding the conversation easing some of his restlessness. They were in New York City and on their way to Manhattan, twelve hours to go before Dante wanted to meet. He could stand to distract himself, at least a little.

"Oh God," Blythe said, clasping her hands over her mouth and staring wide eyed up at Liam.

"What?" A jolt of fear raced through him at the horror in her expression. He stopped mid-step and gripped her shoulders, shaking her. "What is it?"

Blythe lowered her hands, her face oddly pale. "Do you think Capri's gonna get knocked up right away? I don't think I can handle being an auntie just yet."

He would have laughed if he hadn't been so furious with her for making him worry. He let out a whoosh of breath, attempting to calm himself as he slung an arm over her shoulders and continued to walk.

"I don't think Capri getting pregnant is really up to you," he told her, managing a half smile as he looked her in the eye. "Besides, I know deep down that you have a soft spot for kids. And once there's a little blonde haired mini Capri running around, you'll want one of your own."

"Don't even say that," Blythe managed, her hand clutching her stomach as it rolled sickeningly. "The last thing I need right now is a kid."

Because thinking of Blythe and Capri having children automatically made him think of Rhiannon, rosily pregnant with *his* child, he went quiet, hurt by the image. God, he hoped that was still a possibility…if she didn't make it, if Dante killed her, he didn't think he could live with himself. If he failed her, then there was just no point in living anymore…

They made it through the airport and hailed a cab that would take them directly to Times Square. Liam wanted to survey the area first and get an idea of what Dante might be planning.

Why he had chosen such a public place for the meeting, Liam couldn't be sure. Maybe he thought that they would be less inclined to fight back with hundreds of humans in the area, innocents that could potentially be harmed if an all out war started right then and there. Or maybe that was Dante's intention…to cause as much destruction as he possibly could, innocents be damned.

Hopefully he wouldn't expect them to be able to prepare very thoroughly on such short notice, but Thea had already contacted the Enforcers and arranged to have snipers on various rooftops facing the Square, and others to stand by in civilian clothes, ready to rush in if needed. Of course, all of that was in addition to the arsenal his family would be packing as well, and Liam had a feeling that Rian and Brogan were having a field day breaking out all the weapons they had stowed away.

Part of him regretted the fact that Capri and Rian had come home from their honeymoon only to find everything in virtual shambles. But he was sure they understood, and both would be willing to fight if it came down to it. Capri would fight because of Rhiannon, and Rian would fight because it was not only his duty, but because he knew Capri needed him to.

Liam stared out the window of the cab, his eyes scanning the buildings and crowded sidewalks, even as his mind drifted and his restlessness returned.

How many people had he hurt, emotionally at least, while he had been under Vivica's control? He hadn't had time to really stick around and apologize to everyone, or to even show them that he was himself again. But from the flashes of memory that managed to resurface from the last several days, he knew he had ruffled the feathers of more than one member of his family.

Specifically Rohan and his mother. He had this image that kept recurring in his mind of Rohan's face, contorted in violent anger as he lunged straight toward him, intending to hurt and avenge. And then the pain and shock in Clarity's face as he said God knows what to her...

But he would rectify everything once Rhiannon was safe. Nothing else even mattered unless he was able to get her back, unscathed.

"Let us out up here," Blythe said to the driver, leaning toward the front seat. Liam exhaled slowly as they pulled to the curb, reaching into his pocket for cash to pay for their cab.

They got out in front of the Hilton Hotel, and immediately looked to the sky.

Blaring neon signs beamed down at them, blasting streams of advertisements while the streets before them rioted with rush hour traffic.

Liam grabbed Blythe when a frayed looking businessman nearly ran into her on his way into the Hilton, almost knocking her into the gutter.

"Watch where you're going!" Blythe angrily shouted at the man's back, though he either didn't hear her or simply didn't have time to care.

"I don't think I've ever seen this many people in my life," Liam commented, gazing around in a relative daze. "This place is a madhouse."

"It's Times Square, honey," Blythe huffed, glancing around with annoyance in her eyes. "This place is always busy."

"Let's go inside, get cleaned up." Liam pulled her along toward the entrance to the Hilton, dodging pedestrians as he went. "Then I want to walk around, use the scanner and check things out."

"Sounds good to me." Blythe went with him into the hotel lobby. "It feels weird not having Jax here with me..."

Liam snorted out a half laugh and angled his head to look at her, eyebrows raised. "What? I'm not good enough company for you anymore?"

"No, it's not that." Blythe waved his words away, frowning with a heavy sigh. "It's just that being out here like this reminds me of me and Jax hunting for Dante. Only I'm here with you instead. It's just different, ya know?"

"I guess." Wrapping an arm around her, he pulled her close and kissed the top of her head. "Thank you for being here for me, though. You didn't hesitate, not once. It means a lot."

"God, Liam, how could I hesitate?" Blythe looked up at him, clearly hurt. "Rhiannon matters to you, so therefore she matters to me. Okay?"

"Okay." He stopped walking and pulled her in for a hug, suddenly overtaken with emotion. "I love you, Blythe."

"I love you too, dork." She grinned against him even as tears sprang into her eyes, burying her face into his chest. "Okay, okay, enough sappy stuff. Let's get the hell upstairs. I want a damn shower."

By seven o'clock that evening, they had all gathered together at a bustling restaurant in Times Square, ready to formulate a plan of attack.

The Enforcers were already in place on the street and the snipers in strategic locations in the surrounding buildings, scanning for any suspicious activity.

Liam sat at the table in the noisy Italian restaurant, tapping his fingers restlessly against the scarred wooden table top, his eyes constantly flicking from one member of his family to another.

They were all here for one reason, and one reason alone. To save Rhiannon. And he had never been more thankful to any of them in his entire life.

Because he would have understood if some of them had not wanted to come...hell, none of them knew just what awaited them when they went out into the Square. And given

Dante's cryptic message to Burke and Rhiannon just over a month earlier, what they faced in only one hour was likely to be an all out battle.

But they had come anyway…the Muses, the Fates, Clynn and Capri, his father and Brock, Sebastian and Rian, Brogan, Jax and of course Rohan…the only ones who had stayed behind were the ones too young to fight.

As he glanced around at their concerned and worried faces as they discussed just how to approach what they were about to face, he felt a lot of his own apprehensions ease.

They were strong, capable and united. Each with unique abilities and powers, armed with weapons they were trained to use. How could such a group fail?

Well, if they couldn't agree on a course of action then they could fail. And with the way things were going at that moment, bickering back and forth was really all they were accomplishing.

"Look, I know the bastard," Blythe was saying, wagging her fork at Thea and the others, her eyes sharp with determination. "He likes doing things with a bang, flashy and extravagant, with lots of build up and suspense. We've got to expect that he's going to make it seem small and simple, and then somehow turn the tables on us."

"Yes, but he might be doing this to lure us away from Euphora in order to destroy our home," Serendipity put in, glancing around at the others for support. "Sierra is there, I'm just worried for our children's safety."

"There are dozens of Enforcers guarding the castle, they will be more than safe," Thea assured her, before gesturing to the group as a whole. "Dante's main objective is to divide us, plain and simple. If we can stand united, then we shall overcome whatever he throws at us."

"How about I shoot him in the head," Brock said suddenly, leaning back in his chair and sipping beer from a bottle, his eyes flashing with a strange mix of anger and anticipation. "Let him really go out with a bang."

Blythe flashed him an appreciative grin, but Liam and Rohan both glared at him.

"And what happens to Rhiannon if we just kill him like that?" Liam asked heatedly, leaning forward to meet Brock's eyes. "We don't know if he's holding her somewhere or if he's going to bring her with him."

"Rhiannon has to be our first priority," Rohan added, his hand clenching around his water glass until his knuckles were white. "Destroying Dante comes second only to rescuing her."

Brock rolled his eyes resentfully. "I didn't say we wouldn't get your girl back, Rohan. But out of all of us, I think I got the most beef with the asshole and I want dibs on taking him out."

"We don't know how the situation is going to play out, Brock," Sebastian reminded him, hoping to smooth out the tension between the Dryads before it sparked any further. "And we won't know until it happens."

"We have to have a solid course of action for each possibility," Rian suggested, folding his hands in front of him as he stared around the table. "One possibility is that we walk out there, and are ambushed by this 'army' he's claiming he has. If that is the case, then it will be imperative for Liam and Rohan to corner Dante and get Rhiannon's whereabouts out of him, while the rest of us fight."

"I can get on board with that," Liam agreed, looking to Rohan, who nodded curtly, determination in his eyes.

"Now, the second possibility is that we go out there and Dante approaches us directly, with Rhiannon and possibly the Muse. If this is the case, we are going to have to be very cautious, because he will likely have something more planned."

"If that's the case, then I say we grab Rhiannon and take him and Vivica out before he can so much as blink," Blythe told him directly, earning an approving cheer from her father.

Rian looked unsure though, and met her eyes warily. "It may not be so simple, Blythe."

"I don't see why not," she refuted, eyebrows raised. "If we take them out, then whatever else they had planned means nothing."

"Yes but the plan may already be in motion as we speak," Rian said darkly, earning a fearful stare from Capri and a few others. "He's asked us to meet him at an exact time for a reason and it's probably because he has something planned for all of us. It would be foolish of us to assume otherwise, therefore we must take caution and find out what he wants from us when we see him."

Blythe pouted, acknowledging his point as Jax rubbed her back and nodded to his old friend. "There's one thing missing from this whole discussion, something that's likely to change all our plans if we don't give it some thought."

At Rian's questioning stare, Jax continued, eyeing those surrounding him. "We haven't considered just what kind of army he's likely to have, if he even does."

"Demons, I'd think," Blythe suggested, meeting his eyes.

"If all he's got are demons, then why the wait? Why the build up and the suspense?" Jax asked her, shaking his head. "He's used demons against y'all before, and he knows it's not enough. We know how to defeat demons, and frankly, we're pretty damn good at it. I'm willing to bet he's got something else up his sleeve this time."

"Like Vivica." Liam's eyes narrowed bitterly, and he earned a sympathetic glance from Capri from across the table. "He was able to release her from the Underworld. What's to stop him from releasing other monsters?"

"Even Dante doesn't have the power and resources it takes to do such a thing. I'm surprised he was even able to get Vivica out," Thea told him, her eyes darkening with concern and fear. "But evil does not only lie in the Underworld."

"Didn't Burke mention something about that when you spoke with him, my love?" Sebastian asked, his hand finding hers beneath the table and squeezing gently.

Thea sighed. The memory of that particular conversation had been weighing on her mind a lot lately…"Burke said that Dante told him that he had found the evil beings I had locked up throughout the world these last several centuries and that he had freed them."

When no one around the table spoke, but merely sat in anxious silence, Thea continued. "I didn't take it seriously at first, I'll admit. I thought to myself, how could a demon, even one with Dryad blood, possibly unlock the binds that I put in place, meant to last for all eternity? It just didn't seem possible."

"But that was before we knew about Vivica's involvement," Sebastian put in.

Thea nodded, her eyes troubled. "We don't know what she's capable of, but we do know that she has been altered. Her powers have been enhanced, and it's quite possible that she can do even more than the typical Muse can."

"Like break your enchantments?" Capri asked, her brows furrowed worriedly. "How can that be, Thea?"

Thea turned to her, a sad smile playing over her lips. "Despite what you may think of me, Capri, I am not all-powerful. When something that is not of this world, of a much darker, much more sinister evil, is coupled with an ample amount of force and skill…even I can be undone."

"That is why we must not let Dante break us apart," Sebastian asserted, eyeing them all sternly, his wise gray eyes filled with violent storms. "If he has used Vivica to release the monsters we have locked away, then only together will we be strong enough to defeat them."

For a moment everyone was quiet, lost in their own thoughts. Around them, the restaurant buzzed with conversation and laughter as the humans enjoyed their evening, completely unaware of what was coming. How could they know that evil was lurking nearby, and that they would soon be unwittingly in the throes of an all out war of fantastical proportions?

But maybe they wouldn't, Liam thought to himself, his eyes staring unseeingly at the table. If he and his family could somehow prevent it, then the world would be spared the misery and the destruction…

Jax suddenly glanced down at his watch. "It's nearly eight o'clock," he said, his eyes flashing with anticipation as he stared around the table. "Time to find out what goes bump in the night."

Liam watched his family get to their feet and shuffle out of the restaurant, everyone careful to conceal the weapons they carried. He followed them, meeting Rohan's eyes as they emerged out onto the busy street. While the others waited to cross over to the intersection of Broadway and Seventh Avenue, Rohan pulled Liam aside.

"I wanted to apologize to you, Liam," Rohan said, his eyes filled with regret. "I placed blame on you that wasn't deserved."

Liam nodded, feeling regretful himself. "You couldn't have known. If I had been in your place, I would have reacted the same." He shot a glance over toward their family, fighting to keep his emotions in check. "We both love her, Rohan, and we have both lost her before. This time, we'll get her back for good."

The older man nodded, his mouth set in a firm and unwavering line as he patted Liam's shoulder, urging the younger man to look him in the eye. "There was never going to be anyone else for her, Liam. Even though she pretended otherwise, she was destroyed without you. I need you to promise me that when we get her back that you won't let that happen again."

"That's the easiest promise I've ever had to make." Liam held out his hand, shaking Rohan's firmly. "If it's alright with you, when this is all over I'm going to ask her to marry me."

Rohan froze, blinking once with shock. He took a deep breath, his troubled eyes on Liam's determined ones. He nodded once, and finished the handshake with a heavy sigh. "Then you have my blessing."

Liam bowed his head gratefully. "Thank you, sir. I won't let you, or her, down."

"See that you don't." Rohan attempted a small smile, even as the anxiety built up within him again as he steered Liam toward the others, who had begun to cross the street.

It was five minutes till eight.

Chapter Fourteen

Times Square on a Saturday night was a hubbub of frantic activity. Not only was it a center for tourists, locals, and everyone in between to mingle and seek excitement and entertainment, but it was also the self proclaimed crossroads of the world. People of all shapes and sizes rushed around the Square, teeming through the streets in giant waves while the lights dazzled overhead. Booming music, chattering voices, laughter, car horns and screeching tires could be heard all at once, along with the smell of asphalt, sweat, perfume, roasting food, and the overall sizzle of vibrant city life in high summer.

Liam made his way to the head of the pack, trying to keep his family from getting too separated by the crowd. But the problem was that there were just so many people...it was almost impossible to maneuver without getting jostled and shuffled away from the group.

Over the heads of the humans around them, he could see Thea and Jax and a few others who were tall enough to be seen, and he saw irritation and concern about the hoards of humans on their faces as well.

Jax kept glancing down at his scanner, checking for demons in their midst. But from his disconcerted look, he was coming up with nothing.

This could prove to be a serious problem. How could they be expected to fight, if necessary, amongst the throngs of innocent bystanders? But maybe, as he had earlier assumed, this was Dante's intention all along.

He knew that there were Enforcers among them, dressed in civilian wear and remaining casually vigilant. He glanced up at the towering buildings that surrounded them, only to be blinded by the flashing neon lights of the numerous electronic billboards. But somewhere up there, snipers were standing by, ready to intervene if things got out of control.

If Dante was going to bring out his monsters here, in the middle of the busy Square, then he was in for a nasty surprise. Whatever he unleashed would be taken out with bullets from the sky, anonymous and lethal.

He glanced anxiously down at his watch, noting they had but one minute left until eight o'clock. Alright, Dante, he thought fiercely. Give us your best shot.

It was then that he looked up into the crowd and saw her.

It was only the back of her head, but he would know her anywhere. His eyes widened as he frantically stumbled forward, shoving violently at whoever was in his way. He heard a few angry cries and grunts as he went, but he didn't care, couldn't possibly give a damn. Rhiannon was just ahead, he knew it…

He kept his eyes trained on her, determined not to lose sight of her in the crowd. She was swaying and stumbling, heading away from him but at a much slower pace. He didn't even think about it, he just knew he had to get to her.

From behind him, he heard Blythe call out his name questioningly, but he didn't turn around. He was almost there…

He braided through one last cluster of people and reached out for her, grabbing her arm and whirling her around.

She stumbled, her eyes huge, dazed and lost, her face ghostly pale. But it was her.

"Rhia." He pulled her against him and shuddered, feeling her crumble weakly in his arms. Her breath was ragged and uneven, and her heart was racing against his as she fought to gain some semblance of clarity.

"Where am I?" she croaked, her head falling back as she tried to look up at him, her exhaustion so great she thought she'd wither away at that very moment. But there were strong arms holding her, and a scent she recognized, one she knew so well...her eyes burned with tears that came from both terror and recognition.

When Liam stared into her eyes, his hands gripping her arms to hold her upright, he saw with a jolting shock that her pupils were dilated. Cold sweat beaded on her forehead. He was no doctor, but she looked like she had been drugged.

"We have to get you somewhere safe," he began, watching sickeningly as her head rolled on her shoulders again, the drug weakening her system.

"It was Stella..." she battled back against the haze of the drug and stared him in the eye, gritting her teeth and pulling on whatever energy she had left. She had to tell him... "God, it was Stella."

"I know, Rhia, I know. But where is Dante?"

She only shook her head, and suddenly there was a static hissing sound coming from above them, sizzling and jolting in the air as one of the giant billboards exploded, raining sparks down on the crowd. People screamed and ducked, and Liam dragged Rhiannon to the ground and shielded her with his body, fear racing down his spine.

If that had been any indication, he'd say it was eight o'clock on the nose. And that meant only one thing...Dante had arrived.

When the last of the sparks had fallen, he grabbed her and pulled her toward the others, knowing they needed to stick together. He reached Rohan first, who gratefully pulled Rhiannon into his arms. Staying with her, Liam turned and met Thea's eyes. Relief flashed over them as she saw that Rhiannon was with him, but when a few more of the surrounding billboards exploded, her attention was diverted.

The music in the Square ended when the billboards died, and all that was left were the frightened and questioning shouts of the hundreds of people in the area, confused by what was happening. The Square was suddenly much darker than it had been before, lit only by street lamps and what little light came from inside the surrounding buildings.

Taxi cabs were forced to stop when people had poured into the streets, evading the falling sparks. Now their horns could be heard over the din of the crowd, but one voice seemed to resonate above all else. And when he heard it, Liam's eyes shifted and landed on the man himself, and they narrowed with suspicion and intense hatred.

Dante was chuckling as he maneuvered his way through the crowd and appeared before Thea and the others. Because his presence was unnatural and unnerving to the humans, they seemed to part for him, giving him room to stand alone before those of Euphora.

They drew together, standing united as the humans edged out of the way.

Some people were taking pictures, laughing and joking while others were staring fearfully at the strange man, sensing the evil in him. No one could seem to decide if this was just some kind of spontaneous entertainment put on by one of the local theater groups, or the long awaited apocalypse.

"Thea." Dante grinned, stopping before her and lowering into a gracious bow. He lifted his head as he rose again, his eyes intense on hers. "At last."

Thea stepped forward, staring down her nose at him in disgust. "I would say that it is nice to see you again, Dante, had the circumstances been more fortunate."

"And here I was, sincerely looking forward to being reunited with my family," he replied, gazing around at all of them fondly. "For I am still one of you, am I not?"

Thea's eyes narrowed bitterly as Sebastian came up beside her, resting his hand on her shoulder supportively. "You have proven yourself unworthy of the Dryad blood that flows in your veins."

"Ah yes, dirty blood and all that." Dante smiled again, one eyebrow raised in an expression of pure malice. "But you never even gave me a chance to prove myself worthy, did you?"

Thea bristled, despising herself for knowing it was true. But what did it matter when he was bound to have been evil regardless? "You have never belonged on Euphora, Dante. The Dryad in you does not cancel out the demon."

"Instead it makes me stronger, better." He preened, motioning to the expensive black pinstriped suit he wore, complete with blood red tie, as if it showcased his class and power. "I am the only one of my kind in existence; I stand alone, without anyone in this world. And yet all of you fear me…why do you think that is, Thea?"

"Fear is an odd word," Thea began, looking forward to wiping the arrogant smirk off his face. "Generally, we fear the unknown, or the things we do not understand. But I understand you perfectly, Dante. And therefore I do not fear you. I only pity you."

Fury flashed over his face as he sneered at her, his hands clenching into fists at his sides. She had hit the mark. "Even if you do not fear me, surely you must fear what I am capable of…"

His sneer twisted into an evil grin as he started laughing, sensing her uneasiness. Oh, he could hit a mark with her, too. "On several occasions, including most recently, I have had the opportunity to kill members of your precious little family. And I took advantage of the opportunity, twice…" He shifted closer to her, until he was but a foot away, his eyes honing in on her own. "Or have you forgotten the human and your beloved Head Fury?"

He saw her resolve falter as remorse, shame and misery sent a shockwave through to her very soul. How could she forget about Heidi and Roarke?

"And it's been all too easy for me to manipulate those among you...I hear Balgaire is dead but Nyxa isn't. Funny to see her here now, ready to fight against me when I had so graciously assisted her in her bitter revenge plot only a few months ago..."

Nyxa snarled and started forward, only to have Brock grab her and hold her back, his eyes on fire. His hands itched for his weapon, but he refrained, remembering Rian's warning.

"Ah, and my older brother. How lovely to see you, Brock." Dante beamed as he stepped toward him, his eyes glittering cruelly. He paused before Brock, scratching his chin thoughtfully and frowning. "You know, I really don't see the family resemblance. Your vices have destroyed you, brother."

Brock's eyes flashed heatedly as his hands clenched into fists. "You're lucky I don't kill you right now, you sick son of a bitch."

With a derisive snort, Dante waved the comment away and chuckled. "What? And let countless humans perish when everything I've set in motion occurs? Tsk, tsk."

"You've given me back my Dryad, Dante. Now give me one reason why I shouldn't have my snipers shoot you right this moment," Thea called out, causing him to turn back around and face her.

"Your fancy guns and Enforcers don't mean shit, Thea," Dante spat, rounding on her. "I have something you don't– not anymore, anyway. Ah, and here she is."

Vivica appeared from the crowd, strutting forward to Dante's side. His arm slid cozily around her as he grinned at Thea. "You remember Vivica?"

"Her appearance has changed, but yes, I remember." Thea stared bitterly at the woman who had called herself Stella...the woman who had manipulated her way onto Euphora and nearly destroyed everything.

"Yes, isn't she beautiful? I had to secure her a body when I released her from Hell. This poor girl was a runaway from Houston. Amusing, isn't it that humans are sometimes of such great use to us?"

Vivica smiled lustily at him, her eyes filled with admiration and wonder. But when she turned her attention back to Thea, they filled with bitter hate. "Did you miss me, Thea?" she asked with a vicious smile. "I certainly didn't miss you or that god-awful place."

"Life has been better without you," Thea said coolly, staring frostily at the other woman. "I had hoped you were gone for good."

"Very little in this world is permanent, Thea, including death. You know that." Vivica shrugged, cocking her chin arrogantly. "Not to mention your pathetic attempts at imprisoning what should have never been locked up."

"Darling, we mustn't excite them too much, not just yet..." Dante cooed, running his hands down her body seductively. "Play for awhile, first. Have some fun."

"My pleasure." She beamed wickedly at him before stepping forward, her hands on her hips as she stared them all down, confidence and power in her eyes. When she spotted Liam, she smirked and sauntered toward him, her hips swaying and her black leather boots snapping against the concrete. "Liam, Liam, Liam..."

Liam glared at her, instinctively stepping in front of Rhiannon, who was slowly recovering from the drug and hovering silently in her father's arms.

Seeing the woman's face again brought back a flooding wave of memories, mostly of feeling helpless and trapped inside his own mind, of fingers prying and prodding through his thoughts, planting some and disposing of others. The sudden wash of emotions made him instantly sick to his stomach, but he fought back the rush of nausea with the furious anger he had stored within him, waiting to explode.

"Don't look so mad at me, honey," Vivica crooned, giggling at the flash of violence in his eyes. "We had some good times, didn't we?"

"You used me," Liam growled, the urge to throttle her rising within him. But he had to beat it back, knowing one slip up could result in all of their deaths. They still didn't know what kind of plans Dante had in motion…

Vivica laughed, sassily cocking her hip to the side. "Used is such a sad word for what we had, Liam. How can you say that to me, when I got closer to you than anyone ever has…you were willing to leave everything for me, including your little girlfriend. But, then again, blondes are so much more fun, aren't we?"

She shifted toward him, tilting her face up to his as her hands reached out and trailed up his chest. Her blue eyes glittered with feminine mystique and cruelty as her lips curved. "I was so very sad when you broke our connection…you might as well have broken my heart."

Liam grabbed her wrists and flung her away from him, disgusted. "You stay the hell away from me and mine."

She merely laughed again. "But where's the fun in that?"

Suddenly, she looked over his shoulder, her blue eyes sharpening and honing in on her target. But as Liam whirled around to see what it was, Rohan abruptly let go of Rhiannon and charged straight toward Brock, who he cheerfully punched square in the jaw.

"*What the* —?" Brock howled as he held his throbbing jaw, confusion blending violently with his temper. Before he could do more than blink, Rohan swung at him again, a hit he only missed because Brock ducked out of the way. On instinct, his fist flew into Rohan's gut, knocking the wind out of him, but the two continued to attack each other.

They all watched, mortified, while Rohan and Brock beat each other, without any clear provocation. But Liam knew exactly what was happening, and when he whirled back to face Vivica, his hand reached out to grip her by the throat.

"*Get out of his head!*" he bellowed, watching her gasp for air and pitifully try and pry his hand from her neck. When he heard the sound of a barrel cocking on a revolver, Liam's eyes focused on Dante.

"Let her go, boy. We're not finished yet." Dante grinned, the silver of the gun glinting in the orange light of the street lamps.

Liam released Vivica and retreated back, his hands raised in defeat. But he edged toward Rhiannon, who was staring in shock at her father while he gasped for air nearby and clutched his gut.

"Darling, please continue." Dante smiled at Vivica, before aiming his gun at the others. "Anyone who moves will be missing their head."

Liam glanced around at the few dozen curious humans who were crowded around watching the scene unfold. Most had wandered on, thinking there was nothing to see. Around them, Times Square continued on, the city living and breathing despite the turmoil going on at its very heart.

The humans who were watching looked alarmed now that a gun had been drawn, and he had to wonder how long it would be till one of them called the police. He looked at his family, noting their reluctance to draw their own weapons for what he assumed was that very reason, which left Dante successfully holding all the cards, and consequently, all the power. And currently, that power resided directly within Vivica and her destructive abilities...

Without warning, Brock shot a basketball sized ball of fire straight for Rohan, who ducked and in turn shook the ground beneath them, sending a rolling tremor directly toward Brock, knocking him to his hands and knees. People scattered, screaming and shouting, thinking they were experiencing a real earthquake as the ground continued to rock.

They were running scared and Dante looked pleased as he watched them flee. He kept an eye on the group before him, delighted to have them so easily under his control. They were armed, he knew that much, but did they have the nerve to open fire on him when there were so many innocents around? He thought it highly unlikely…but good for him, as he didn't care about human casualties. In his mind, it was just part of war.

Vivica stood at his side, her eyes focused intently on Rohan and Brock, bringing out all of the hate, jealousy, and malice she knew lurked within both men. How easy they all were to manipulate, like little puppets on a string she could dance across the stage, reciting lines that harbored none of the caution or hesitation usually used to keep such vile hatred at bay.

No…she had unleashed the beast within both men, and she planned to do the same with the others…

"You couldn't let me have her, could you?" Rohan snarled, rounding on Brock as the tremors subsided, malevolence in his eyes. "You always had to have everything for yourself."

"She was mine first!" Brock growled, getting to his feet and clenching his fists. "You stole her from me!"

"She came to me of her own free will because she was sick of you. What was I supposed to do, turn away the one woman I'd always wanted just because you had her first?"

"She never wanted you, her father just convinced her that you were better than me." Brock got directly in Rohan's face, years of pent up aggression pouring out all at once, all aided by Vivica's gentle, mind probing fingers… "But I was the one she really craved. She never got over what I could give to her in bed…"

Rohan's face flushed with fury as he swung out at his arch rival once more, making contact with the other man's face. "I gave her everything and I was faithful to her. You, on the other hand, are incapable of being anything more than an asshole."

"Coming from the biggest asshole I know." Brock shoved Rohan back, startled suddenly when Serendipity pushed her way between them, her hands raised in a gesture of sovereignty.

"*Stop!*" she ordered, and immediately she placed her hands on both men's chests, closing her eyes and concentrating, fighting to break Vivica's hold on them. She focused on Brock first, since he was more violent, and struggled to push Vivica from his mind.

Brock fell to his knees, gasping for air and clutching his head. Nyxa was at his side in an instant, pulling him away from Rohan protectively.

But Vivica was stronger, and slyly slipped into Serendipity's mind, causing her to clutch her head and let out a panicked shriek. Within mere seconds she had lost the fight, and when she turned on Rohan, the others watched with stunned bewilderment.

"Brock's right, Rohan, I never really wanted you."

"Well, then we're even, because now I don't want you," Rohan shot back, getting in her face, his hands trembling at his sides. "You cold, cruel, worthless woman."

"Boring, unfeeling, pathetic man!" Serendipity reached up and slapped him hard across the face.

As they continued, Liam held Rhiannon against him and watched warily as others in his family began to turn on each other. Unable, as of yet, to use the weapons they'd brought, and emotionally on edge, they made for easy targets.

Lucian turned on Clarity, Thea shoved at Sebastian, Blythe and Brogan went to sudden blows. Clynn and Rian began to shout at each other, with Capri in the middle, her face twisted in an angry snarl as she attacked them both. Jax had fallen to his knees, attempting to fight back against Vivica's attempts to get into his mind, but from the way his hands were shaking as they clutched against his head, Liam wasn't sure he was winning the fight.

"I didn't think she could control more than one person at a time," Liam managed, clutching Rhiannon and staring around at his family anxiously. "God, I should have known…"

"Liam…" Rhiannon tilted her head to look at him, fear in her eyes. "What's happening?"

"I think we're losing," he murmured, at the same time wondering why Vivica was sparing him and Rhiannon from the feud she'd created. But maybe she wanted him to suffer while he watched everything he cared about burn…

"Why are they all fighting?" she asked, her mind still a bit fuzzy and dazed. Her ears were ringing and her vision was blurry but she finally felt she could stand on her own two feet and not stumble.

"She's inside all their heads, bringing out their rage and hostility and forcing them to fight," Liam said simply, his eyes darting from one violent brawl to the next. Maybe this was to be the end…they would quite simply kill one another, and then there would be nothing left of any of them…

"How is that possible?" Rhiannon gripped his shirt, meeting his eyes and trying to focus.

"She can control people, Rhia."

"I don't understand." She trembled, wondering if this was somehow just a strange dream that she would awaken from any moment…

"She was controlling me the entire time, just like she's controlling all of them now." He turned to her, feeling the old pain return to his chest. "None of what I've said to you the last several days has been me, Rhia. She used me to hurt you, to hurt everyone. I finally broke free of her, but by that time you had already gone."

"God…" She shut her eyes, needing to breathe to calm her furiously beating heart. "Dante told me that you had really fallen for her. And I believed him."

"Well, this is proof of what she's capable of." He gestured to the group, watching as she stared at all of them, fear in her eyes. "We didn't come here to hash out our own rivalries. We came here to save you and to destroy Dante. But now…now I don't know what's going to happen."

"Then it's up to us, Liam." She straightened her shoulders, regaining some of her strength thanks to the determination that his words had given her.

Nodding, he stared at Dante, who was watching the crowd with obvious pleasure. Beside him, Vivica was silent and fierce, her eyes nearly glowing with power as she worked the entire crowd into a frenzy.

Liam suddenly made up his mind. He knew what had to be done, what was inevitably going to happen anyway...

Over the din of shouting, roars and snarls, he called out to Dante. "Alright, Dante, enough of this!"

Dante glanced over, amusement flashing in his eyes as he began to chuckle. "You mean you're not enjoying yourself?"

"I mean you should stand up and fight like a man instead of letting your girlfriend do all the dirty work," Liam growled, stepping toward Dante fearlessly. "C'mon, let's go. Just the two of us, right now."

In response, Dante obligingly aimed his revolver straight at Liam's heart, one eyebrow raised as his lips curved into a wicked grin. "I'm afraid you don't stand much of a chance, boy."

Gritting his teeth, Liam closed the distance between himself and Dante until his chest was pressed up against the tip of the gun, the bullet inside directly aimed at his heart.

Dante merely grinned. "Feeling suicidal?"

"More like disappointed that you won't face me without hiding behind a gun. What are you afraid of Dante? After all, you're a Fire Dryad, why don't you use your powers? Or are you afraid because you know that fire stands no chance against water?"

Dante's head fell back as he laughed, his body shaking with glee as he lowered his gun. He looked briefly at the glittering Rolex on his wrist, laughter still bubbling from his throat as he glanced back at Liam.

"Lucky for you, it's nearly nine o'clock. Well, it's six o'clock where we're going, but what does it matter?" Dante turned to

Vivica, placing a hand on her shoulder. "Darling, it's time. But you've had fun, haven't you?"

Vivica nodded, her lips spreading in a sadistic grin. "Lots. Pity, I would have loved to watch them attack each other for a bit longer."

"I know. I just love to watch the empire crumble over petty arguments and jealousies. It's so...dramatic." Dante looked back at Liam and winked. "If you thought this was fun, just wait until you see what's coming."

Liam's brow furrowed as he backed up toward Rhiannon, suspicious of the maniacal gleam that suddenly appeared in Dante's eyes. Without warning, he went from a sadistic and violent man to a demonic monster. And when his eyes flashed red, Liam pulled Rhiannon against him protectively, unable to fight back the instinctual shudder that raced down his spine.

"Goodbye, Times Square. It's been fun." Dante glanced around at the frightened looking humans as police sirens began to hauntingly sound in the distance.

And then the world went dark, and all they could hear were the screams.

Chapter Fifteen

In a finger snap, the darkness vanished. For Liam, it was like opening his eyes for the first time, sensing light and shrinking away from the startling brightness of it.

The sudden absence of screaming echoed hollowly in his mind as he fought to grasp what had just happened.

He wasn't alone. Rhiannon was still pressed against him, her breathing shallow and forced as her entire body shook in a violent shudder. But she wasn't hurt.

His family was there around him, and they were all clutching their heads and groaning, trembling as if waking from a nightmare. From his own experience, he gauged that they were no longer under Vivica's control, and were suffering from the aftereffects just as he had when he had broken free.

It was that thought that had him glancing around for Dante and Vivica, only to see them standing some yards away, arm-in-arm like proud parents overseeing their children playing in the yard. Disgust warred with confusion as he realized that they were standing in a grassy field in an enormously wide open valley. In the distance, mountains speared up toward the sky, snowcapped and majestic, shadowed by the sun that had begun to descend beyond their peaks. The wind whipped around them, flowing through the grass so it appeared as if they were standing in a sea of shimmering green waves.

Somehow, they had all been transported from Times Square to this location, wherever it was, and Liam had a sickening feeling that things were about to get worse...

"Are you okay?" he murmured to Rhiannon, tilting her chin up so he could see her face. She was pale and frightened, but she nodded.

"Yes." She turned away from him, searching for her father. She spotted him collapsed against Brock, both men fighting to catch their breath. She hoped since they were no longer fighting that it meant Vivica had released them, along with everyone else.

Taking a deep breath, she linked her hand with Liam's and looked at him again, meeting his eyes. Even without saying it, they understood each other. They would stand united, no matter what happened...

Thea and Sebastian surfaced from the haze of Vivica's spell first, and they both stood tall and faced Dante, stone cold and furious.

Thea's chin tilted up defensively as she sneered down her nose at him, livid at having been taken advantage of. Beside her, Sebastian glared with equal defiance.

"Alright, Dante. You've proven that in a crowd of innocent humans you have the upper hand on us. We shall see how you fare now, without them as leverage," Thea bellowed, power flashing in her eyes as she seemed suddenly larger, somehow fiercer and more intense. Sebastian equally appeared to glow with an ethereal power, drawing in on the energy from the churning wind and cloudless sky above them.

Dante seemed less than impressed as he chuckled. "Thea, darling, having the humans around was only for fun. I just love to see the fear on their faces, to listen to their terrified screams as they run frightfully from what they do not understand." His eyes darkened maliciously as he grinned toothily at Thea, all but licking his lips in hunger and delight. "But it's time to up the ante. I think you'll enjoy what I have planned for all of you...it'll be the ultimate test in your allegiances to one another. Though if earlier is any indication, I'd say there's far too much hostility and resentment within your own ranks for you to be successful."

Behind Thea and Sebastian, the rest of the group recovered and gathered together, a strong and united front. They all unearthed the weapons they carried, aiming guns and brandishing swords that flashed in the dying light of the sun.

Liam and Rhiannon stood beside Capri and Rian, near Blythe and Jax, all of them staring mercilessly at Dante and Vivica. A collective anger and resentment resided over them all, each with their own reasons for wanting justice and revenge. Perhaps it was fitting that they were all together, here in what was surely meant to be a battleground, armed and ready to destroy him by any means necessary.

Thea glanced over her shoulder at all of them, her lips curving into a proud and fierce smile. "We are united, Dante. You will not win."

"Oh, I beg to differ." His eyes flashed to the open sky once before he glanced down at the watch he wore.

Liam watched Dante curiously, wondering how long they were going to chat with him before Thea gave the orders for them to fight. Surely it wouldn't take much to take him and Vivica out; most of his family had either a pistol or a sword in their hands...

It was then that he remembered the monsters.

Fear raced down his spine in one swift jolt, but by the time he glanced around, searching for any sign of something dark and unnatural that Dante might use against them, there was a deep, resonating cracking sound that seemed to come impossibly from the sky above.

"It's time." Dante threw his arms out triumphantly as he watched them gape up at the sky, where the cracking sound only grew louder and harsher. His eyes flashed wickedly as he pulled Vivica against him, enjoying catching them off guard. They could not have expected this…oh no, this was to be his moment, the cherry on top of the sundae of destroying everything they were, bit by glorious bit.

Liam stared in the direction of where it seemed the sound came from, which was somewhere near the mountains that crested in the distance. But it wasn't until he saw the seam that he knew exactly where it was…

A jagged crack had formed in the blue of the sky, splitting in a rough circular pattern, as if being sawed by something on the other side…and as he stared at it, the line seemed to widen and deepen, until the cracking sound boomed across the valley, shaking the ground as the piece of sky that had been cut suddenly began to tumble to Earth.

Down it fell, like a puzzle piece shaken free of its proper place in the picture, leaving a gaping hole that opened to nothing but cavernous blackness. When the piece of sky smashed into the field roughly a mile away, it sent a rumbling tremor through the ground that nearly knocked him to his knees. All he could do was clutch Rhiannon and stare uneasily at the hole in the sky. What the hell was going to come out of it?

"Get ready for it, Thea." Dante clapped his hands giddily, his excitement mounting. "You'll enjoy this."

Thea glared at him before turning back to the gaping hole, anxiously linking her hand with Sebastian's. Beside her, he was trembling with fury and disgust. How dare Dante damage his beautiful sky this way? The man would pay for it, and dearly.

But when three dark figures descended from the opening, something akin to pure horror could be felt resonating in the air.

Something wicked and unnatural had come through, and as the creatures flew straight toward them, Thea's eyes widened and she whirled around to face Dante.

"*Damn you!*" she shouted fiercely, her hands clenched tightly at her sides as her face flushed with violent anger. Her wild dark curls spun in the air around her as the magnitude of what Dante had done hit her in waves.

Dante stepped toward her, laughing boldly and clasping his hands together merrily. "Ah yes, you remember the harpies, don't you?"

Thea gritted her teeth and whirled around when a shrieking cry echoed across the field, resounding through the swirling wind and sending shivers down to her bones. Her eyes followed the three creatures as they flew overhead, circling like vultures craving a dead carcass.

At first glance, the harpies looked like dark haired women with enormous raven wings and steel gray scales covering their bodies. But when one of them extended their legs and launched itself down upon them, its fierce hawk-like talons flashed in the sunlight, wickedly sharp and deadly.

It swooped down and nearly clipped Brock, who shot a fireball at it, catching its wing. But it flapped away and resumed circling with its sisters, screeching in outrage.

"It's been quite some time since they've seen the light of day...centuries really, so I expect they're pretty hungry," Dante quipped, beaming up at them. "And they are probably not too pleased that you locked them up in that dingy, remote castle in Slovakia, either. Oh, look, I think they remember you."

The three harpies were staring at Thea, crying out threateningly as they began spiraling downward toward her. When they were close enough, their vivid orange eyes flashed and they dove straight for her.

Sebastian leaped and shoved her to the ground, covering her body with his as the shrieking creatures swooped down upon them. She heard his sharp intake of breath as one of them managed to scrape his back with its claws before they soared back into the sky. Tears of guilt and rage brimmed in her eyes, knowing he had taken the brunt of the attack for her.

She rolled over and sat up, cupping his face in her hands as he panted, wincing against the shock of pain. Pressing her forehead against his, she shut her eyes tight so the tears would not fall, not wanting to show weakness, not now. "I'm so sorry, my love…" she whispered, pressing her lips briefly to his before rising to her feet and helping him up, noting he was pale from the pain, but not mortally hurt. He nodded to her determinedly, clenching his jaw fiercely as he glared at Dante.

"Just what are you trying to prove by releasing these creatures, Dante?" Sebastian asked, suddenly throwing his hand out toward the sky where the harpies were circling. The wind that had been blowing around suddenly seemed to curve up and aim directly for the creatures, knocking all three of them into a spiraling cyclone. Their frightened shrieks rang out with the howl of the wind, and when Sebastian brought his hand down swiftly, the wind carried the creatures straight into the ground. They smacked violently into the grass, cutting off their shrieks instantly as they lay writhing in agony some yards away.

Everyone stared wide eyed from the creatures and back to Sebastian, who slipped his arm around Thea and turned his attention back to Dante.

"Well?"

Dante looked toxically furious for one flickering moment, but then he brushed off the incident with a sneering laugh. "So you took down the first batch, that's fine. They were only the warm up, anyway."

He glanced down at his watch once more, and grinned. "Our timing is quite impeccable today…"

The ground suddenly began to violently shake, and the Earth below them split into a gaping crack, dividing them. Liam grabbed Rhiannon and dragged her back from the hole, even as Capri, Rian, Blythe and Jax ended up on the other side. Liam's eyes shot briefly to meet Blythe's, and for a moment she almost looked as though she was going to jump over the crack to get to him. But before she could, Jax caught her and yanked her back at the exact moment something black leapt out of the dark hole, its howl piercing the air.

What looked like an oversized black dog landed gracefully some yards away, accompanied by a sweeping black fog that seemed to follow its every movement and swirl menacingly in the air around it. The dog growled at them, baring its sharp teeth in a maniacal snarl. Its muscles were bunched with strength and ferocity as it stared them down, red eyes glowing with malice and hunger.

"My personal favorite!" Vivica gushed as she nodded to Thea. "Don't you remember the Black Dog, Thea?"

Thea turned from the dog to Vivica, her eyes as hard as agate and her temper sparking. "You used it to strike fear into the hearts of men as they went into battle, or as they lay dying from the wars you created. It was one of the many reasons why I banished you and locked the creature up in the remote English countryside, where it belonged. I never thought you would have the power to release it."

"Well I'm not the same Muse I once was. I've changed in ways that would curl your toes." Vivica began to laugh lustily, her eyes suddenly flashing to the dog and honing in on it sharply, her blue eyes appearing to glow with power as she spoke. The southern lilt of her voice deepened demonically when she uttered the single, alarming word. "Attack."

The dog leapt over the hole it had emerged from, heading straight for Rian and Capri. Rian shifted in front of Capri protectively and aimed his .50 semi-automatic pistol at the creature, firing at it almost instantaneously. The bullet struck the dog in the shoulder and it faltered momentarily, but when it kept coming for them, Jax lifted his shotgun onto his shoulder and fired. Before the bullet could make contact, the dog vanished in a sweep of billowing, black smoke, appearing several yards away, growling threateningly. Jax tried to fire once more, but the dog disappeared again and then reappeared behind Dante and Vivica, where it began to pace back and forth, glaring at them with glowing eyes.

"Damnit," Jax cursed, frowning at Rian, unsure what else to do. Beside him, Blythe was rubbing her hands together, thinking she'd light a fire under the damn creature and see if he'd burn. Before she got the chance, however, storm clouds appeared on the horizon, thunder rumbling and lightning crackling. The storm was rapidly approaching, much faster than was natural, and they all stared at it apprehensively.

"What now?" Rhiannon murmured, her eyes glued to the raging clouds.

"God only knows." Liam let out a huff of breath as he shot a glance over at Vivica and Dante, who were beaming at the storm expectantly. If he could just get Dante alone, away from Vivica, then he might be able to play their little game right back at them. There had to be a way to drive a wedge between them and pit them against one another so they were distracted and divided. It had worked with his own family, up until now. He just needed to figure out what would set them off...

"There it is." He heard Rhiannon gasp, covering her mouth with her hands as she gawked at the clouds, terror in her eyes. He followed her gaze, spotting what was descending from the storm clouds on black leathery wings.

It was a goddamn dragon. And it had three heads. He felt his heart sink in his chest as he watched it soar down toward them, teeth bared as it growled deep within its throat. It was not much larger than a pickup truck, but there was something about it that terrified him more than the harpies or the dog had...dragons, if he remembered right from his stint in reading folklore and myths, were not easy to destroy. And there were just so many different types, who knew just what kind Dante had released, and from where...

"Everyone, stay together," Thea called out, motioning for those on the other side of the crack to walk around and rejoin the group.

She had locked away many dragons in her time, but this particular one she remembered disturbingly well. It had wrought terror and destruction in Eastern Europe for years before she had managed to catch it and imprison it within the confines of an enormous mountain, where she had thought it would remain for all time. But somehow Vivica had been able to find it and release it...

With her family all together and at her side, Thea watched the dragon land before them, and its three heads turned as one to eye her intensely. Its black scales glittered in the flash of lightning as the storm clouds continued to rage overhead, and its three sets of beady yellow eyes seemed to stare directly at her, as if recognizing her as the one who had captured it all those centuries ago.

"Bet you weren't expecting a dragon, were you, Thea?" Dante shouted over the din of thunder and the dragon's heavy, growling breath. There was a sick, demented laughter in his voice, and a giddy pleasure at seeing them squirm with discomfort and fear. "Vivica, darling, tell the dragon to attack Blythe. I think this will be proper punishment for her reckless disobedience."

Vivica nodded and grinned as Blythe bared her teeth in a wild snarl, barely resisting the urge to charge at Dante. "We may be related, asshole, but that doesn't make me your damn slave!"

Dante's eyes flashed with a mixture of loathing and stunning desire as he began to walk toward her, clearly drawn to her defiance. She was the spitting image of his mother, Bristol, even if she was unfortunately a whore...

"Dearest Blythe..." His lips curved slowly as his eyes flashed brutally red, filled with malevolence and evil. "Think of the life we could have had..."

On impulse, she spit at his feet, her lips curled into a disgusted sneer as Jax stood at her side, his shot gun pointed directly at Dante's chest. Dante chuckled darkly, shaking his head at the two of them. "You made your bed, darling. Now it's time to sleep in it."

He stepped back as the dragon suddenly lurched forward, one of the three heads lunging out, jaws wide, intent on biting Blythe. But she ducked and Jax fired off a round from his gun, severing the dragon's neck in two. The head fell limply to the ground, and the body of the dragon and remaining two heads writhed and roared in pain and anger. Jax pulled Blythe back, but she smacked at him bitterly.

"Damnit, don't you understand dragons at all?" she spat, furious with him. He stared at her in disbelief.

"I just saved your neck. You just can't give me credit for anything, can you?" Jax shot back, temper flaring.

"Okay, I'll give you credit for giving the dragon an extra set of teeth. Thanks, cowboy," Blythe said sarcastically as she pointed to where the dragon was flailing around wildly, the neck that had been severed suddenly healing with two heads rapidly sprouting up to take its place.

When Jax realized what was happening, he paled, his eyes wide with horror. "Well, shit…"

"Lesson learned. Don't go for the neck, and avoid its blood. It's poisonous." Blythe grabbed him around the neck and dragged him down for a quick kiss before she charged at the dragon, hands raised and a warrior's cry on her lips.

Fire shot from the palms of her hands, scalding the dragon as it reared up and soared into the sky, fleeing the flames. It swooped overhead, circling as it glared down at her. She shot a fireball up at it, but it was quick enough to easily dodge it before abruptly diving down toward her.

It was so fast that she didn't have the opportunity to build up enough fire to shoot at it, so she fell to the ground instead and covered her neck with her hands, the whoosh of the dragon's body as it flew mere inches above her roaring in her head. When it rose once more into the air, she glared at it resentfully, only to have Jax gather her up into his arms forcefully and carry her back toward the group.

"Foolish, crazy, stubborn brat," he grumbled, the fear clenching his heart violently as he held her against him, ignoring her attempts to release herself.

"Put me down, I was able to hurt it! Let me try again." She smacked at his chest, but the realization of just how close she'd come to being dragon food hit her in a sweeping wave that had her stomach rolling weakly. "God, okay. Just let me catch my breath." She pressed her face into his neck as he brought her back to group.

Thea turned to Brock, who was watching the dragon circle overhead, his hands clenching and unclenching at his sides. "Brock, you know what to do." She nodded when he glanced down at her, and he grinned darkly.

"Yes I do." He tilted his head back and braced himself, his hands held out and a massive fireball beginning to build between them, glowing white hot at its core. He swung back and hurled the fireball up into the sky toward the dragon, and it soared through the air like a meteor. But before it could make contact with the dragon, another fireball shot out and struck Brock's out of the sky, both plummeting to Earth in raging flames.

With a violent growl, Brock glared over at Dante, whose hands were out and held together, his face contorted with fury and triumph. He let out a relieved laugh, his body shaking with it as he looked at Brock.

"I can't let you do that, brother," Dante told him, brushing his hands together as if to clean them off. "Blythe has earned the chance to take on the beast herself."

Before Brock had a chance to retort, a series of shrieking screams echoed from behind them as the harpies flew up into the air once again, recovered from their fall. They dived down, one by one, so swiftly that there was no option other than to run.

Liam grabbed Rhiannon's hand and pulled her with him, shooting a glance over his shoulder and seeing the harpies rise back up into the sky, only to dive again, lethal talons bared.

He stopped and pushed her behind him, keeping her shielded as his family began firing up at the creatures, thunder rumbling and lightning flashing against the churning dark sky.

On instinct, he shot a glance over to Vivica, who was staring up at the harpies intently, her blue eyes glowing with power. He could tell that she was controlling the harpies, most likely to keep them focused on the attack. And she had clearly been controlling the dragon and the dog as well, who now both swept in to attack his family.

It suddenly dawned on him what he could say to sever the tie between Dante and Vivica…it was all so obvious now. Whirling around, he met Rhiannon's eyes firmly.

"I want you to talk with Vivica, egg her on, find something to use against her. Make her realize that she's being used by Dante and that he doesn't really care about her. Whatever you have to say to rile her up, just make it happen. Okay?"

She nodded, but her brows furrowed in confusion when he started to leave her. "What are you going to do?"

He reached for her hand, lifting it to his lips in a brief moment of tenderness, fighting back the urge to just take her away from all the destruction and flee. His family, his home… they all needed him to finish this. And he knew what he had to do now.

When he released her hand and met her eyes once more, there was a fire in them she recognized as bold fearlessness… here he was, standing before her as war raged mercilessly behind him. Not just a boy, not a man, not even a Dryad. He was a hero.

"It's time Dante and I had a personal chat," he said simply. He nodded to her before he turned around and stalked over to where Dante was standing with Vivica. He unsheathed the revolver Rian had given him from the holster at his belt, and aimed it directly at Dante's chest as he approached.

Dante glanced over, surprise flickering briefly in his eyes before he recovered with a smile.

"Ah, Liam." He lifted his own revolver, touching the tip to Liam's gun with a metallic click. One dark eyebrow lifted tauntingly as he stared down his nose at the younger man. "Do you even know how to use a gun?"

"Pull the trigger and bang," Liam shot back with a sneer. "But that's not why I'm here. I want that one-on-one we talked about earlier, Dante. Just you and me, no guns."

"And why should I agree to such a proposal?" Dante asked curiously, his eyes flashing with humor. "What's to stop me from just killing you right now and saving myself the trouble of a dirty fight?"

"You won't kill me because that's not enough of a challenge for you." Liam lowered his own gun and shoved it back into his holster, then held his hands up in surrender. "C'mon, I'll make it real easy. Just pull the trigger, and then I'm gone."

Dante considered the situation for a moment, his tawny eyes betraying nothing as he stared directly at Liam. But when his lips twisted into a grin, Liam knew he had him.

"I suppose the proposition has some merit," he said as he tucked his revolver into the holster beneath his suit jacket. "But perhaps it will be more interesting if no one is around to save you the moment before I kill you."

Liam paled slightly as Dante turned to Vivica and murmured something in her ear.

The last thing Liam saw was Vivica snap her fingers as the world went dark once again.

Chapter Sixteen

In the blink of an eye, Liam found himself on the cliff's edge on one of the mountains that overlooked the valley, his feet teetering over the edge dangerously. He jolted backwards, arms flailing as he whirled around, searching for Dante. He spotted the other man hovering in the shadows nearby, leaning casually against the rocky mountain face, a lit cigarette in his mouth.

Letting out the breath he'd been holding, Liam glanced back over his shoulder at the valley far below, where his family was fighting the monsters. He could see Vivica, standing tall as she wielded the creatures, controlling their actions. Near her, he spotted Rhiannon. He had to trust that she would make good on what he had asked her to do. It was going to be crucial for his plan to work...but then again, this was Rhiannon, the person he trusted most in the entire world. With her sharp mind, he knew she'd get the job done.

He watched the battle for a few moments, lost in thought. Then, to his horror, a group of at least fifteen men appeared out of thin air behind Vivica, men he could only assume were demons she had summoned to join the fight. He watched, mortified, as the men sprinted into the fray of the battle, guns blazing and bullets flying. Unable to watch any longer, he whirled around to face Dante, fury in his eyes.

"How many more surprises are you gonna pull on us?" he shouted, desperately wishing he hadn't left Rhiannon by herself. Hell, he might have just made a drastic and terrible mistake...

Dante took a drag on the cigarette and exhaled, the smoke billowing around him. Then he dropped the cigarette to the floor and snuffed it out with his black snakeskin boot before stepping toward Liam and grinning.

"I'll take it the demons have arrived." He peered over Liam's shoulder to get a look of the destruction himself, pleased at the results. "You know, I don't think this whole plan could have worked out any better."

Liam's eyes narrowed as he tucked his hands into his pockets, needing to do something with them so he didn't strike out prematurely. God knows he was mad enough at that moment...

"Are there more coming?"

Dante grinned. "Even if there were, I doubt we'd need them. Apparently my rather small army has been effective enough to destroy the prestigious people of Euphora..."

"The fight isn't won yet, Dante," Liam reminded him, attempting to hide the relief that flooded through him at that moment. At least this was it... "If you think Thea is going to sit back and let you take control, you're sadly mistaken."

"She thinks she's so smart," Dante spat, scowling bitterly. "But I've outwitted her time and time again, so what makes you think she'll get the upper hand on me this time?"

"Because you've screwed up. Big time," Liam said casually, grinning at the confusion and denial that flashed over Dante's face. "Oh, you don't think so?"

Dante stared him down, trying to determine what kind of game Liam was playing. "The last time we met, boy, I told you I was your worst nightmare. It would do well for you to remember that now when you're trying to screw with me." He got in Liam's face, his eyes ripe with rage and arrogance.

Liam merely shrugged, fighting to maintain nonchalance. He knew indifference would only piss off Dante further, but that was exactly where he wanted him.

"I'm just trying to be honest, Dante. But if you don't want to hear it…"

"What the hell do you know?" Dante growled, stalking off to stare over the cliff's edge toward the battle, his hands clasped regally behind his back. Everything was going according to plan…and soon they would be dead. Then he could watch Thea suffer, knowing she had no one and nothing any longer. Just like she had taken everything from him, he would take it all from her…

"Tell me, Dante, I'm curious…" Liam began, shifting to stare at the demon's back, pleased when he stiffened at the words. "Would you take Vivica over Blythe?"

With a fierce laugh, Dante whirled around, eyebrows raised. "What kind of a question is that?"

"I was just wondering because I know how badly you want Blythe…if you could have either of them, which would you choose?"

"Blythe betrayed me," he snapped, glaring at nothing in particular as he pondered the question. "But she's blood. She's the spitting image of the only person I ever gave a damn about. My obsession with her knows no bounds." His eyes widened a bit as madness flashed over his face. Liam had to bite back his discomfort at seeing the pure fixation in the other man's expression.

"But Vivica seems okay," Liam put in, fanning the flames of Dante's temper, bit by bit. Oh, and it was working.

Dante's head snapped up as he glared at Liam. "Vivica's a fool. Albeit a useful fool, but nothing more."

"Then why the charade, Dante? If you don't love her, and you don't want her, then why lie to her?"

"Women are swayed by such things. It was simply too easy." Dante shrugged, grimacing. "Shaking her won't be easy once this is done."

"See, that's the mistake you made," Liam pointed out with a grin.

"What is?"

"You gave her too much power." Liam chuckled, shaking his head as if it should have been so pathetically obvious. "Haven't you ever read Shakespeare? Hell hath no fury like a woman scorned, Dante. First rule of seducing women is to maintain control. But you've gone and made her so important, so crucial, that you simply can't succeed without her. And what's worse is that she knows it. Tsk tsk."

Dante waved the thought away, turning around to pace. But the seed was planted, and now it was growing into an entire garden of uncertainty and panic in his mind. How had he over-looked that? In his mad rush to overtake Thea and Sebastian, how had he slipped up so horrifically?

"So I'll kill her," Dante decided, still pacing and running through the options in his head. "We'll finish all of you, and then I'll put a bullet in her brain. Case closed."

Liam rolled his eyes dramatically with a frustrated sigh. "Did you not hear me? She's too strong, she has too much power. All she has to do is get into your mind before you have the chance to pull the trigger, and then poof! You're her own personal slave until the day you die. Don't think she won't do it, the bitch is crazy and you know it."

Dante's eyes widened as he cursed under his breath, furious. "So I'll drug her, and then shoot her. Hah! Reason your way out of that one, boy!"

Smirking now in triumph, Dante cocked his chin up arrogantly at Liam, tucking his hands into the pockets of his pinstriped slacks.

"Really? You don't think she's expecting something like that? Women like to be seduced, but they're not stupid. For all you know, she might be planning on offing you and taking over when all this is done."

"That's absurd. She's obsessed with me," Dante argued, refusing to acknowledge the idea that Vivica would turn on him. "No…I have her right where I want her."

"Alright, it's your grave you're digging. No skin off my nose." Liam turned around to stand at the cliff's edge once more, his eyes on the battle.

Behind him, he heard Dante begin to laugh. The sound was beginning to grate on his nerves. He whirled around, prepared to square off with the man once more but a rapid burst of fire had him falling to the ground to avoid getting burned. Dante continued to laugh as the fireball he'd launched at Liam sailed out and dissipated into thin air some yards away.

"This is what you wanted, wasn't it?" Dante charged, watching Liam get to his feet and meet his eyes defiantly.

"I just hope you're ready to drown, asshole," Liam muttered through gritted teeth as he shot a fierce stream of water straight at Dante, knocking the man back into the mountain face, causing rocks to tumble down around him. Dante managed to dodge out of the way, shooting out a fireball as he sprinted to the side. Liam extinguished the ball of fire midair with a second burst of water, a grin curving over his lips. "That the best you got, Dante?"

Dante shook his head as he rubbed his hands together manically, his eyes lit with glee and adrenaline. "You forget, boy, that I have one distinct advantage over you."

"Fire doesn't stand a chance against water and you know it."

Dante's head fell back with a quick and fierce laugh, his eyes flashing a murderous, bloody red as he smiled. "But I wonder how water will fare when confronted with a demon?"

And then, almost in an instant, the man evaporated into nothing but a black, shadowy mist, out of which emerged a shadowy serpent that crawled horrifically toward Liam, vivid red eyes glowing through the darkness.

It had taken Rhiannon more than a few moments to deal with the fact that Liam had quite simply disappeared into thin air along with Dante. God knows where Vivica sent them, or if he would ever return…

But she had to have faith in him, just as he had faith in her. There was nothing she could do for him now, other than what he had asked of her before he had left.

The sudden appearance of brute looking humans possessed by demons had thrown her off kilter, but thankfully they had launched themselves into the group of those already fighting and had paid little attention to her.

In fact, she was currently the only person other than Vivica who was not fighting. And up until the moment she wandered into Vivica's line of sight and broke the woman's concentration did Vivica even realize she hadn't been alone.

Vivica jolted, almost losing control over the monsters, who momentarily paused fighting and nearly collapsed. But she merely scowled and swiftly regained control before turning to Rhiannon.

"Shouldn't you be out there with the others, little girl? Or are you too scared?" Vivica challenged, smirking at Rhiannon as she planted her hands on her hips and cocked her chin up condescendingly.

Rhiannon's eyes narrowed as she stepped closer. "It would be nice to know just who I was fighting against. You're getting into their minds, controlling them…how?"

Vivica rolled her eyes as she laughed. "You mean they didn't take the time to fill you in?"

"Between the kidnapping and the drugging, no, there hasn't been much time for explanations. But from what I've gathered tonight, you used to live on Euphora, and Thea banished you."

"I was a Muse," Vivica revealed proudly, tossing back her long locks of blonde hair as she smiled. "Nearly a hundred years ago I lived on Euphora. But apparently my…methods were not appropriate in Thea's eyes."

"From what I heard, you used your powers to hurt people. I can see why Thea didn't appreciate that," Rhiannon said, crossing her arms over her chest and eyeing Vivica strangely. "But what happened to you when you were banished?"

"I experimented, mostly." Vivica frowned, those days dark and distant to her now. "Voodoo became an obsession of mine. It was a way I could influence others that Thea had no control over. But one night…things got carried away." She clenched her teeth, the memory of the horrific pain and confusion coursing through her. She had to fight back the nausea she felt just from thinking of it. "I conducted a ritual with some of my followers and we opened a portal, allowing a demon to come through. I was in a trance, seduced by the magic and the music, and because of it the demon was drawn to my weakness. He possessed me, and used me to attack my followers. And, as a result, they murdered me and the demon inside my body, not truly understanding anything more other than that they had released an insurmountable evil."

Rhiannon's eyes widened. "If you died, then how are you standing here?"

"Ah, now that's the most interesting part." Vivica smiled wickedly, her eyes flashing with power and pride. How desperately she wanted to brag… "When they killed me, the demon dragged me down with him to Hell, giving me no choice in the matter. Though I must say, it worked out nicely because I was something of a commodity in the Underworld. You see, very rarely does a Muse, or anyone from Euphora, end up down there in death. And so they used me. They took what I was and made me better, stronger, more powerful. And then they waited for the right person to come along and release me. Dante was just the right man for the job…"

Rhiannon chewed her bottom lip for a moment, thinking through all the new information. "So Dante released you and then used you to release the harpies, the Black Dog, and the dragon?"

Vivica sneered, insulted. "He didn't use me. We're partners. I just happened to be extraordinarily useful to him, but without his knowledge on where the creatures were contained, I wouldn't have known where to find them."

"Yes, but without you, he would have never been able to construct this army of his." Rhiannon motioned to the battle waging on beyond them with her arms, shaking her head. "So really, you are more valuable to him than he is to you."

"No." Vivica let out a huff of breath, suddenly annoyed by the direction the conversation had taken. "Dante released me, therefore I would still be in Hell if it wasn't for him."

"I'm sure it was only a matter of time before someone suitable came along. Maybe someone who would truly appreciate your talents." Rhiannon held Vivica's eyes, woman to woman. This was the way to get to her, she was certain of it. She just had to keep pushing...

"Dante does appreciate me," Vivica replied haughtily, sneering at Rhiannon. "What do you know, anyway?"

"I know that I see you doing all of the dirty work, while he sits back and takes the lion's share of the credit. Like back at the Inn, when you kidnapped me? He had you destroy the room, didn't he? And I'm assuming it was you who somehow located me and you who drugged me. It was you who had to spend time on Euphora, spend time with Liam, convincing everyone that you were just a normal, human girl. And then it was all up to you to get into our heads and force us to fight. It was you who had to transport us here from New York. And now it's you who has to control the monsters you released from their prisons, all while he gets to sit back and chat somewhere with Liam. And did he ever once give you credit for any of that? Not really, not in the way you deserve. No, it's all about him and it's always been all about him. This is his war, his revenge, and his emotional baggage."

"Shut up, what the hell do you know, you little brat," Vivica snapped, the urge to strike Rhiannon in the face rushing through her in a wave of sudden violence. But, just as it had been with Dante, the seeds were now planted, and they were growing whether Vivica wanted them to or not.

Turning away from the girl, Vivica focused back on the battle, closing her eyes to center herself. She was still in full control of the beasts, but from the looks of it, they weren't winning.

Two of the three harpies had been shot down from the sky and were lying dead in the grass, while the third one circled overhead, grieving and vengeful over the deaths of her sisters. Nearly half of the demons had been destroyed, with the human's they'd possessed being treated and put into a deep, comforting sleep by the Muses under a tree some yards away.

The dragon, the Black Dog, and a handful of demons still remained in the fight. And from the looks of it, those on the Euphora side were hardly wounded.

Annoyed, Vivica upped the ante and urged more aggression in the dragon, knowing it was their best bet. And as she did so, she felt some of her own strength leave her as she concentrated more of her mind on the creatures, and yet she couldn't help but think of Dante and what the hell he was doing up there on that cliff.

Having a fine little chat, that's probably what he's doing, she thought bitterly, her eyes flashing as they opened to stare out at the battle once again. The man certainly loved to talk. In fact, she was certain this could have been pulled off much more effectively had they not been so theatrical about it. They should have ordered Thea and her posse to show up or they would kill the girl, and then she could have used her control to keep them submissive while Dante simply shot and murdered them all. Then they could have left Thea and

Sebastian to wallow in the blood of their family, and she and Dante could have stormed Euphora and taken over.

But no...Dante had wanted excessive dramatics. Like forcing them to bicker amongst themselves, and scare a handful of humans with exploding lights and earthquakes. And goddamn monsters that she honestly didn't know what they were going to do with once the battle was over. She wasn't capable of locking them up again and she couldn't control them forever. Eventually they were going to have to be released and she'd be damned if they'd turn on her.

Feeling suddenly incensed, she glared over at Rhiannon, who had been watching her quietly, her arms still crossed protectively over her chest. The girl was just weak, she didn't even want to fight with the others. How pathetic.

"Do you know why Dante is the way he is, Vivica? Why he's so angry with all of us?" Rhiannon said suddenly, sensing she had given the woman enough time to stew over what had previously been said.

"He hates you all for the same reason I do. Being banished creates resentment," Vivica responded confidently.

"It does, yes. But that's not everything." Stepping closer, Rhiannon let her arms fall to her sides in a gesture of trust and openness. Woman to woman... "Did he tell you the reason he didn't want to just kill us? Why he insists on always toying with us, using our insecurities so we fight with each other while he gets to watch from the sidelines?"

"He enjoys the theatrics of it, that's all." Vivica brushed the thought away callously.

"It's because he's obsessed with us." Rhiannon's own eyes widened as she acknowledged the complete and utter truth behind her statement as she said it. Of course...it was so obvious to her now...

Vivica snorted out an impatient laugh, hiding the fact that the girl's words had sent an unpleasant shiver down her spine.

Inspired, Rhiannon continued. "His entire life he's been told that he's one of us, and yet he can't be with us. His mother was all he had, and I'm sure she told him countless stories about Euphora, and about Thea and Sebastian. He grew up craving nothing more than being in his true and rightful home. But he also had to understand that that was never going to be a possibility for him, because of his demon blood. And so he resented us, but along with that resentment came his obsession. He obsessed over his mother, because she was his only link to us. And when he got old enough and smart enough, he understood that he could manipulate us, that we weren't perfect and that we could be weakened. So that became his hobby, his life's goal…to get so ingrained in our lives that we would have no choice but to accept his existence. That's all he's ever wanted…our acceptance."

"Bullshit," Vivica managed, though the word had no feeling behind it. She had gone rather pale while Rhiannon had spoken, her anger diminishing and confusion and turmoil replacing it. "Dante wants to destroy all of you, he wants to make Thea suffer."

"I don't think he even truly understands what he wants, Vivica." Shaking her head, Rhiannon frowned. "He thinks that what will ultimately make him happy is to see us all dead. But in reality, he quite simply cannot exist without us. We are everything to him."

"No, no, I don't believe you," Vivica stammered, her hands shaking as she ran them through her hair, clutching her head as she fought to steady her breathing. "This has not all been for nothing. This has been for the purpose of destroying all of you and getting revenge on Thea for banishing us. Dante loves me."

"None of that is true, and you know it," Rhiannon argued, stepping up the heat now. "He's only using you. He's using you to play his game, to create more havoc for us. Don't you see that? If he loved you, he would have told you the truth. But instead he's lied to you."

"*No!*" Vivica struck out then, her hand swiping viciously across Rhiannon's cheek in a stunning slap. Rhiannon stepped back, holding her face and wincing from the stinging pain.

"If you don't believe me, then go find out for yourself," Rhiannon managed, looking up to meet Vivica's angry eyes as her hands fell down to her sides. "Go to wherever you sent them, and force him to tell you the truth. That's how it works, isn't it? You get inside a person's head and you force what's really in their minds out of them?"

Vivica seemed to think about it for a moment, weighing the pros and cons in her mind. Surely it wouldn't hurt to go find out the truth...and the girl was right, she was easily capable of it. And really he ought to be carrying more of the burden of pulling off this whole scheme of his...

"Fine. But you're coming with me," Vivica decided, grabbing Rhiannon's arm suddenly and yanking her against her harshly. "I don't want you skipping off to freedom just yet. You're still good leverage."

Rhiannon's eyes widened, but she nodded, steeling herself against the fear. They were going to where Dante was, which meant that Liam was there too...and the thought of seeing him suddenly lifted her spirits and gave her strength.

Vivica didn't even spare one last glance at her monsters and demons as she snapped her fingers and plunged them both into darkness.

Liam clutched his pistol in his hands, his heart pounding in his chest and his eyes trained on the shadowy serpent currently slithering in circles around him, preparing to attack.

So far, his bullets had been utterly useless. How was he to know that lead bullets did next to nothing to a demon? He had never been trained in fighting demons before...

And apparently, demons were impervious to water, because dousing Dante had done little as well. The only thing that had seemed to have any effect whatsoever had been attempting to shower Dante in ice and freeze him, but he was so quick that it was near impossible for the ice to settle long enough to solidify.

So they were squaring off, and Liam felt pathetically useless. He hadn't expected Dante to transform, but now that it had happened he realized what a foolish assumption that had been. Of course Dante would play dirty, that was how he did everything.

But…he had an idea on what might make Dante transform back into Dryad form. After all, the man was a conversationalist with a monstrous ego. Playing into that ought to do the trick…

"Did you know that Blythe wants to marry the bounty hunter?" Liam began, keeping his gun pointed at Dante even though he knew it was virtually useless. "She wants to have kids with him and everything."

Dante let out a guttural hissing sound that sounded threatening, so Liam happily continued. "You really screwed things up with her, buddy. If you had played your cards right, she might have chosen you instead of him."

Dante let out another low, aggressive noise, but Liam only smiled. "I'm sorry, does the realization that it's your own fault you lost her to another man bother you? I guess it would bother me to know what a loser I was."

For whatever reason, those words worked like a charm because Dante reared up and let out a manic hiss, only to suddenly transform from a sweep of black smoke into his Dryad form, his face contorted with jealousy and wild rage. *"You insufferable piece of—"*

Before he could finish his sentence, he was jolted by a sudden flash of white light that blinded them both for a flickering moment. When it cleared, Vivica and Rhiannon appeared in front of them, side-by-side.

Liam gaped, terror gripping his heart and thinking that everyone else was dead and Vivica was only coming to tell them the news. But he could still hear the commotion from down below in the valley...he met Rhiannon's eyes, and she nodded very slowly, as though to say that she knew she was doing.

And when Vivica suddenly burst forward and stormed up to Dante, pressing her hands against the sides of his face with madness in her eyes, Liam stepped aside and backed toward Rhiannon, watching the scene unfold before him.

Dante's surprise gave Vivica the time she needed to get into his mind, and when his expression of shock faded to one of blank indifference, it was clear that she had him.

"*Why did you release me?*" she bellowed, her eyes boring into his as he hovered before her, helpless under her control.

"To use you," Dante said placidly, his deep voice oddly haunting without his usual bite.

"*Why?*"

"Because I wanted to step things up a notch and really hit Thea where it hurts. You were the perfect tool. You're not only powerful, but you had a unique history with Thea that no one else has, and a thirst for revenge that I could influence and use."

Vivica's hands began to tremble but she held firm, determined to hear it all from him as her fury began to build. "Were your intentions really to kill them all and destroy Euphora?"

Dante shook his head, his lips curving into an eerie smile. "If they die, then it's all over."

"What's over?" Vivica demanded.

"Everything."

Dante's eyes closed peacefully as Vivica covered her face in her hands and let out a raging scream that echoed forcefully off the mountain side and down into the valley below.

Chapter Seventeen

Capri clutched at a stitch in her side as she fought to catch her breath, having just been chased by the remaining harpy as it had flown through the air with a god awful vengeance. She had tried to trap the creature in a tunnel of wind, but instead it had managed to evade the cyclone and launch itself straight for her, fury in its bright eyes.

If she hadn't fought back her instinct to flee and boldly reached for the sword Rian had given her, whirling around to plunge it deep into the belly of the monster, she might not have survived. But now she stood before the creature as it died in the grass at her feet, her arms wrapped around her torso as she fought to catch her breath and come to terms with the knowledge that she had actually killed something.

But she also knew that if the harpy hadn't died, then she most certainly would have.

It was then that she heard the echoing scream of rage coming from somewhere near the mountains, and her head jolted up at the sound. Her breath caught in her throat as an unwelcome shiver raced through her. God…what a horrible sound…

"Capri!" Rian called out, rushing to her as his gun tumbled from his hands to land with a thud on the grass. He scooped her up into his arms, hugging her and lifting her clear off the ground as he buried his face against her neck and shuddered.

She welcomed him in, trembling from the adrenaline that came from facing death and conquering it, and knowing just what could have been. Her hands fisted in his hair and she breathed him in, shutting her eyes tight so she wouldn't have to face the bloody carcass at their feet.

She fought to calm her rapidly beating heart as he lowered her to the ground. "What was that scream?"

He shook his head, his eyes troubled. "I don't know. But Vivica and Rhiannon are both gone."

"Do you think they went to wherever Vivica sent Dante and Liam?" Capri asked, her eyes searching his.

In response, he stared over her shoulder toward the mountain range, even though he could make out nothing but the rocky cliffs and snow capped peaks.

"It sounded like it came from the mountains. Maybe they're up there," he told her, clutching her shoulders tightly in his hands. "Either way, there's nothing we can do for them. Our obligation is to win this fight."

Capri nodded, but her chest ached horribly at the thought that Liam and Rhiannon could be hurt…or worse, dead.

Disturbed, she surveyed the battle scene around them. So much destruction…so much violence, anger and bloodshed…the grassy field that had started out as a beautiful prairie now resembled a mine field, with smoke streaming up from the ground and storm clouds that continued to rage mercilessly overhead. She'd used those clouds herself to send bolts of lightning down upon their enemies, which she spotted her father doing now. Lucian was beside him, adding water to the electricity to brutally electrify the Black Dog. Clearly they had discovered this was the secret to the dog's demise, as it was instant and exacting and much harder to evade than the bullets had been.

Blythe was with Jax and Brogan as they tackled a few of the remaining demons. Brogan forced the demons from their human hosts and Jax fired liquid nitrogen bullets into the serpents. Blythe followed up with a pistol loaded with lead bullets that shattered the demons into a million pieces, bursting in a cloud of glittering glass.

The Fates were wielding swords and attacking those demons that tried to interfere with the destruction of their own, thus guarding Blythe and the others, while the Muses tended the human hosts, careful to aid whatever wounds they could patch up while urging them into a peaceful sleep. They would need to be returned to a safe zone, where they would be left to awaken, their memories cleansed of everything they had witnessed. Near them, Thea was with Sebastian, tending to the deep scratches on his back.

"It looks like Brock and Rohan need help," Rian said suddenly, nodding to where the two men were struggling to tackle the dragon, which they had managed to ensnare in thorny vines attached to the ground. But it had reared up and snapped some of the binds, and was flapping its enormous leathery wings in a desperate attempt to get back into the sky.

"Go, I'm going to see if Thea needs me." Capri attempted a small smile even as her brow creased with worry and fear. "Please, be careful."

In response, he cupped her face in his hands and kissed her briefly on the mouth, his serious eyes filled with grit and courage. "This is what I was born to do."

With that, he picked his gun up from the grass and charged for Rohan and Brock, leaving her standing alone to watch him go. He was right, she thought to herself proudly. He was a warrior, and this was his purpose and his true passion. He would come back to her safely, that much she knew. He always did.

Taking a deep breath, she turned away from the battle and jogged over to Thea where she was rubbing salve that the Muses had brought onto Sebastian's bare back. Capri blushed a bit at having intruded on what appeared to be an intimate moment, but Thea welcomed her over regardless.

"Capri." Thea's face was strained with concern and rage as she glanced up from her lover's wounds. "I need you to finish treating his back, he's in more pain than he's stubbornly going to admit."

Sebastian winced and shot her an irritated look. "It's not that bad of a cut, my love. I can fight."

"Harpies have toxins on their talons, Sebastian, and you know it. If we don't treat the infection now, it will spread and who knows how long it will take you to recover," Thea snapped, but Capri could tell that her sharp tongue was not born out of annoyance, but out of guilt and fear. It struck her to the core to see Thea so vulnerable...

"I'll do it, Thea. Don't worry," Capri reassured her, already kneeling down in the grass and smiling sweetly at Sebastian.

"Good." Thea rose to her feet and stared off in the distance toward the mountains, her eyes narrowing with fury as her long black dress blew around her in the gusts of wind that came from the storm above. "If that scream is any indication, they're up on that mountain somewhere and Vivica is upset. It's about time I take control of this situation and end this once and for all."

"What are you going to do?" Capri asked curiously, already beginning to rub more salve on Sebastian's back as she looked at Thea.

Thea pursed her lips, her eyes flashing dangerously as she glanced down at her Air Dryad, the urgency and anticipation of power already beginning to flood through her system in pulsing waves. Her hands trembled at her sides, and in response she clenched them tightly into fists and felt her lips curve into a dark and knowing smile.

"When I told you I wasn't all-powerful, Capri, I didn't mean that I couldn't *become* all-powerful."

Capri only shook her head, confused, as Sebastian let out a hiss of breath and glared up at her.

"Thea! You can't be serious?" he asked harshly, attempting to turn around but faltering from the sharp pain that came from shifting his back. Fighting against it, he met her eyes. "It's dangerous!"

"I know what I'm doing, Sebastian. Vivica is much stronger than any of us expected and the only answer is to become what she cannot control. I won't be long."

With a flourish of skirt and billowing black curls, she whirled around and glided out across the grass, heading away from the battle to an area that was wide open and empty. Her bare feet connected her with the rich and fertile soil below, while the bare skin of her arms and face embraced the feel of the wind and storm above. The grass brushed against her legs as she walked, and the sensation blended beautifully with the thrumming song of the Earth in her veins. When she came to a stop, she immediately dropped down to a crouch, her eyes closing as she dug her hands into the soil, absorbed in the feel of it as she let her head roll back on her shoulders and the gift within her summon the power from the very Earth she stood on.

She felt the ground shudder beneath her, trembling from deep within as she released the dirt from her hands and rose once more to her feet, her arms stretching up toward the sky, her eyes still closed.

Her feet felt it first, the answering shimmer of power that rose from the core of the planet to merge with her very body, sliding its way up her legs and toward her belly. She inhaled slowly and exhaled even slower, almost as if she were meditating, allowing the ancient energy of the Earth to come inside of her and make her stronger.

If she took too much, she knew she could destroy herself... therefore she couldn't be greedy. The feeling was incredibly seductive and addicting, the need for it almost impossible to ignore once it began. But she had to maintain control, had to take only what she needed, or the very Earth could cease to turn and the damage it caused would be irreversible.

Shimmering waves pulsed through her body and she welcomed the power that had reached her heart, thudding along with the blood that ran in her veins. In her mind, she almost pictured her blood glowing white hot inside of her as it moved beneath her skin. The urge to keep going, to keep taking and taking until she could take no more was thundering within her, but she knew she had to push back...she couldn't keep going... only a little more...

No. Stop. Now. She opened her eyes, exhaling and purposely stepping back from the rooted spot where she had been, clutching her body and writhing from the sudden absence of feeling. Her body was numb and dulled, as if she'd never feel again...

But as she righted herself and released another heavy sigh, she smiled, knowing she had succeeded. She stared down at her hands, saw them glowing with a vague, ethereal golden light, and she beamed with a sense of power and contentment. Yes...now she was ready.

With one last glance over to Sebastian and Capri, Thea spread her arms out wide and in a blinding flash of light, she disappeared.

Liam nudged Rhiannon behind him as Vivica writhed with rage and agony, her body shaking with barely restrained violence as Dante suddenly seemed to awaken from under her control, and stumble back from her.

Shaking his head in an attempt to clear it, Dante tried to stay on his own two feet as he stared cautiously at Vivica, completely at a loss over what had just transpired.

"Vivica, darling..." he began, reaching out for her. But she swatted his hand away angrily and got in his face, her eyes menacing.

"*You lied to me!*" she shrieked, losing all control as she started clawing at his face and hitting him. He fought back, his own temper flaring violently as he shoved her away from him, grinning as she stumbled to the ground.

"You shouldn't have made it so easy, darling." He chuckled, pulling his pistol from the holster under his suit jacket, his eyes shining with madness.

But before anything could happen, a glowing ball of bright white light appeared between them, growing in size before flashing blindingly. They all cowered away from it, not understanding what was happening, as Thea suddenly appeared. The light faded, but she remained glowing...

Liam and Rhiannon gawked at her, unsure if it was really Thea they were seeing, or some kind of glorious mirage. While she looked like Thea, there was something much more to her, something more powerful, more ethereal and bright, as if she had been forged from the Earth itself and glowed with absolute power. Her hair appeared to billow around her despite the eerie lack of a breeze, and her dark eyes glittered against a face that shimmered like golden dust. The skirt of her dress flowed as though she were immersed in water, and when she spoke, her voice resonated through to their very bones, as if echoing through every cell in their bodies.

"This ends now," she bellowed, her eyes honing in on both Vivica and Dante, who cowered before her, stunned to silence by the very presence of her.

They both suddenly realized they were no longer dealing with Thea...they were now confronted with Mother Earth herself.

She went to Vivica first, her hand suddenly reaching out to grasp the woman by the throat as she lifted her from the ground, her eyes filled with terror as Thea cut off her breath. She gasped desperately for air, pawing at Thea's iron grip uselessly as her legs flailed and kicked beneath her. Thea smiled and loosened her hold just enough so Vivica could breathe, but not enough for her to struggle free.

Before Liam or Rhiannon could stop him, Dante pulled his revolver and fired a demon bullet directly at Thea, where it exploded against her side in a burst of fiery flames. She barely flinched, however, and merely stared down at the fire as though it was nothing but an insignificant nuisance.

With her free hand, she brushed at the flames, instantly extinguishing them. A black burn mark and the bullet embedded in her side remained, but she felt no pain. Her body was filled with an undeniable power and she was virtually indestructible. Dante's petty demon bullets could do her no harm.

Her eyes shot over to meet Dante's stunned ones as her free hand reached out and pointed to him. Glowing golden ropes shot from her palm and circled around him like rapid fire, binding his arms against his body as he fell pitifully to his knees. The ropes continued to wind around him until he couldn't move, leaving only his shoulders, head, and lower legs exposed.

He glared at her when she finished, but along with the loathing was also a kind of eerie possessiveness, as if he rejoiced in the fact that she was here, in his presence. His eyes were glued to her, visually lapping up every detail, absorbing her into his memory.

"I'll get to you next, Dante. And don't think about transforming, as you won't be able to now." Thea tilted her head and eyed him sternly, the power coursing through her body in rushing waves. Turning back to Vivica, her lips curled into a cruel snarl, her anger sparking. "I'm going to destroy you, Vivica. I have no other choice."

Vivica let out a manic laugh, straining against Thea's hold on her throat. "You can't kill me, Thea. I'm one of your creations. I'm a Muse. Or did you forget?"

One of Thea's dark eyebrows raised as she glared down at the woman. "What you seem to forget is that you died, Vivica, and were reconstructed and altered in the Underworld. You are no longer one of my creatures, but instead a dark creation of Hell. Therefore, it will be my pleasure to destroy you."

Vivica's face went ghostly white as her eyes widened fearfully. "P-please, Thea, don't do this…"

"Why shouldn't I? You have proven yourself incapable of being anything more than destructive and evil. The world would be a better place without you in it."

"He tricked me," Vivica panted, her eyes darting over to Dante, who was still staring at Thea, mesmerized. "He used me, Thea…he fooled me into doing all of this. I was weak at heart; I always have been. You remember that."

"If I don't destroy you, then what do you propose I do with you?" Thea asked inquisitively.

"Show mercy, Thea, please…" Vivica begged, tears streaming down her cheeks.

Thea released Vivica, letting her drop to her knees and rub her aching throat, her chest shaking as she sobbed uncontrollably. Liam and Rhiannon watched with wide eyes as Thea held her hands out, palms spread, over Vivica's head.

"Lucky for you, destroying you does not mean killing you, Vivica," Thea said, inhaling deeply and gathering the power within her, focusing it on the task at hand. "But rather, destroying what's left of the Muse in your blood and banishing the evil from your body, leaving you nothing more than a human. Consider it my one last gift to you."

"Thank you, Thea, t-thank you," Vivica stammered, still sobbing as Thea's hands hovered over the crown of her head.

"When you awaken, you'll know nothing of who you were. Goodbye, Vivica."

Thin tendrils of white light seeped from the palms of Thea's hands, swirling through the air to wrap around Vivica's head. They snaked across her skin, spiraling around her to enclose her in a glowing white cocoon. Thea's head fell back as the power trembled inside of her, her lips parting as she released a smooth, contented breath. Within seconds, Vivica's entire body was wrapped in the cocoon and she ceased to move inside, as if she had tumbled into a deep slumber.

Suddenly, black smoke began to seep from between the threads of white light, dripping down to fall on the ground and disappear into the soil. The cocoon trembled once as the last of the darkness released itself from Vivica, and then the cocoon began to fade away.

Thea kneeled down and cradled Vivica's seemingly lifeless body tenderly in her arms, like a mother would with a child. She inhaled deeply, calmly, and when she exhaled, Vivica vanished from her arms, fading into nothingness.

For a moment, Thea was still while she sat on the ground, her hands on her knees and her eyes closed. Her body continued to exude a shimmering glow as the power inside of her settled and calmed.

The first task was done.

Her eyes flew open and she got to her feet gracefully, suddenly gliding toward Dante as if she were cruising through smooth, glassy water. Her dark eyes flashed dangerously as she cupped his face in her hands, noting the way his amber eyes filled with longing and fury all at once.

She stared at him for a moment, thinking of all the things he had done, all of the horrors he had caused...and how the pity she felt for him overshadowed nearly all of the anger. Certainly, he had killed members of her family, and he had terrorized others and wreaked enough havoc for an entire century. But he was only a man, honed by a lifetime of rejection, confusion, and resentment over what he was. He hadn't asked to be born to a Dryad mother and a demon father...but here he was regardless.

However, that was where her pity ended for him. She believed in personal responsibility and choices, and he had done nothing but make all of the wrong ones. He used his hatred and his obsession to strike fear into the heart of everyone she loved. But all of that was going to stop now, and she relished in knowing the end was finally here.

"Dante..." she murmured, leaning in toward his face, her dark eyes holding his, searching. He seemed to freeze, never having been so close to her before, the power she resonated shuddering through to his very core. He wanted nothing more than to reach out to her, to simply touch her skin and know what she felt like. His eyes widened with madness as he struggled against his bonds, but she simply backed away, leaving him wanting.

"*Damn you!*" he screamed, gnashing his teeth as he tried to inch toward her.

She shook her head, her face stern and serious as she continued to stare at him. "Unlike Vivica, I cannot kill you. But also unlike Vivica, I will not be showing you mercy," she began, turning to look at Liam and Rhiannon, who were hovering nearby, frozen in place and stunned. "Come closer, please."

Without hesitation, they both moved toward her, just as drawn to her as Dante was. Mother Earth was at the heart of everything, and the power she was radiating seemed to transfer into their own blood and simmer there, building up and making them fuller, stronger…

"For this, we will need the other two Dryads, as well," Thea declared, turning from them and walking toward the cliff's edge, where down below she could see the rest of her family, finishing the battle.

On the ground, Blythe stood beside Jax. Her pistol was clutched in her hands as she shot a round into the last demon, enjoying the shimmer of glassy dust as it exploded into pieces. Finally…it was over.

"We make a good team, cowboy." She grinned up at Jax, pulling him down by the collar of his shirt so she could kiss him. In response, he tugged her against him and deepened the kiss, his emotions ranging from thrilled to exhausted to relieved, coupled with immense pride at seeing his girl kick so much ass.

He broke the kiss and smiled back at her, his green eyes darkening with a rushing intensity. "There is nothing sexier than watching you kill demons, darlin'."

She snorted out a laugh, enormously pleased. "Maybe we should go hunt down some more, then."

"We have all the time in the world for that." Jax pulled her against him again, pressing a firm kiss to her forehead.

"We do?" Blythe asked shakily, blinking back her confusion as she struggled to find the meaning behind his words. She looked up at him, and suddenly realized he looked just as startled as she was by what he had said.

"I…" he began, his brow furrowing as he tried to find the words to say. Damnit, he knew what he really wanted…

"Is that your weird way of asking me to marry you?" Blythe managed, her eyes wide as she stared up at him, her system rocked by a sudden, stunning emotion.

But before he could respond, panic filled his eyes as he noticed she was starting to quite literally fade away. "Blythe, what the–?"

She stared down at her hands, and the fact that she could suddenly see through them had her mouth falling open and her eyes bulging.

With a frantic look at Jax, she felt the world around her going dark. She called out his name as everything suddenly went to blackness.

Several yards away, Capri was standing with Rian, Brock and Rohan, the dragon dead at their feet. Its body was charred and burnt to a crisp, and tightly bound to the ground by thick, thorny vines. Capri wrapped her arm around Rian as she watched Brock and Rohan for the first time in over twenty years actually smile and laugh with each other.

"I still can't believe that worked," Rohan said, patting Brock's back and letting out a shaky laugh.

Brock grinned in return, positively beaming. "Couldn't have done it without you, buddy. Trapping it with those vines was a great idea."

"You would have just kept tossing fire at it while it flew out of reach." Rohan chuckled, surprised when Brock let out a hoot of laughter.

"Yeah, but without my fire, you would have just grown a couple of plants and prayed the beast had allergies."

Rohan laughed so hard he had to grip Brock's shoulder to keep from toppling over, and the two men enjoyed the friendship they had long ago forsaken.

Serendipity and Nyxa approached, huddled together, eyes wide with curiosity and caution. They weren't sure what to make of Brock and Rohan's sudden friendliness, and weren't sure if it was something that was only temporary, or perhaps for good…

"Rohan?" Serendipity said softly, watching as he turned to look at her, his smile fading a little. Her heart broke to see it, and she felt a single tear fall down her cheek. Seeing it, Rohan left Brock and went to his wife, gathering her in his arms.

"Everything is going to be fine," he murmured, letting out a heavy sigh. "None of us are perfect, but I think it's time we stopped this foolishness."

His eyes shot to meet Brock's, who had his arms wrapped around Nyxa. Brock nodded firmly, his lips flashing into a humorous grin.

"Hell, we took out a dragon together. I'd say that's enough to make anybody friends."

Rohan smiled. "I'd say so too."

Capri watched the scene unfold with misty eyes, sniffling as she tilted her head to look at Rian.

"Isn't it wonderful?"

His lips curved slightly as he looked down at her, pleased to see the older Dryads making amends. But when he saw her face, his entire body went cold and his eyes widened with alarm.

"Capri!" He stared at her body helplessly as she suddenly began to fade away, and her smile faltered as she looked down at herself and realized what was happening.

She reached out for him desperately in fear and shock as her vision went hazy and she swiftly lost herself in sudden darkness.

Chapter Eighteen

Up on the cliff in the mountains far above, Thea waited patiently for Blythe and Capri to arrive. Liam and Rhiannon stood behind her, awaiting her instructions on what they were to do with Dante.

When the two girls suddenly appeared before them, arriving with a flash of white light, Thea smiled warmly.

"I'm sorry to pull you away, girls. But this is of the utmost importance," Thea told them, motioning to where Dante was on his knees and bound by golden ropes, his eyes fiery with rage and passion.

Blythe and Capri both looked down at their hands and then at each other, confusion and relief rushing through them. When they followed Thea's motion toward Dante and spotted Liam and Rhiannon, they seemed to understand.

"You need the four of us to destroy him," Blythe murmured, turning to Thea for confirmation as her eyes lit up.

Beside her, Capri nervously chewed her bottom lip, her brow furrowed in confusion. "What do we need to do?"

She glanced over at the others questioningly and seemed to draw them in, until they were huddled together, solidly united.

Thea watched her four young Dryads with satisfaction, pleased to see Liam take his place at the back, as though representing the strength and backbone of the group. Blythe and Rhiannon flanked his sides, the heart and the soul. And Capri naturally went to the middle front, reaching for both girls' hands, the glue that held them all together.

Very few other Dryad groups embodied the strength and unity that this one did, including their parents. And though they had their fair share of troubles and differences, somehow they had managed to overcome the obstacles better than most.

And perhaps it was fitting that this group would be the one to end it all, as they were the most devastatingly affected from the very start. Surely, if anyone deserved to harbor resentment and to administer justice, it was them.

"The time has come for you to finish this," Thea began, looking at each one in turn. "As you all are aware, I cannot destroy him myself, but I can instruct you on how to imprison him where he will never be able to escape or be found. It will require maximum effort, an enormous amount of focus, and most of all, it will only be possible if the four of you are fully and unrestrictedly united." She paused, letting the weight of her instructions take root. They had to know just how important their next steps would be, or else they would fail miserably. "Are you ready to do this?"

Liam's hands came up to rest on Blythe and Rhiannon's shoulders as he met Thea's eyes. "We're ready."

The three girls nodded in agreement at his words, fiercely determined and unafraid. Thea's lips curved into a soft smile, immensely proud of them. And even though she knew what was to come would test the strength of their bonds and attempt to weaken them, she also knew that they, more so than any other group, could handle it.

With a subtle bow, she motioned for them to approach Dante, who glared at them with madness in his eyes.

"You all think you're so special…" he snarled, his eyes darting back and forth between them, as if trying to find some way to slither his way in and manipulate with words to somehow spare his life, his very existence. He knew just what was coming, he was no fool. He knew where they thought they'd send him, and he'd be damned if he'd go out without a fight. "Just because you get to live on Euphora, you think you're better than me. But I'm stronger than all of you combined, and you know it! I was able to outwit each and every one of you, and it is only now that Thea has caught me that you are even able to face me without me slaughtering you."

"You wouldn't kill us even if you had the opportunity, Dante," Rhiannon said suddenly, earning a questioning stare from the others.

"Hah! I wouldn't bet on that, sweetheart," Dante retorted, chuckling to himself.

"Then why didn't you kill Capri when you possessed her in her bedroom earlier this year? You easily could have. And why didn't you kill Blythe when she came to you in the alleyway in Richmond? Or me when you had me tied to a chair at Burke's home? You even had the chance to kill Liam the entire time you had him alone up here on this cliff, and yet you didn't. Why, Dante?"

"Each time there was a bigger plan…it wouldn't have suited my interests to kill you then," Dante reasoned, rolling his eyes dismissively.

"But why all the plans? If you hate us as much as you claim, then you would stop at nothing to kill us all off," Liam put in, catching on to what Rhiannon had started. He remembered Vivica questioning Dante about this very subject just moments before, though it hadn't made much sense at the time…

"Like a cat, I wanted to play with the mouse first before I ate it." Dante's lips spread into a wide and wicked grin as he started to laugh, amused by his own metaphor.

"But what happens to the cat when every last mouse is gone?" Rhiannon asked, her eyes hardening as they focused directly on his, forcing him to look at her. He did and his smile faltered under the weight of her stare. "The cat dies, Dante. When all the little mice are gone, the cat has nothing left to live for if not for the hunt."

"That's a cute theory," he murmured, his voice cracking as he cleared his throat and looked at Capri, who was staring down at him cautiously. "But there is only one end goal to a hunt...and that's the death of the prey."

His eyes flashed a brief and vivid bloody red, and Capri felt her rarely used temper sparking within her. This monster was the reason she would never know her mother and had nearly missed out on the life she was meant to have... "You are so pathetic," she snapped, her face flushing with resentment and indignation. "Rhiannon's right, you could have killed the four of us in the past, and yet you didn't. But you did kill my mother and Roarke, because doing so directly hurt us Dryads. And then you spared my life when I was three years old, and I thought it was just because your mother had told you to. But now I wonder if you even had the nerve to do it in the first place."

Dante's lips curled into a cruel snarl, violence washing over him as he struggled against the golden ropes, aching to attack. "What makes you think I wouldn't have done it? You were nothing, you are nothing, and killing you would have been a pleasure."

Capri shook her head fervently, pale blonde strands of hair falling down over her cheeks as she leaned in, getting right in his face, appalled and excited by her own daring. "No, Dante, I'm not nothing. Especially not to you."

"You said so yourself, Dante," Liam said suddenly, glaring down at the man, enjoying the flash of panic in his eyes. "If we die, then everything is over for you. Though you might not remember that since Vivica was in your mind exposing the truth at the time."

"*No!*" Dante growled furiously.

"You know, this has all been really cute, but I think it's time we take out the trash once and for all," Blythe said, resting a reassuring hand on Capri's shoulder as she eyed them all, her lips curled halfway between a smirk and a sneer.

"Darling Blythe…" Dante hissed out, chest heaving as he stared at her obsessively, shoving aside his fury to focus solely on her. "You wouldn't send your own flesh and blood away…"

"Jesus, you never shut the hell up, do you?" Blythe spat, reaching out to violently slap her hand across his face, before suddenly leaning close to him with fiery heat flaring in her eyes. "You can't possibly understand the joy I'm going to get from knowing you won't be coming back from where we're sending you. I am sick and goddamn tired of your stupid mind games and your creepy obsession with me and my family. You're done, Dante. It's over for you."

He lifted one dark brow indignantly and sneered at her, as if truly insulted by her words. Incensed, she nearly smacked him again but Liam pulled her back, urging her to settle down.

Thea cleared her throat and they all turned to face her, looking guilty. She only smiled.

"While this has been more than interesting, Blythe is correct. We need to, ah…take out the trash, and sooner rather than later, please."

"Let's do this." Blythe bounced once on the balls of her feet, clapping her hands together as adrenaline and fury mixed to pump beautifully through her blood. Beside her, Liam and Rhiannon merely eyed each other valiantly, and Capri attempted a small smile, determined and ready to do what needed to be done.

"Circle around him, and take each other's hands," Thea instructed, watching as they followed her command and took their places around Dante, who sneered at each of them furiously. But behind the fury, Thea knew there was fear. And even though a part of her pitied him, she felt his punishment was rightly deserved, and a long time coming.

Liam stood between Rhiannon and Blythe, with Capri across from him. He took their hands and eyed each of them in turn with a confident smile. Blythe flashed an answering grin back at him, and Rhiannon's lips curved up ever so softly. Across from him, Capri exhaled slowly in an attempt to steady herself as she met his eyes, filled with quiet power. But though they were all running on adrenaline, nerves and a sense of purpose, there was relief in knowing it was nearly the end.

"I want you all to close your eyes and clear your mind of all thoughts...you'll need a clean slate as you focus all of your attention on the unique element that swims in your veins. Air, Fire, Earth, and Water...search within your mind and your heart for the essence of your gift, and bring it out, letting it fill your entire body, consuming you until you are nothing but your element, and that element alone."

Liam shut his eyes and concentrated on the darkness behind his eyelids, imagining the glowing ball of blue light swimming near his heart, the Dryad gift that resided within him. He pictured it flickering and expanding, resembling water as it glistens in the sunlight, filling the dark void that was his body until there was nothing left but Water, surging through his bloodstream and breathing with the very breath he exhaled. It felt like shimmering waves rushing all over him, rising and falling like the tides of the ocean, until it almost seemed as if he could hear the crashing waves of the sea resounding somewhere deep inside his heart.

For he was the very water that made the waves, the very water that pooled in the chasms of the Earth and gave life to every living creature. He was the rain that fell in soft patters to the ground, and the fish that swam with the sighing current.

His body felt loose and light and free, as if he were floating, and until Thea spoke again, he thought he was submerged in the ocean somewhere, enveloped lovingly by the water...

"Open your eyes please, and look to one another," Thea commanded, her hands clasped together in front of her as she admired the beauty of them as they lost themselves to their inner gift, their innate power and true identity...

Liam heard Capri gasp, and Blythe curse numbly under her breath, and so he opened his eyes as well and took in the sight around him.

He had heard of auras before and had never believed in them. But it struck him now that an aura was exactly what was surrounding each of them now.

It seemed as though his entire body shimmered with a glowing bluish light, bright and iridescent, as if somehow emanating from his very skin. Across from him, Capri was staring at her arms with wide eyes, the silvery radiance shining in her lovely gray eyes. Blythe's lips had curved into a childlike grin as she examined her own golden ethereal glow that sparkled with a tinge of fiery red. And when he turned to Rhiannon, he saw that she was inhaling and exhaling slowly, fighting to calm the frantic beating of her heart as the truly supernatural appeared to be occurring. But he knew that she could no more deny the power coursing through them at this moment than he could. He thought she looked incredibly stunning, her body surrounded by a vivid green light, gleaming with hints of brilliant gold.

Through their joined hands, it felt as though the power they'd drawn from their elements pulsated, uniting them together. And though there was no wind, not even a breeze, it felt as though the air had turned to a smooth and sultry fluid around them, flowing over their clothes and hair until it looked as if they were suspended in water.

A strange, static humming sound resonated through his ears and in his mind, and the anticipation of what was to come thrummed through his very veins.

"I know this all seems very strange to you, but it is as natural as breathing," Thea said, noting the tension behind Rhiannon's eyes and the nerves in Capri's. At their feet, Dante was staring up at all of them in stunned disbelief and eager jealousy, as though he wanted nothing more than to join them, to be one of them... "I want you all to repeat after me."

When they looked to her and nodded, she tilted her head up grandly and beamed with sheer control and purpose. And when she spoke, the words seemed to flow toward them, and pour right back out of their own mouths in unison, as if she were speaking straight through them.

"We four, the elements, Air, Fire, Earth and Water, unite to destroy this evil, this monstrosity of darkness, and banish him from this world to the place where demons may not arise. So it will be, for all eternity."

As they finished repeating the enchantment, their words seemed to echo and resound forcefully off the mountainside and in the air, loud and thundering, filled with absolute power. And as the words struck out into the air, Dante began to laugh.

His chin was resting on his chest as the laughter began, bubbling in his throat and coursing through his blood, the very actions happening against him so unbelievable and yet so forcefully desired that he couldn't even begin to understand it all. All he could do was laugh.

His head fell back as the laughter burst from within him, no longer a chuckle but now a raucous release of humor and petrified horror. The golden ropes that held him began to glow even brighter, blinding him so that he had to shut his eyes, but he continued to laugh, boldly and madly.

The ground at their feet began to tremble, and a misty rain suddenly began to fall from nowhere. A howling wind began to rush around them, a cyclone of roaring power. And when flames burst from the ground beneath Dante's knees and enveloped him in fire, his laughter was drowned out by the roar of the wind, and it seemed as though the world was on the verge of annihilation.

But instead, a vivid flash of golden light exploded from the flames, and before they could do more than blink, everything was gone, leaving behind nothing but obscurity.

The next thing Liam knew, he was lying on his back, his head pounding dully and his body aching with a deep and hollow pain. His eyes flew open as he gasped for air, his hand flying out to clutch at his chest, his lungs gratefully drinking in clear, fresh mountain air with greedy gulps. He stared up at the clear, blue sky above him, momentarily stunned and lost.

Suddenly, Rhiannon's face came into view as she leaned over him, her sage eyes filled with worry. When her hands fluttered over his cheeks they were trembling and weak, as if all of her strength had been ripped from her body.

"Liam, are you okay?" she asked, her voice breathy, alarmed tears swimming in her eyes.

"I'm fine." He tried to sit up, his arms shaking pitifully as he balanced them on the ground beneath him and rose into a sitting position. His eyes darted over Rhiannon's shoulder. Blythe and Capri were both lying on the ground as well, hands still clasped and breathing heavily as they came to. Clearly, whatever power they had harnessed had whiplashed back at them and knocked them off their feet.

Turning back to Rhiannon, he managed to pull her into his arms, his eyes shutting tight as a wave of dizziness washed over him. What had happened to them? Was Dante gone?

"I'm sorry, I should have warned you that this was a possibility," Thea's voice echoed somewhere in his head, causing him to open his eyes and look up, only to see Mother Earth standing over him. "I'm afraid sometimes powerful enchantments such as that one can have a devastating effect on those who perform it.

But you'll all be fine, just give yourselves a moment to recover your strength."

"Damn, that was intense…" Blythe murmured, clutching her head and sitting up, her eyes shut tight against the tension straining behind them. One moment, she had felt like some kind of goddess, all-powerful and filled with vigor and vitality. And now, it felt as though she had been sapped of all her strength, drained dry of every last drop.

Beside her, Capri moaned as she rested her forehead against her knees, wrapping her arms around her legs and fighting back the nausea swimming miserably inside of her. But when she remembered Dante, her head whipped up and her eyes darted around, searching for him.

"Is he gone?" she whispered, her voice hoarse and desperate, her eyes wide and wild.

"Yes," Thea said, kneeling down to cup the girl's face in her hand to steady her. Capri's eyes met Thea's and held, and seemed to calm somewhat at the assurance in the other woman's voice. "He is gone, forever, to a place where demons do not resurface. You will never have to worry about him hurting you ever again."

Capri's eyes filled with grateful tears. "Thank God…"

"Thank God, indeed." Thea smiled, helping Capri to her feet. "Now, I don't know about all of you, but I'd like to be reunited with the rest of my family."

For Liam, coming home to Euphora was like returning from an epic, year long war. Even though the entire ordeal had only lasted several hours, it felt as though it had been several months. He was exhausted; his nerves frayed and his body sore and used. He wanted nothing more than to crawl into bed and sleep for a thousand years, maybe two.

Rhiannon refused to let him carry her, but instead insisted on walking by his side, holding his hand in her own as they went into the castle together with the others. While the Muses and Fates reunited with their children, others came together to share battle stories and a sense of triumph and victory. The rest drifted off in search of a bath or a bed to collapse into.

Liam was pleased when Rhiannon simply followed him up to his room, not saying a word as he opened the door to let her inside. She continued her silence as she shrugged out of her dress and climbed into his bed, curling up under his blankets and resting her head comfortably against his pillow.

He glanced over at his dresser and spotted the engagement ring, where he had left it before going out to find her. He slipped it into his pocket once again, unsure what she would say if she noticed it lying there in plain view. It was probably best to hold off on the whole thing for just a little bit longer...

He crawled in beside her, pulling her against his body so he could enjoy having her safe in his arms. They both exhaled a deep and contented sigh before tumbling into a wonderfully dreamless and long awaited sleep.

Chapter Nineteen

"I can't believe you're seriously pissed off about this."

Jax rolled his eyes, crossing his arms over his chest and grunting. "I'm not pissed off, I'm just jealous."

Blythe let out a husky laugh and punched him playfully in the shoulder. They were seated together on one of the lounge sofas in the parlor, and at his heated look she leaned into him to nibble delicately at his ear, grinning. "C'mon, cowboy, don't be mad at me for doing what needed to be done…besides, now you can fantasize about me slapping Dante in the face."

"God, I wish I could've seen that," he mused, tilting his head to grin at her wickedly. "I bet it was damn priceless."

"Of course it was. Everything about me is priceless." She preened, laughing at herself as she cuddled against him, happy for the first time in what felt like forever. They were home and they were both safe…

She looked up at his face, noting the scar that trailed down his cheek, marring his once ruggedly handsome face. But to her, it was a symbol of the horrors they had been through, and a reminder of what he had sacrificed to be with her. This wasn't his war, but he had fought beside her regardless, because he was just that way...

"I can't get over you just fading away like that," Rian said suddenly, the memory haunting him as he looked down at Capri, who was cuddled up in his lap in an adjacent armchair to the sofa.

"That was downright bizarre," Jax agreed heatedly, frowning down at Blythe. "It was like you girls were a mirage or something."

Capri frowned, sincerely sorry. "I feel so bad, if there had been some way for me to let you know I was okay..."

"No," Rian assured her, pressing a soft kiss to her forehead. "You did everything right. You destroyed Dante, baby."

"It was about damn time, too," Blythe chipped in, stretching her arms up over her head and yawning, leaning away from Jax to smile at him. "Betcha wish you'd seen me glowing all gold and red and stuff, huh?"

Jax cleared his throat, tugging at the collar of his shirt and looking oddly uneasy. "You know, darlin', the more I try and pretend that you're normal, the more you remind me that you're the furthest thing from it."

"How true." She beamed at him fondly, patting his cheek as she laughed.

"I wonder how much longer Liam and Rhiannon are going to sleep in," Capri said, glancing down at her watch and frowning. "It's been fourteen hours since we got back."

"That's probably because they're not sleeping," Jax suggested, earning a swift punch in the arm from Blythe.

"Ew!" she grunted, scowling at him. "That's my brother and therefore gross."

Jax just shrugged and grinned at her. "What? That didn't stop us."

Capri burst into giggles, and Rian eyed Jax sardonically, his lips curving. "We're all tired after yesterday."

"Ain't that the truth," Blythe agreed, releasing a heavy sigh. Then her eyes shot over Capri's shoulder and her face broke into a grin. "Speaking of the lovebirds!"

Liam and Rhiannon walked into the room, both looking fresh and well rested. Blythe jumped to her feet and sprinted to Liam, bounding into his arms. He lifted her up and spun her around, laughing as he set her back on her feet and tweaked her nose affectionately.

"How's my girl?" he grinned, ruffling her mass of fiery curls until she smacked his hand away.

"Fine. I slept like the dead. Damn, Liam, just damn!" Blythe bit her bottom lip and jumped up and down, fist pumping the air excitedly. "Can you believe what the four of us did? I can't get over it."

Liam chuckled, smiling over at Rhiannon. "It was... interesting."

Rhiannon shrugged, trying to keep a clear and logical head about the whole thing. "Thea explained it all to me as we were leaving, and it's really very simple and natural. All we did was harness energy from our individual elements and use that energy to fuel the enchantment. It's really not that extraordinary."

Blythe rolled her eyes, though the meaning behind it was less sarcastic and more affectionate. She had come to oddly appreciate Rhiannon's practical and efficient way of overanalyzing things.

"Even if it was simple, it was still badass," Blythe told her, throwing her arm over Rhiannon's shoulder and beaming at Capri and Liam. "The four of us really made it happen. All of us, really." She nodded to both Jax and Rian. "God, and our dads took out that friggin' dragon! I'd almost forgotten about that."

Rhiannon smiled, remembering how her father and Brock had looked laughing together for the first time ever in her lifetime. "They really bonded over it, for whatever reason."

Blythe looked at her thoughtfully, her lips curving. "I think it was only a matter of time. I mean, really, who goes their entire lifetime holding a grudge?"

Rhiannon's eyebrows raised as she stared down at Blythe skeptically. "You're telling me that if none of this had happened, you would have still gotten over hating me and been my friend?"

Blythe thought about it for a moment. "Mmm...I'm sure eventually we would have gotten over whatever it was that got between us."

"You stole Liam from me. That's what got between us," Rhiannon reminded her, though Blythe looked insulted.

"No I didn't! You were more than welcome to come play with us. You were just a brat."

Rhiannon pulled away and crossed her arms over her chest defensively. "I was not! Just because I actually cared about school-work and learning doesn't make me a brat."

"That's right, it makes you a nerd." Blythe grinned, her eyes glittering with humor. "Whatever, we're over it now, aren't we?"

Rhiannon sighed, pushing aside her indignation for the sake of being civil. After all, she was usually the mature one of the group, and seeing Blythe taking a more adult stance on this one subject was irking her. "Certainly. One hundred percent over it."

Capri sprung to her feet and danced over to them, wrapping them both in a hug. "Isn't it so much easier being friends?"

"Yes, mom." Blythe poked Capri in the side and grinned. "So Vivica's a human now, huh?"

"Thea said she sent her to California, memory erased and all her powers gone." Rhiannon confirmed, leaning into Liam when he wrapped his arm around her. "I suppose she felt it was a more fitting punishment than destroying her."

"Thea is not always merciless," Capri chimed in, smiling sadly. "I think we all sometimes forget that she's not perfect, and that she makes mistakes and feels guilt and remorse just like anyone else."

"True, and she made things right in the end, which is what matters," Liam agreed, turning around as Brogan appeared in the doorway to the parlor, his quietly poetic face unreadable.

Rhiannon started to step toward him, but he went straight to Liam, his hand outstretched in a sign of diplomacy.

"I'm sorry that this is a bit delayed…but I owe you an apology," Brogan said firmly as Liam accepted his hand. Beside him, Rhiannon was watching Brogan curiously, unnerved at seeing the two of them together.

Liam smiled politely. "You don't owe me anything, Brogan. It's all over now."

Brogan didn't look convinced. "If I had given you the location where she was staying sooner, it might not have been too late." He turned to Rhiannon, regret and misery filling his eyes. "I'm sorry, Rhiannon. I feel like I let you down."

"Oh, Brogan," she managed, breaking away from Liam to hug her old friend tightly, tears swimming in her eyes. "It's not your fault, please don't blame yourself. I shouldn't have left in the first place."

Brogan released a heavy sigh as he pulled away from her, his hands on her shoulders as he stared into her eyes. "I'm glad you're safe."

"Me too." She sniffled, feeling foolish as she wiped the tears away from her cheeks. She let out a half laugh and glanced over her shoulder at the others, who were watching quietly. "Blythe, do you still have a few girls in mind for my good friend? He deserves only the best."

Brogan flushed a bit with embarrassment, especially when Blythe let out a hoot of laughter and grinned.

"Whenever you wanna take a trip down to El Paso, honey, we'll go," she declared, beaming up at him warmly.

Brogan nodded with a shy smile. "Alright."

"Speaking of El Paso…" Jax said suddenly, rising to his feet to pull Blythe into his arms. She tilted her head back to look up at him, her lips curving into a wicked grin.

"What about El Paso, cowboy?" she murmured, nuzzling his nose with her own, which caused Liam to groan uncomfortably.

"If you're gonna hit on my sister, Jax, you should at least do it someplace where I can't see or hear it."

"Oh, get over yourself," Blythe shot back with a laugh, sticking her tongue out at him. "I'm happy, and that's…hey, wait, I just remembered something."

"What's that, darlin'?" Jax asked, distracted by the smooth curve of her shoulder and the freckles that graced it.

Blythe chewed on her bottom lip for a moment, as if wondering whether or not to say the words. Because this was horribly unlike her, Jax felt a strange uneasiness in his gut. "Blythe?"

She met his eyes and tried to look nonchalant, but there was this crazy hope and desperation bursting within her all the same… "Are we, like, engaged now, or something?"

Capri let covered her mouth with her hands excitedly as Rian rose to his feet to stand behind her, a questioning smirk on his face. Rhiannon's eyebrows raised curiously while Liam merely grinned.

Jax froze, his breath halting in his chest as he stared down at her, panic setting in. Okay…they'd had that conversation moments before she'd disappeared into nothing, and then he'd pretty much forgotten about it, as it had been pretty low on his list of priorities at that time. But now…

"Do you want to be engaged?" he asked, fighting to keep his voice cool and calm, even though he knew she could read the heat in his eyes.

She shrugged, feigning indifference. "I don't know, do you?"

"I don't know."

"Well, then."

For a moment, no one said anything, and the silence hung heavy and undeniably awkward in the air.

"God, just say yes and be done with it," Liam burst out, rolling his eyes.

"Say yes to what? He hasn't technically asked me yet, not really anyway." Blythe crossed her arms over her chest and stared up at Jax, one eyebrow raised skeptically. "I just want to know if this is a go or not."

Jax let out a huff of breath, running his hands through his blonde hair and glaring around at the others, looking irritated. "You sure lit a fire under my ass, didn't you?"

"Okay, fine. I'll make it easier for you," Blythe charged, cocking her chin up defensively. "Will you marry me, cowboy?"

"Damnit…" he cursed under his breath, clutching his head in his hands and turning away from her, beating back against all the caution and uncertainty in his mind. He knew what he wanted, and there was no point in denying it any longer. She was it for him, it was just that simple. Whirling around, he scooped her up into his arms and kissed her fully on the mouth, enjoying the fire of it as she vibrated with adrenaline against him. Breaking the kiss, he stared down at her, his lips curving into an arrogant grin. "What the hell. Why not?"

Blythe shut her eyes and let out the breath she'd been holding, silently thanking God as she smiled. "Good, because if you'd said no there would have been hell to pay."

"Oh, I don't doubt it."

While the others laughed together and congratulated them, Liam watched the scene with thoughtful eyes. After all, he had his own proposal that he'd been meaning to make…and when he glanced over to Rhiannon, who was hugging Blythe happily and smiling, he knew that all he had been doing was wasting time up until this point. He couldn't waste it anymore, not after nearly losing her again.

He stepped toward Rhiannon and reached for her hand, pulling her away from the others.

She glanced over at him questioningly, but after seeing the intense look in his eyes she gave in, letting him lead her from the room without a single word.

He pulled her out into the corridor and toward the back doors that lead out into the silent and still gardens that grew wild behind the castle. The gardens that had, over so many years of knowing her, become somewhat of a secret place for them. It seemed only natural to head there now, when so many important words needed to be said...

But as they were walking, he could feel her hand warm in his, could hear her breathing softly beside him, and this rushing need hit him all at once, mixed with desperation, fear, and unshakable guilt. Whirling around, he backed her suddenly up against the stone wall of the corridor and crushed her mouth with his own, unable to explain the unfathomable emotions that were coursing through him at that very moment.

But, God, he'd nearly lost her again...and knowing how much pain he had unknowingly caused her tore through him so furiously that the only way he could release the frustration was by showing her now that she was it for him. It had always been her, and for that scheming Muse and vile Dante to try and get between them...

"I love you, Rhia," he groaned, his heart racing and his breath catching in his throat as his mouth trailed along the skin beneath her ear, reveling in the feel of her hands clinging to his back.

"I know," she whispered, feeling tears come into her eyes and burn there beautifully. She clung to him, hating that she had ever believed he would have betrayed her so callously. "I'm sorry I gave up on you, Liam."

"What are you talking about?" he asked, pulling away to stare into her eyes, his hands cupping her face delicately.

She avoided looking at him, feeling ashamed even though she knew he would never blame her. "I didn't believe Blythe when she told me you were under some kind of spell...I just assumed the worst, thinking it was better to just accept and move on versus risking disappointment…it was stupid of me. I should have fought for you, like you've always fought for me. But I didn't."

For a moment he said nothing, he only stared at her and pondered what to say. It hurt to hear the truth directly from her. Then again, for someone who had so recently discovered sharing their heart blindly and unrestrictedly, he supposed she had fared better than most would have.

"Rhia, you did what you had to do to survive, I can't blame you for that. And for someone as practical and logical as you, I can't imagine it would be easy to accept the notion that I was under that woman's control. It doesn't make you a bad person."

She met his eyes sadly. "No, but it makes me a fool."

"No one's perfect all the time." He pressed his lips to hers in an attempt to comfort, hating to see her upset. "Including me. None of this would have happened if I hadn't gone down to New Orleans by myself to fix that oil spill."

"If it hadn't been then, it would have been another day, Liam," she asserted, needing him to understand. "Vivica and Dante told me that they had caused the oil spill in an attempt to lure you away from Euphora. If you hadn't gone, or if you'd been with your father, then they would have simply caused some other kind of distraction to drag you away. It was only a matter of time."

"But I let her get to me, I let her use me to hurt you, to hurt everyone," he reminded her, misery in his eyes. "After everything that we had gone through, all the progress we'd made together, I was going to lose it all because of them. It makes me sick to think of how you must have felt when you saw me in that stupid club, or every time after that with Vivica. I don't know how you stayed put as long as you did."

"I stayed because Capri needed me," she said firmly. "Though really it was the wedding itself that did me in…"

"We were standing at the altar," he said then, the memory flashing back to him suddenly. "You were across from me, wearing that dress…I remember feeling like I'd woken up or something just looking at you, and seeing you there had been almost like this great relief…"

"You called me Rhia," she whispered, her throat tightening, choking off her breath. "It scared the living daylights out of me."

"I remember that." He frowned, searching through what little he could remember from those horrid days. "You looked at me as if you'd seen a ghost."

She nodded, a tear slipping down her cheek miserably as she rubbed at her heart, the pain still echoing dully there. "And then it was as if it had never happened. Your face went blank and you smiled, but it wasn't the same. God, I don't know why I was in so much denial over it. That should have been the biggest indication…"

"Don't," he growled, grabbing her shoulders firmly and shaking her. "It doesn't change anything now, so please don't."

She reached up to touch his face, knowing he was right. As she did so, he spotted the scarring wound on her hand where Dante had cut her, and seeing it staggered him.

Gripping her hand, he looked up from the healing cut to her eyes, seeing the hesitation in them. So far she'd been able to keep it from him, as if it hadn't mattered. But, damnit, it did matter…

Releasing her hand, he let out the breath that had gotten stalled in his lungs moments before, running his hands through his hair and avoiding looking at her. She would never be able to understand, just couldn't possibly fathom just how agonizing it had been to walk into that room and see her blood spilled on the floor, smeared over the walls…

"He was a monster, Liam," she said, her serious eyes firm as they found his. "But he's gone. He won't ever be able to get to us again."

In response, he simply pulled her against him and held her, needing to remember the truth behind those words. Dante was gone…it was done.

Somewhere nearby, someone cleared their throat in a polite attempt to interrupt. Liam turned around and saw his parents approaching, holding hands. His eyes widened at the sight of it, but he kept his mouth closed for fear that he was reading too far into what probably meant nothing…

"Hey there, boyo," Lucian greeted, grinning ear-to-ear as he patted Liam on the back companionably. His eyes shifted to Rhiannon, and warmed as he nodded to her. "Nice day for a stroll through the gardens…don't you think?"

"That's where we were heading," Liam told him, honing in on his mother. "You guys too?"

Clarity smiled at him timidly, as if she was unsure if he approved of her or not. "I think we all deserve a walk in the sunshine after the day we had yesterday."

Because he couldn't have agreed more, Liam smiled affectionately at her. "Thank you both for being there, it meant a lot."

"You're our son, how could we not be there?" Clarity said assertively, bristling a bit at the notion even as she glanced up at Lucian, who beamed at her before looking back at his son.

"She's right, Liam. We would do anything for you." He wrapped his arm around his wife and held her close, something Liam hadn't seen him do in years.

"You guys look…happy," Liam managed before he could stop himself, feeling oddly confused and pleased at the same time. He wanted to still be angry with his mother over everything that had happened before, but somehow things seemed different now…

"We are happy, aren't we, love?" Lucian grinned down at Clarity, who smiled prettily up at him.

"It's never too late to be happy," she said simply.

Liam suddenly felt like he and Rhiannon were intruding on some kind of moment between his parents, so he motioned to her to continue on down the corridor.

"We'll just let you two get going." He waved absently and hurried Rhiannon along, unsure what to make of the situation that had just unfolded before them. Rhiannon started laughing as she fought to keep pace with him as he all but ran toward the doors that led to the back gardens, shoving them open and leading her out into the glorious morning sunlight.

"Liam, slow down." She pulled back on his arm to stop him, wondering why he was acting so strangely. Sure, she knew what had been happening between his parents, she had witnessed it herself...but if they were happy now, then clearly they had come to some kind of resolution. "What's wrong with you?"

Liam sighed and collapsed onto the top of the stone steps that led out into the wild blooming garden, waiting until she sat beside him to speak.

"That was just...weird."

"Why?"

He shook his head, not even really knowing the answer. "It's just that, I've never really seen them look at each other the way they just did, and I can't seem to wrap my mind around it. It's always been that they were like two separate people. Sure, they were my parents, but they weren't a collective 'parents' the way most are. They were just like parent one and parent two. Does that make sense?"

"No." She bit back a laugh as she studied him, amused that he was having such a hard time understanding what seemed so obvious and natural to her. "Look, I know how you feel in a way, because my parents were never very close either...but it shouldn't upset you to see your mother and father actually acting like they love each other. It should make you happy."

"It does," he decided, turning to look at her. "Of course it does."

"Then what?" She nudged him playfully with her shoulder, laughter in her eyes.

He took a deep breath, frowning as he fought to come to terms with everything... "I don't know. Whatever, I should just be glad they're happy, right?"

"Yes you should." She leaned in to kiss his cheek, pleased to see him relax a bit. "My parents are working through their issues, too. They even slept in the same bed last night."

Liam snorted and eyed her curiously. "How do you know that?"

"I saw them both come out of his room together this morning while you were still sleeping. They both scurried back inside like guilty children. It was actually quite amusing." She grinned at him, enjoying knowing that her father had managed to find the happy in-between of being his wife's slave and being a wild and carefree bachelor…

"You know, it's astonishing how one epic battle can suddenly have everyone making amends," Liam mused, peacefully gazing out at the wild grasses and roses in the garden.

"I suppose a true life or death situation puts things into perspective," Rhiannon suggested, sighing deeply and laying her head on his shoulder. "And now we have another wedding to plan."

"Mmm…two weddings, Rhia," Liam told her, his arm wrapping around her shoulders casually.

"Two?" Rhiannon's brows furrowed together as she tried to think back, wondering if something had happened while she'd been away… "Blythe and Jax are engaged now, but who else is there? Brogan's not with anyone yet, and Tobias and Sierra are too young…everyone else is already married. Oh! Nyxa and Brock must be getting remarried. That makes sense."

Liam rolled his eyes and grunted. How could he have forgotten about that one… "Okay, three weddings then."

"Three?" Rhiannon pursed her lips, fully confused now.

"Good Lord, you are not this dense, Rhia." Liam chuckled, meeting her eyes and shaking his head. "I was talking about us. We are the third wedding."

"Us…" She blinked, her breath clogging in her throat as she fought to process what he meant. But when he reached into his pocket and pulled out the ring, she felt oddly dizzy. "Oh."

"Yeah. Oh." Liam held out the ring so she could take it, and watched with guarded eyes as she held it in her fingers, examining every detail of it in the light. The sapphire stone flashed vivid blue and the diamonds glittered beautifully in the white gold band. Her face was completely unreadable. "Do you not like it?"

She shook her head, her eyes taking in every glorious, beautiful aspect of the ring even as her heart began to swell in her chest. Pressing her lips firmly together in an attempt to stem back the flow of tears she knew was coming, she started to hand the ring back to him.

He stared down at it, confused, before she realized that she was supposed to accept it.

"Is it too soon?" he asked, frustrated by her reaction. He'd expected her to joyfully accept and leap into his arms, all smiles and fulfilled dreams…but instead she just looked shell shocked, and it was impossible to determine just what she was feeling.

"No…no, it's not too soon," she said in return, staring down at the ring again. "It's just that I think you're supposed to be asking me something right now. That way I can respond and then this will be over."

"Okay…" He tried not to focus on the word *over* too much as he reached for her face to tilt it toward him so he could look at her. "Will you marry me?"

"Yes," she said simply, her expression completely serious as she pulled away from his hand and slipped the ring onto her own finger. She examined it once more now that it was on her hand, and seeing it there broke the dam of civility and proper manners within her.

Her lips spread into a wide smile as she turned to him, cupping his face in her hands and kissing him.

"Thank you…it's beautiful," she said breathily between kisses as her lips pressed against his cheeks, his chin, his forehead, his nose…anywhere she could reach. "I love you."

He pulled her into his lap and held her close, catching her mouth with his eagerly. "I know, Rhia. I'll make you happy, I promise."

"You've made me happy my entire life." She breathed in his scent as she buried her face in his neck, needing a moment to regain her composure. God, was this really happening?

"In case you cared, I got your father's approval already." Liam grinned, noting the surprise on her face.

"Really? When?"

"In Times Square, right before we found you," he told her, running his free hand through her length of brown hair absently.

"I see.." Rhiannon murmured. "So I suppose this is our happy ending, then?"

"Yeah…yeah, I think it is," he replied, his lips curving into his trademark crooked grin.

"Good." She rose to her feet and reached out for his hand, the still and silent garden stretching out behind her. Her smile spread warmly as he took her hand and stood up beside her. "Let's go for that walk now. It's the most beautiful day."

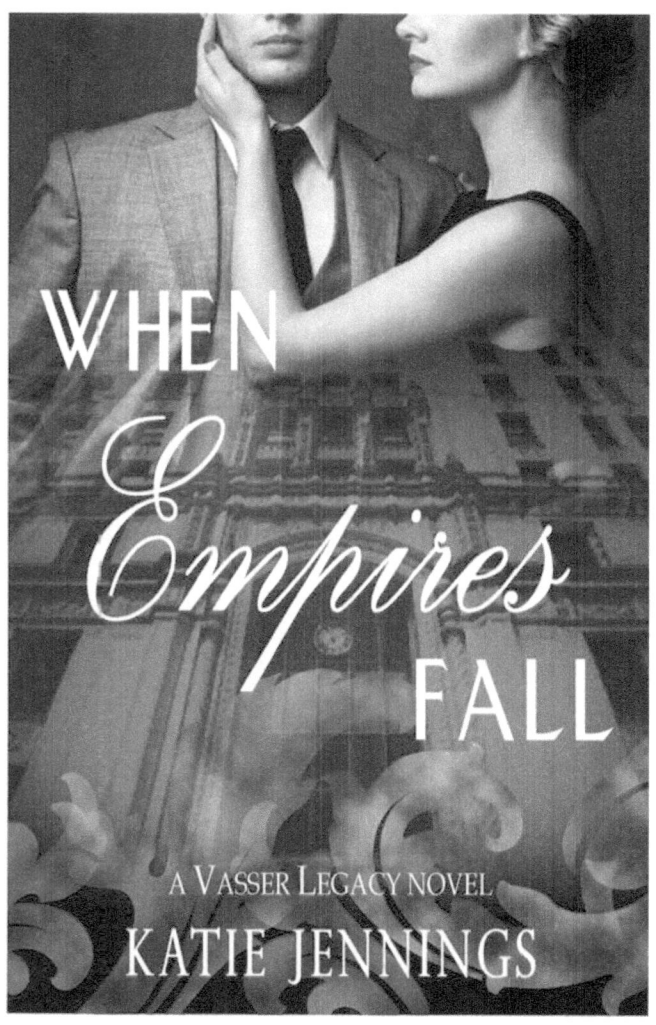

WHEN

Empires

FALL

A VASSER LEGACY NOVEL

KATIE JENNINGS

THE VASSER LEGACY SERIES - BOOK ONE

PROLOGUE

I f someone had compared him to the great Captains of Industry who had built America from the ground up, he would have laughed. Surely he was no Rockefeller, and he'd be damned if they likened him to Carnegie, the bighearted fool. But perhaps there was some truth to the statement, if one considered hotels to be of equal importance to railways and steel.

And to Winston C. Vasser, hotels were everything.

In his old age, he now understood that hotels had not given the country the same core benefits that other industries like steel and railroads had, but he and his father before him had recognized that where there was money to be made, there was also money to be spent. And the men who profited from luck and good old American ingenuity needed a place to spend the riches they had accumulated. Hence, the luxury hotels of America were born.

And by God had it boomed. What had started as a single hotel in 1899, housed inside a building that had once been a coat factory in midtown Manhattan, had paved the way for an empire the likes of which America was rapidly becoming known for. It was a country for men with big ideas and great dreams, and the willingness and tenacity to make them come true.

Which was why Winston knew he would live out his remaining days right there in New York, the most magnificent city the world had ever seen.

If only he knew how limited those days were to be.

He settled in to his plush desk chair in the center of his quiet study, his eyes drifting to the view of the city lights beyond his window, the dark scene spotted with falling winter snow. It was picturesque, as the view always was from the suites of the Vasser Hotel, and rather calming to him despite the circumstances.

He was, in many ways *un*like his father before him, an honest man. Winston prided himself on being straight with people, and on his word being as solid as a firm handshake. Which was perhaps part of the reason why the deception he had begun to weave was so troubling to him.

In his prime he had been sturdily built and taller than most, with a clear, booming voice and enough charm to outwit even the stealthiest of opponents. Generally that charm was used to get what he wanted, and he was damn good at it most of the time.

He had managed to take what his father had started and ride on the growth of the country as it exploded into the robust 20th century. One hotel had quickly become two in the United States, with a third and fourth abroad in Europe. And he was thrilled to imagine a day when there would be a Vasser luxury hotel in every worthwhile major city across the globe. After all, the century was only half over, and God only knew what lay ahead for the Vasser Hotel empire, and for the greatest country the world had ever seen.

Tucking his warm, royal blue velvet robe closer around his aging body, he turned to face his heirloom oak desk, currently littered with scattered papers, well worn books, glossy black and white photographs, and an ancient deck of cards he'd had since he was ten years old.

Thoughtfully, and a bit wearily, he reached for them, running his thumb over the surface of the box that held the yellowing cards, its edges tattered and worn from time. The front was graced with an image of the American flag, Old Glory. Seeing it brought back the onslaught of pain, along with the furious denial and shuddering disbelief.

The last time he had held that deck of cards in his hands had been when the Army men had come, carrying three flags and three sets of dog tags, inscribed with the names of three of his seven sons. It had been one of only two times he had ever cried in his life, the second being when his youngest son, Cyrus, the fourth to have gone to fight the Nazis, came home miraculously unscathed and a lavishly decorated war hero.

That had been the day he had learned humility and the true measure of sacrifice. After all, the war his generation had fought seemed somehow less frightening, less deadly. He supposed Americans had film to thank for the violent images that surfaced from the war that had claimed his sons, the scenes of destruction and death, of France and the rest of Europe reduced to rubble. His ancestors had come from France, and it was a place he had known well as a boy. And to see it ruined, to know his sons had perished protecting it, had done more damage to his soul than could have ever been repaired.

Feeling sick with grief, he yanked open his right hand desk drawer and tossed the cards inside, slamming the drawer shut again. He didn't want to think about it, couldn't bear to imagine the horror of it now. He had no time for it, not when he had to act swiftly and secretly to ensure that his legacy, and that of his father, would not be tainted. After all, as his father's only child, he was head of the family empire now, and had been for some time.

He had four surviving sons who had given him ten grandchildren and three great-grandchildren, with surely more to come. They all benefited from the fruits of his labor, and from the legacy he would pass on to them when he died.

But none of them would, in the foreseeable future, anyway, take his place as patriarch of the Vasser Hotels. He simply just could not allow it to happen.

Rummaging through the assorted papers on his desk, Winston came across one that was blank and he hastily pushed the rest out of the way, clearing space enough for him to write. He grabbed his polished black fountain pen from its holder and pressed the tip to the paper, his mind swirling with hope and regret and fear.

This was serious, of that much he was sure. He could not afford to make mistakes, not when so much was riding on this decision. It had to be Rosalie. She was the only person he could trust, the only person who had never let him down. He owed everything to her for uncovering that dark and heinous secret, the one he shuddered to even imagine now.

His pen scrawled over the page in his practiced cursive, spelling out the new terms for his soon to be rewritten will. Rosalie Owens would, upon his death, take control of the hotels, the accounts, and the employees, including his own children and grandchildren. She would be in charge of ensuring the future of the company and the prestigious reputation of the Vasser Hotels.

His hand paused as he finished the sentence, his pale blue eyes scanning the words through his wire-rimmed glasses, over and over, cementing them in place in his mind. Yes, this was the only answer, the only solution. His soon to be ex-wife wasn't going to be happy about him leaving the entire family legacy to his mistress, but what did he care? It was not for her to decide, nor to judge. What he did with the empire he and his father had single-handedly built was entirely up to him. Certainly it was uncommon for a *woman* to run a company such as his, but he knew without a shadow of a doubt that she could do it, and that she would be the only one to respect his vision for the Vasser legacy.

He began to scribble down more words on the page when there was a sharp knocking on the door to his room. Beyond the entrance of the study, he could see the door to the suite, shrouded mostly in shadows since the only light source came from his desk lamp. A sense of unease settled over him as he wet his lips, feeling the need to moisten his suddenly dry throat.

"Come in," he called out, annoyed when his usually jovial and clear voice seemed to crack with anxiety. Surely there was nothing to fear; he was in no danger...not yet, anyway.

The door opened slowly and a man walked in, looking oddly calm and collected. Winston attempted a smile as the man quietly shut the door until it was merely cracked behind him before proceeding forward into the study.

Winston immediately flipped the paper he'd been writing on over, concealing the words. God knew he couldn't let the news get out, not yet, anyway, that his will was to be changed.

"Shouldn't you be at home with your family?" Winston asked the man, his feathery white eyebrows raised in curiosity laced abruptly with a bone-quaking fear. He had a right to be afraid, though the reasons for it both pained and infuriated him.

"There are some important matters I need to attend to first," the man replied, stepping into the room, the light from the desk lamp glowing gold over the sharp lines of his face. It only served to heighten the dangerous gleam in his cold, calculating eyes and darken the hollows his brows made over them. They were eyes that seemed unnaturally dark now, and eerily devoid of any emotion other than carefully controlled rage.

Winston thought consciously of the .22 Derringer pistol hidden in the drawer to his right, wondering if he would need to use it. Good Lord, use it on his own flesh and blood...

"What sort of...matters?"

The man grinned, though the gesture lacked even the tiniest scrap of humor. No, it was a smile like that of a hunter scenting prey, stalking dangerously in the shadows, primed to pounce.

"I think you know." Chuckling, the man stood before Winston's desk, his dark trench coat brushing against his long legs and his hands tucked discreetly in its deep pockets. "Then again, you've always been a little slow on the uptake, old man. So perhaps you need a detailed explanation on why I feel you've fucked me. So to speak."

"Now, look here-" Winston began, only to be cut off when the man raised one hand up harshly, palm spread, to halt the words. His eyes glittered with impatience and a malice Winston had never before seen. Or perhaps he had simply ignored it, all these years...

"I know you plan to leave everything to the whore," the man growled, his voice tinged with cold violence. "You intend to bypass your own heirs to give the bitch everything that should be rightfully mine. After everything I have sacrificed, you still choose to dishonor me this way."

Winston inhaled sharply, his own temper flaring as indignation coursed through him. He glared at the man as if he were a stranger, feeling suddenly choked with despair and fury over that one, horrific truth...

"Sacrifice? Surely you have sacrificed nothing but your soul. God will punish you for what you have done to your own flesh and blood, your family!"

"Fuck family," the man hissed, keeping his voice low and level despite the sudden urge he had to tear every inch of the man in front of him to pieces. "If my actions to ensure my success mean I have sold my soul, then surely you have sold yours in the name of that whore, Rosalie."

"This discussion is over," Winston grunted angrily, only to bite back confusion and fear as the man suddenly skirted around the desk to approach him, his face glazed with a chilling frost, his dark eyes betraying nothing. Those eyes held Winston's as the man came closer, coming up behind his chair and resting his hands companionably on the top edge of the backrest.

"I don't know what made you think you could cross me and get away with it, old man," the man said conversationally, reaching down to scoop up the paper Winston had been writing on. He lifted it up to eye level and glanced at what was written on it before stuffing it swiftly into his inside coat pocket.

Winston only shook his head, knowing now exactly what was about to befall him. He should have expected it, should have known it would end this way. There was nothing he could do at this point to dissuade the man, not now. And surely he was no match physically for someone nearly forty years younger than he, stronger and with a fiercely determined will that he had never seen in any other man.

This man had killed before. He would easily do it again...

The truth of it had resurfaced, but now it would perish with him. And God knows what would happen to Rosalie. He would probably target and kill her too.

"How could you do it? I just need to know," Winston murmured, his head still shaking back and forth in disbelief and dull fear. But it was the fear that had him abruptly reaching out to wrench open his desk drawer and desperately fumble around for his pistol, only to discover it missing. The man behind him let out a dark laugh, and pulled the very same pistol from his coat pocket, showing Winston over his shoulder.

"I have always been resourceful. I do what needs to be done to get ahead, no matter the cost."

Winston eyed the pistol with a newfound shock racing through his blood. Good Lord, he was going to be murdered with his own gun. What terrible misdeeds had he committed in his life to deserve such a fate?

"You monster," Winston choked out, clutching his robe around his midsection, his eyes glued to the gun. He didn't think he could bear to look at the man's face, only to have the image of those horrifying eyes be the last thing he would ever see...

"Turn your head, old man. And look straight ahead," the man instructed, pressing the pistol to the side of Winston's head. "It'll all be over soon."

"Monster," Winston repeated as he shut his eyes tight, feeling tears brim hotly behind his closed lids, the cold steel of the pistol like sharp white frost against his temple.

Outside, a child watched the scene unfold through the barely open door with wide, terrified eyes. When the blast of the gunshot resounded through the room, Winston collapsed over his own desk, his blood spilling to soak through his papers and books.

Almost instantly, the child shot out into the hallway, fleeing like a rabbit to safety, a frightened scream held back only by a pure, unbridled terror that the monster was coming for him next.

It was a fear he would live with for the rest of his life.

Nothing can compare to the exhilaration of discovering, at last, a mode of release for the imagination. Mine came, after years of struggling to visualize my creativity, in the form of the written word. I found myself with my nose constantly in a book, absorbing the life of the characters and the beauty of the setting. It was intoxicating, to say the least, and the only thing I knew was that I wanted to give writing a shot, and take the thousands of characters and storylines in my head and put them down on paper and form them into something real and compelling.

In truth, I'm just a girl from a small town north of Los Angeles with an imagination for days and thank goodness a keyboard at my fingertips. And even though my husband thinks I'm a nerd and my mom is undoubtedly my biggest fan, at the end of the day I'm loving life and enjoying giving breath to the characters living in my heart and sharing with others all of the creativity I can harness.

I believe in true love and I've always believed in happy endings. And that is just the beginning of the story.

K